RÜTZ

I.M.O.N

ISBN: 979-8-9927275-4-8

Dedication

To Tajah Monet Williams, my guardian angel. Protector of my family. My one and only sibling. I share you with the world. To be remembered. Loved. And embraced. We Miss You.

Acknowledgment

My Supporters

Ravaunte Hutchins

Deneka Johnsom

Joyce Williams

Jesus Perez

Annalisa Morin

Jacob Benedict

Damon Morton

My Best Help

Shawanna Forrest

Darvin Moore

Demecko Riley

Juaron McKinley

Table of Contents

Dedication...3

Acknowledgment...4

About the Author...6

Awakening the Beast...14

Dreams and Nightmares.......................................27

Seeds of Evolution..41

Freedom Fighters..57

The King's Fall...74

A Bright New World...102

New Beginnings...199

One Step Closer..218

About the Author

Whispers of ink and echoes of forgotten tales weave together the storyteller known only by the shadows of their words. A traveler through realms unseen, a keeper of ancient truths, and a seeker of the unknown, this author remains hidden in plain sight—woven into the very fabric of the world they create.

Born where the sun kisses the earth and raised among towering steel and whispered winds, they have walked through struggles unseen, forging their voice in the fires of experience. Some say their footsteps linger in the streets of the past, while their soul resides in the boundless possibilities of tomorrow.

Their words are not just written; they are discovered, waiting for those who dare to seek. Hidden within the pages of this book are the breadcrumbs—clues that lead to the RÜTZ.

Will you unravel the mystery? Or will you, too, become part of the legend?

Generations ago, Heaven and Earth collided, birthing a fractured world where every Era coexists, blending past, present, and future into a single, chaotic timeline. This cataclysmic event bestowed god-like abilities upon all living humans. With each life's end came the dawn of a new existence. As souls departed their mortal shells, they swiftly entered the cycle of reincarnation, their essence weaving through the fabric of time to be reborn anew.

The world now comprises seven distinct Zones, each a vast continent with unique characteristics and inhabitants. Of these, five are well-known, while two remain shrouded in mystery.

In the Seventh Zone, whispers of ancient beings and forgotten civilizations echo through desolate landscapes. Few dare to venture into its depths, for tales of unspeakable horrors and eldritch entities abound. In stark contrast, the First Zone is an uncharted paradise, a utopian realm said to be untouched by conflict or decay, where the very air shimmers with ethereal light, and harmony reigns supreme. Both Zones, though vastly different, share an enigmatic allure that few have the courage to explore.

The Sixth Zone, known as the Land of The Gods, stands as a testament to divine power. Towering temples and majestic citadels reach toward the heavens, where beings of immense strength and wisdom rule over domains of unimaginable beauty and wonder. Beyond the Land of The Gods lies the Fifth Zone, the Dragon Dynasty, a realm where majestic beasts soar through the skies and mighty dragons guard ancient treasures hidden amidst mist-shrouded peaks.

At the world's nadir resides the Fourth Zone, the primal Animal Kingdom, a savage wilderness where prehistoric creatures roam freely and the laws of nature reign supreme. Here, amidst dense jungles and treacherous swamps, life teems in all its primal glory, untouched by the influence of man.

The Third Zone houses the Middle Ages, a realm of knights and castles, where chivalry and honor are upheld as sacred ideals. Amidst rolling hills and fertile valleys, feudal lords vie for power and influence while brave knights embark on quests of valor and heroism.

Finally, there's "The City," located in the Second Zone, an urban marvel shielded within an energy dome—its final dome yet to be erected. Here, towering skyscrapers and bustling thoroughfares form the heart of civilization, where the pulse of industry and innovation beats ceaselessly. Governed by authorities who claim the outside world is filled with peril, citizens toil endlessly in exchange for paper currency, their labor sapping their vitality as they sustain the dome's power. Only the city's soldiers wield their god-like abilities, augmented by machinery and cyborg enhancements, as they stand vigilant against threats both within and beyond the city's walls. Civilian use of these powers, without approval, warrants imprisonment, or worse, death, as the iron grip of authority tightens its hold over the populace.

On an unusually somber night, the City plunged into darkness, heralding the arrival of Thoth, a superpower of wisdom, traversing the cityscape through dreams. His quest was to find two chosen individuals. Amidst his search, he stumbled upon a dream steeped in anguish and despair. The dreamer, Omni, harbored a monstrous soul bereft of love, his powers spiraling out of control, manifesting as nightmares.

Driven by an unexplained force within Omni, Thoth awakened the latent beast. Meanwhile, he sought out the two beings he needed. First, Keem, a young captain disillusioned by the government's injustices toward its citizens. Thoth revealed a vision of a massive conflict, with Keem leading a small band to victory. Simultaneously, Thoth whispered cryptic words to Nakh, a man of intuition and martial prowess, urging him to leave the city and protect its Society from the looming threat.

As Omni's fury unleashed devastation upon the city's outskirts, Nakh and Keem sprang into action. Racing toward the chaos, they encountered the wreckage of Omni's home. Keem, suspicious of Nakh's presence, interrogated him. Before Nakh could respond, a rumble echoed from the city's edge, drawing their attention to a breach in the dome.

Locking eyes with concern, Keem warned Nakh of the consequences—banishment or death. Undeterred, Nakh resolved to face the unknown beyond the dome, driven by a sense of duty to protect the city's inhabitants.

Nakh grinned. "See ya on the other side!"

Once beyond the wall, Keem and Nakh dashed through the newly torn-down forest, finally reaching Omni's unconscious form. As they approached, Omni jolted awake, confusion etched across his face.

Omni exclaimed, "Where am I? Who are you? And what happened to my clothes?"

Nakh stepped forward. "I'm Nakh. I woke up to destruction and followed its trail to the edge of the dome."

Keem interjected, "You heard it too! It seems the rest of the city heard nothing. I encountered no one on my way here nor near the dome's edge."

Omni, bewildered, demanded, "Wait, what happened?"

"We don't know," Nakh replied.

Keem suggested, "But neither of us can return now. Let's set up camp elsewhere for the night and strategize before the city dispatches a search party for the culprit behind the chaos."

With a resigned sigh, Keem tossed Omni a pair of pants from his bag. As they walked away, Omni lowered his head, muttering, "Now I'm a fugitive. Nothing ever goes well for me."

They continued through the wooded area until they reached the border of the Unknown Zone Two.

"Can we please stop now? We don't even know where we're going," Omni pleaded.

Keem shot him a disapproving glance, his thoughts echoing, 'lazy bastard,' but agreed to set up camp near the border. Meanwhile, Omni focused on the ground, and to the amazement of Nakh and Keem, a cannabinoid plant sprouted seemingly out of thin air.

"You can manipulate plants?" Nakh asked in astonishment.

Omni grinned. "Just a little something."

As Omni's plant finished rolling itself, Keem tossed him a lighter. "Well, lucky we're not in the city, or they'd have us locked up anyway."

They laughed together as they passed the night, the glow of the fire casting flickering shadows around them.

Awakening the Beast

The next morning, Keem jolted awake, feeling an intense energy pulsating above him. His eyes darted skyward to witness a majestic sight—a white dragon gracefully circling in the early dawn's darkness. Urgently, he nudged Nakh awake.

"Get up! Get up, man... Look at that!" Keem exclaimed, pointing excitedly to the sky. Nakh stirred from his slumber, still groggy.

"Where's the other guy?" Nakh mumbled, looking around.

Keem whirled around, searching the surroundings. "Yeah, where did he disappear to?"

Nakh, still half-asleep, pointed to an unusual sight: a large boulder that 'had not been there the previous night. "There he is, inside that rock!"

The boulder suddenly split in half, revealing Omni standing in its midst.

"So, you control rock too?" Keem asked, astonished.

"Anything of the earth is mine to manipulate," Omni replied casually.

"What happened to our boulder fort?" Keem questioned.

"Gone with the wind, I suppose. I don't know," Omni shrugged.

As they ventured further into the arid landscape of the Middle Ages, marked by sand dunes and scarce vegetation, Nakh observed the dry terrain. "This land is much drier than the outskirts of the city," he noted.

Meanwhile, Omni concentrated, summoning a tree bearing ripe fruits from the barren ground. He carved his name into the trunk, imbuing it with life as cannabinoid vines began to weave around its branches. "As long as we have sustenance and a means to relax, we should be fine. Though, I can't shake off the city's warning about a looming threat. We must be prepared to defend ourselves."

Keem noticed a distant town on the horizon as they walked along a dusty trail, passing a lighter to Omni.

"By the way, I'm Omni," he introduced himself.

As they approached the town's only tavern, Nakh shared snippets of his background, hinting at hidden truths and his family's pursuit of knowledge while pondering the absence of his usual source of distilled water.

Upon entering the tavern, Omni burst into laughter, causing the room to fall silent as all eyes turned toward the group.

"HOLY SHIT! It's like a pirate, a cowboy, and a man in tights walked into a bar! Where are the cameras?"

His laughter echoed through the room, but the outlaws at the nearby table began to scowl.

Nakh thought to himself, *this doesn't seem like any act I've ever seen.*

Keem, trying to defuse the situation, stepped forward. "Omni, maybe tone it down a bit."

But Omni continued to laugh, oblivious to the growing tension. "Why? This is too funny!"

The tavern patrons began to rise from their seats, moving threateningly toward the group.

"These three think there's something funny. Let's see if they're still laughing after we cut them a bigger smile and see if we think that's funny," a pirate snarled.

A knight drew his sword, flames dancing along its edge. "How about we just burn their insides!" he threatened.

Before the situation could escalate further, Keem intervened, creating a powerful gust of wind that extinguished the flames and pushed back the advancing crowd. Meanwhile, Nakh rushed toward the knight while Omni conjured spiky thorns from the ground to fend off the remaining attackers.

Nakh engaged the knight in combat, skillfully dodging his fiery strikes. With a swift kick, Nakh disarmed the knight, causing the flames on his sword to sputter and die.

"That's a fancy sword you have. I can't wait to see how it handles in my hands," Nakh taunted.

"Death will be the only feeling you take away with this sword," the knight retorted, intensifying his sword's flames as he lunged at Nakh. The knight swung and slashed several more times. Nakh dodged all the attacks with a smirk on his face. Nakh kicked the sword out of the knight's hand, and the fire went out.

"Let's see how much of a chance you have on the other end of the blade," Nakh said as he picked up the sword.

Keem fought off the crowd with wind-combined attacks that cut sharper than the sharpest blades. Keem and Omni finished off the last of the crowd as Nakh got closer to the knight.

"What's going on here?" Nakh demanded.

"What do you mean? We are living! It's been this way for years now," the knight replied.

"But there is not supposed to be conscious life out here," Nakh stated, puzzled.

"Well, you are looking at it. So are you going to kill me or keep belittling me with these damn questions?" the knight yelled, standing defiantly.

Amidst the chaos, the tavern door swung open, and a figure stepped into the blinding sunlight. The man wore a pirate captain's hat, and the knight immediately dropped to one knee in deference.

"Who's this?" Omni asked.

"How many people get drunk during the day around this town?" Omni said while shading his eyes from the sun. The man had on a vest with a pirate captain hat. The knight lowered back down to one knee to bow his head.

"What the hell is his problem?" Omni muttered.

"This must be their leader or something," Keem speculated, preparing for another attack.

Wait, I know that face! Nakh thought to himself.

18

"I am weak, sir!" the knight shouted out. "Help us, Marius!"

"Nakh!" Omni and Keem's eyes widened as if they saw a ghost. Then, the three all looked at each other as Hutch walked closer out of the blinding shining sun.

"You two know him too?" Keem asked.

"That's my cousin. But weren't you... incarcerated?" Nakh said, looking at Hutch with joy.

"He's like a brother to me. But the rumor I heard was different. They said you had a medical problem and couldn't control yourself," Keem said as he shook Hutch's hand.

Hutch turned to Omni with a casual air, his eyes scanning the surroundings as he spoke, "Roll one of those up, Omni, while we walk and talk. I was headed out anyway."

He addressed the knight who had accompanied them, handing back his sword that Nakh had taken earlier. The knight nodded solemnly, "Right away, Marius," and dashed back toward the tavern.

Omni, feeling drained from the earlier fight, replied, "I only have enough energy to roll up one."

But before he could reach for the nearby well, Nakh intervened urgently, "STOP!"

His voice cut through the air with a sense of urgency that made Omni pause in his tracks. Nakh stepped forward, explaining, "That's not the water you should drink. It's hard water, unhealthy for the pineal."

Taking charge, Hutch strode over to a nearby bucket and picked it up, placing it carefully beside Omni. With a confident gesture, he extended his hand over the bucket, and clear, clean water began pouring out, as if from an invisible faucet.

Omni's eyes widened in surprise as he watched the water fill the bucket. He leaned forward, scooping some of it into his hands and bringing it to his lips. "You used to have the foggiest water when we were growing up. This is very different," he remarked.

Meanwhile, Keem, intrigued by the conversation, inquired, "Now, what's this about a pineal?"

Nakh seized the opportunity to educate them. He explained, "The city gave us fluoride water to harden our pineal and block us from using our energy. The Pineal is the third eye and the main source of God-like ability."

As they continued walking and conversing, Omni grew another cannabinoid plant, pondering the implications of Nakh's words. "So the foods from the earth will not be all I need to be at my max potential?" he mused aloud.

Nakh shook his head, a grave expression on his face. "No," he replied solemnly, "You may have power, but no control. Even worse, your energy doesn't even last long. There are many more things you must learn and implement."

Hutch, drawing from his own experience, interjected, "I've been out here for nine months. One day, while studying at Nakh's home, we were all learning about the benefits of distilled water. About five days passed after drinking only it, I felt my abilities begin to rise out of proportion, but I had control over it. That night, I had the most descriptive dream. It felt as if I were being talked to in person. I was told to leave the city but stay close. Train until I meet three strangers with familiar faces. The next day was a holiday, which meant the majority of people in the city didn't work, so the dome's energy wasn't as strong. When I arrived near the dome, two others were there. We escaped and have been here getting stronger. One of the two was my friend Dallas, the first mate, and the other one died in battle once we got to the second zone. We became stronger outside of the kingdom, that's how I got the name Marius. It means of the sea."

With his tale concluded, Hutch glanced ahead, noting the dark forest looming on the horizon as they walked.

As they delved deeper into the forest, the atmosphere grew increasingly eerie. Shadows danced among the twisted branches, and a sense of foreboding hung heavy in the air. Omni's unease was palpable, his instincts warning him of impending danger.

"There aren't any lions, tigers, or bears in this forest, are there?" Omni asked nervously.

Hutch's reassurance did little to quell Omni's growing apprehension. Despite the captain's confidence, the oppressive atmosphere seemed to amplify their vulnerability.

"I've never had a problem in this forest. I may be on the world's wanted list, but hey, a man's gotta make a living," Hutch said nonchalantly.

Omni's distrust only deepened as they pressed onward, the mist thickening around them like a sinister shroud. "I don't trust it," he muttered.

Suddenly, as if summoned by Omni's misgivings, a swirling mist enveloped them, obscuring their surroundings. From the heart of the fog emerged a figure, dark and menacing, his presence exuding an aura of malevolence.

"I am Fie, and I come for the darkness within you," the figure declared, his voice echoing ominously through the eerie silence.

The group exchanged wary glances, unsure of how to confront this unexpected threat.

"I can sense a great dark power, and I want it. More dark energy, and we can rule this world," Fie proclaimed, his laughter ringing out like a chilling prophecy.

Nakh's mind raced, grappling with the implications of Fie's words. Who was he referring to when he spoke of "we?"

"We have no problems with you," Hutch tried to reason, his voice steady despite the tension.

Fie advanced, his intentions clear. Hutch and Keem braced themselves for an imminent attack, but Fie's sudden disappearance left them on edge, uncertain of his next move.

Fie's insidious influence soon became apparent as Omni writhed in agony, his mind besieged by dark forces beyond his control. Desperate cries filled the air as Omni's transformation began, his body morphing into an instrument of destruction.

"He's releasing his Monster!" Hutch exclaimed, recognizing the gravity of their situation.

"Our only hope is to reach safety before Omni's rampage spirals out of control," Hutch urged. "My ship is not much further. We must tire him out, or we could lose our lives."

With spiked thorns sprouting from Omni's form, their peril grew more imminent by the second. Nakh knew that every moment counted as he resolved to divert Omni's attention, buying his companions precious time to escape the encroaching darkness.

"I'll distract him!" Nakh volunteered, his voice filled with determination.

As Nakh ascended to a higher branch, the weight of his responsibility pressed upon him like the dense fog creeping through the forest. Is this the monstrous entity foretold in his unsettling dreams? How does one confront such a formidable foe? These questions echoed in Nakh's mind as Omni's form shifted, morphing into an amalgamation of Earth's elements.

Meanwhile, Hutch, ever pragmatic, forged ahead toward the safety of the ship, with Keem in tow, each step a resolute stride toward escape. But Omni's transformation into an unstoppable force drew Nakh's attention like a moth to flame, his determination to protect his companions unwavering.

As spikes erupted from the ground where Nakh had stood moments before, he realized the futility of facing Omni head-on. Yet, a sense of duty propelled him forward, his agile movements akin to a dancer's grace amidst the chaos of the forest.

Dodging a barrage of debris launched by Omni's earth-shaking blows, Nakh sprinted toward Keem and Hutch, desperation lending wings to his feet. With a sudden tackle, he propelled them forward, narrowly escaping the deadly onslaught trailing behind.

As they regrouped, Hutch's crew hurried to their captain's side, their loyalty evident in their eager inquiries and offers of retribution. Hutch, commanding and composed, issued orders with precision, directing his crew to retrieve Omni's unconscious form and hasten their departure.

Amidst the flurry of activity, Keem's voice cut through the tension, demanding answers about the enigmatic figure known as Fie. Hutch's response, laden with uncertainty, hinted at the deeper mysteries lurking in the shadows, fueling their resolve to seek enlightenment.

With Dallas joining their midst, the final pieces of their party assembled, each member poised for the journey ahead. Hutch's resolve remained unshaken, his gaze fixed on the horizon where the island of knowledge beckoned, promising answers to their burning questions.

Dreams and Nightmares

Nakh joined Hutch and Keem on the captain's deck, the weight of their recent encounter heavy upon them like the oppressive humidity of a summer night at sea.

"So, have you seen that before? He was unstoppable," Nakh inquired, his fingers absently plucking a piece of fruit from his backpack.

Hutch's expression softened, tinged with concern as he replied, "I've seen it many times, but not that bad. He usually causes a little damage, and then we hide him before the soldiers come looking for him. When he purposely uses his ability, he tends to have more control. But anger or other deep emotions tend to bring the monster out of him."

Keem's voice sliced through the air, laced with anger and frustration. "Well, he is dangerous. He could have killed us all. He is the reason we are in this predicament now!"

Nakh's mind churned with the implications of their discussion. The warlock's interest in Omni's uncontrollable power hinted at deeper machinations, perhaps a sinister purpose lurking beneath the surface. Protecting Omni's life seemed paramount, a realization that settled heavily in Nakh's gut as he tossed his apple core overboard.

Hutch's decisive tone broke the tension, his words a beacon of pragmatism amidst the storm of emotions. "I'll have my men show you to your cabins. Let us get some rest for the night and worry about it tomorrow."

As Hutch departed, leaving them to their thoughts, Omni's dream swept him into a tumult of despair and anguish, the flickering flames of a burning city reflecting the turmoil within his soul. Amidst the carnage, lifeless bodies sprawled across the scorched earth, a haunting reminder of the devastation wrought by his inner turmoil.

"Why?" he cried out, his voice echoing into the abyss. "Why must I be a monster? What purpose does this darkness serve?" Tears streamed down his face, mingling with the ashes of his shattered dreams.

With trembling hands, Omni reached out to the lifeless forms of his family, their faces contorted in silent agony. "Did... Did I do this?" he murmured, his voice choked with guilt and sorrow.

As his sister's form dissolved into ash, slipping through his fingers like the sands of time, a celestial figure emerged from the darkness, bathed in ethereal light. Clad in robes and adorned with a mask reminiscent of a dog, the figure exuded an aura of serene wisdom.

"Every life has a meaning," the figure intoned, its voice resonating with the weight of ages. "Even amidst darkness, you have the power to create light. Good and evil are two sides of the same coin, each shaping the other in an eternal dance."

With a final admonition to "find your heart," the enigmatic being ascended into the heavens, leaving Omni to confront the depths of his soul. Awakening from his turbulent slumber, he found himself bathed in sweat, his heart racing with the echoes of his dream.

Beside him stood Nakh, a beacon of calm amidst the storm. "I had a feeling you were about to wake," Nakh said softly, offering Omni a cup of water. As Omni drank, the cool liquid soothed his parched throat, easing the lingering tension in his body.

"Where are we?" Omni asked, his voice still heavy with the weight of his dream.

"We're aboard Hutch's ship, headed toward the Island of Knowledge," Nakh replied, his tone reassuring.

As Omni tended to his cannabinoid plant, finding solace in the familiar rhythm of life, he couldn't shake the feeling that his dream held a deeper significance. With Nakh's reassurance that Keem and Hutch were safe, Omni felt a glimmer of hope amidst the darkness that threatened to engulf him.

"He disappeared, and then you turned into an unstoppable monster. I didn't let you hurt anyone, though. Keem and Hutch are safe," Nakh said, blowing out a cloud of smoke.

"It's like you knew that I was going to ask you if I hurt the others. I do not want to be the guy who has no control. It hurts me more to unknowingly hurt the people I love, trust, and care about," Omni said, taking the plant Nakh passed back to him.

"Do not worry. I will protect the people, and we will work together on helping you take full control of your abilities. I don't fear you, I accept you," Nakh said, walking out of the room.

Omni's face reflected shock as the wind blew out the flame of the lantern.

As the sunrise painted the sky with hues of orange and pink, Keem stood at the back of the boat, a fishing rod in hand. Hutch joined him, taking in the serene morning.

"Wish we could smoke this beautiful morning," Hutch remarked, casting his line into the water.

"I'll go wake up Omni," Keem said, starting to reel his line back in.

"No, no. Let him rest. We can go without for now. Want to have a friendly competition to take our minds off of it, like the old days?" Hutch suggested, stopping Keem.

"Well, it is getting closer to the time when everyone wakes up. How about whoever catches the most fish wins," Keem proposed.

"You're on!" Hutch declared, already feeling a tug on his line. He swiftly reeled in a fish, a triumphant grin spreading across his face. Keem frowned as Hutch cast his line again, laughing.

"That's one to your none," Hutch teased, clearly enjoying his lead.

Keem focused his intent on Hutch's hook, forming a circular motion of wind around it under the water. No fish could get near Hutch's hook now.

"This feels like a big one!" Keem yelled out, reeling in a fish even larger than Hutch's catch. Hutch shook his head and laughed.

Hutch focused his intent on Keem's hook as soon as he cast it into the water, removing a full circle of water around it. Keem became furious.

"You cheater! I'll win without a rod," Keem yelled, standing on the ledge and plucking fish from the water with great gusts of wind.

"Now, this is my type of game," Hutch said, joining Keem at the side.

The two started filling their area with tons of fish, their powers creating huge, vicious waves. The boat rocked harder and harder, prompting everyone to come out of their cabins to investigate the commotion. Omni and Nakh emerged to see a large tidal wave approaching.

"What the hell? That's bigger than the boat," Omni said, growing a cannabinoid plant beneath him. Nakh yelled to Hutch and Keem, "Stop the wave. It's getting closer!"

Dallas stepped up past Nakh and Omni, putting both hands out and closing his eyes. Omni and Nakh exchanged confused looks. When Dallas opened his eyes, they had an ice-cold glare, and his breath was visible as if it were snowing. He reached his arms out and spread his fingers.

"FROST," he commanded, and the wave began to freeze. All the surrounding water instantly turned to ice.

"Dammit, Dallas! Now you have the boat stuck in the ice, you damn show-off. You're lucky the island is right there," Hutch said, annoyed.

"So now we have to walk," Omni said with disappointment.

"Well, does anybody have a lighter? I'm ready," Omni added, jumping off the front of the boat onto the ice.

As the group approached the island, a curious sight awaited them: a large smoke cloud rising in the distance, signaling a welcoming party of sorts. Nakh couldn't help but voice his curiosity. "There's a welcoming party as if they were waiting for us. Why is that, Hutch?"

"I do not know. This is my first time here. I just always knew where it was," Hutch replied, his tone tinged with uncertainty as they continued their journey.

As they drew closer, the sound of enchanting music filled the air, and the sight of people dancing greeted them. Omni, ever eager for a celebration, wasted no time joining the festivities. "Now, this is more my speed. I love a good party!" he exclaimed, dancing his way into the heart of the gathering.

"Welcome!" the islanders greeted them warmly. "I'm Sir Winston, and today is our harvest. You are welcome to stay, eat, and party. What's ours is yours."

Keem wasted no time getting to the point. "Could you take us to your source of information? We have many questions to ask."

"You must wait until sunrise again, sir. The elders do not like to communicate after dark. But they are expecting you," Winston replied.

Meanwhile, Omni distributed his cannabinoid plants, urging Keem to relax and enjoy the festivities. "Let us enjoy ourselves and respect the elders. Plus, I haven't seen such pretty women since I met you," he quipped.

Keem handed Omni a lighter, his skepticism evident. "Since when did you become so noble?" he teased.

Noticing Dallas's proximity to his sword, Nakh couldn't help but inquire about his prowess. However, Hutch quickly vouched for Dallas's skills before Nakh could press further. "He's the best with any weapon you put in his hand. He's just not big with words," Hutch interjected before wandering off to join the others.

"I'll teach everyone a few things tomorrow. For now, let us have fun," Dallas declared as he finally joined the group, ready to embrace the festivities.

As the sun rose, awakening the island and its inhabitants, Keem found himself roused from sleep by a mysterious figure named Taki. She wasted no time informing them of the elder's summons.

One by one, Keem roused the others from their slumber, each awakening in their own unique manner. Finally, Omni joined the group, unfazed by the laughter surrounding him and ready to face the day's challenges with his usual nonchalance.

As they approached the hall of the elder's, the rising sun cast its golden rays upon the mirrored walls, creating a breathtaking display of light and shadow. Within, the three elder's awaited them, each bearing marks of wisdom and experience. Taki, their guide, offered a brief introduction, emphasizing the importance of paying attention to the elder's words and actions. With anticipation mounting, the group prepared to face the mysteries that lay ahead.

As they arrived at the hall of the elder's, the first rays of dawn began to illuminate the room. The sunlight danced off the mirror walls, casting ethereal reflections throughout the space. Three elder's sat at a round table, each bearing unique features that hinted at their wisdom. One elder's eyes were missing, another had no ears, and the last elder's mouth was tightly wrapped in cloth.

Taki stepped forward, addressing the group. "Our Elders are wise," she began, her voice echoing in the chamber. "You must pay close attention to their words and actions. They possess knowledge beyond our understanding, and they will reveal what you seek without you needing to voice it. But feel free to ask each elder one question."

The group exchanged glances, sensing the weight of the moment as they prepared to engage with the enigmatic elder's.

Nakh approached the elder with no eyes and asked, "What is this world?" He walked closer as the elder pulled out a scroll, which Nakh accepted before returning to the others.

Omni suddenly burst out, "Who is Fie?"

The reaction was immediate and intense. Two of the elder's eyes widened, and they abruptly stood from the table, striding past the group toward the exit. Once outside, the elder with their mouth tied up, pointed to the highest mountain.

"What an answer," Omni murmured under his breath.

Finally, Keem asked the last elder his question. "Where do our paths take us from here?"

The elder with no ears responded solemnly, revealing the dire situation their people faced. "Most of our people have been taken and placed into bondage inside the kingdom. The King and his men are preparing to wage war on us and take over the entire zone for themselves. Your path will be determined by the choices you make. Will you join forces with a group of strangers to protect a land that is not your own, or will you mind your own business and take your own route?"

With those words, the two elders walked back into the building, leaving the group to ponder their next steps. Taki then led them back down the path.

"What does it say on the scroll, Nakh?" asked Hutch. Nakh unrolled the scroll and placed two stones on the ends.

"It's a map. It shows the lands that the elders have viewed. It shows four different zones," Taki explained.

"But the elder was blind, and the mute one just pointed. The one who couldn't hear anything said the most. It's just confusing," Omni remarked.

"It says the city does not exist," Keem added.

"What city are you talking about?" asked Taki. Keem explained how they all came from the city and there was supposed to be no one living outside of it. The group then started walking away, escorted by Taki toward the training grounds.

Omni remained, looking up at the mountain with curiosity. "I must know what's up there," he thought to himself as Keem stood by his side.

"Let's find out what's up there," Keem suggested.

"We will meet you all back at the training ground," he told the group as he and Omni ran off and up the mountain.

Meanwhile, at the training ground, Nakh was beginning to learn a few lessons in swordplay.

"Here!" Dallas said, throwing a sword at Nakh.

"Heads up!" Hutch added, tossing another sword.

"Hutch told me a lot about you. And I saw what he meant when you went to get that scroll. The elder didn't even move, and you walked up knowing he was going to give you something," Dallas remarked as he made a few attacks at Nakh.

Nakh smirked as he blocked the attack with one sword and swung the other sword at Hutch before he could react.

"There is no reason fighting him with his eyes open; give him real training!" Hutch exclaimed, frustration evident in his voice as he threw his sword down and stepped aside. Dallas retrieved a cloth from his pocket and proceeded to blindfold Nakh. With focused intent, Dallas extended his hand and whispered, "Frost." Ice began to form from the ground, shaping itself into the likeness of a soldier.

"Now, since you can see with your intuition, can you feel with it as well?" Dallas questioned as the ice clone stood before Nakh.

Meanwhile, Omni and Keem reached the entrance of the cave. Darkness enveloped them, accompanied by a palpable energy.

"I felt this energy before, the morning after the dome," Keem remarked.

"Why didn't you tell anybody you felt such a strong force then if you did?" Omni questioned as they ventured further into the cave. The silence grew heavy around them.

"Hey, Keem. Let me see your lighter," Omni requested, flicking it, but it refused to stay lit. Before Keem could respond, Omni sparked the lighter again, revealing a colossal white dragon with fiery eyes. Frozen in fear, Omni couldn't move as the dragon unleashed a torrent of blue flames toward them.

"MOVE!" Keem shouted, pushing Omni out of harm's way.

"GOOO!" Keem yelled as Omni narrowly avoided the flames.

"NOOO!" Omni cried out, reaching back for Keem as he fell. Keem's piercing scream of agony reverberated through the cavern, causing Omni to lower his head, overwhelmed by the weight of his friend's pain.

"Not again," he whispered, his voice trembling with anguish. Tears welled up in Omni's eyes, tracing a path down his cheeks as he grappled with the helplessness of the situation. The echoes of Keem's suffering etched a haunting melody in Omni's mind, a stark reminder of the consequences of their perilous journey.

Seeds of Evolution

As Nakh continued to train on the ground, Dallas orchestrated his progress, summoning more ice soldiers to test Nakh's skills further. Amidst the flurry of icy attacks, Nakh demonstrated remarkable agility, evading most of the projectiles with ease.

His frustration bubbled to the surface as the first sickle of ice grazed his arm. "HEY!" he exclaimed, his voice echoing across the training ground. "If you think it's going to be a walk in the park, think again!"

Approaching Nakh with purpose, Dallas extended a unique-looking sword toward him. "I have something special from our sword collection that might interest you," he said, his tone filled with anticipation. "This one's tailored to your vibrational ability. It amplifies your power on contact and creates a sensory field within a fifty-foot radius, perfect for detecting nearby threats."

Taking the sword with a determined grip, Nakh felt a surge of confidence. With Dallas's guidance, he removed his blindfold, ready to embrace the full potential of his newfound abilities.

Determination etched on his face, Nakh stood poised for the challenges that lay ahead, eager to push himself to new heights.

Dallas, observing Nakh's progress with a keen eye, summoned ten ice soldiers to encircle him. "Use the sword as an extension of yourself," Dallas instructed, his voice steady with confidence. "Let it become your brush, painting a masterpiece for the world to see. These clones will test your speed and precision, so show them what you're made of."

With that, Dallas stepped back, leaving Nakh to face the onslaught alone. The ice soldiers moved with lightning speed, their movements a blur as they closed in on him.

Reacting with instinctual grace, Nakh leaped back, spinning around to strike down two clones behind him. The sword hummed with power as it sliced through the icy figures, scattering them into pieces. A low frequency emitted from the sword, resonating with Nakh's senses alone.

Sensing the approach of two clones from above, Nakh leaped into action, intercepting their attack with a daring maneuver. Using the first clone as a springboard, he propelled himself upwards, delivering a devastating blow that shattered both assailants.

As Nakh descended to the ground, he plunged the tuning sword into the earth, unleashing a powerful shockwave that reverberated through the ground, incapacitating the remaining clones.

Standing amidst the aftermath, Nakh couldn't resist a touch of sarcasm. "How was that for art?" he quipped, a smirk playing on his lips as he surveyed the scene of his triumph.

While Nakh honed his skills at the training ground, Omni grappled with his inner turmoil atop the mountain. Tears streaked down his face as he berated himself for his perceived failure. "Why did I freeze up? I could have moved out of the way, and Keem would still be alive," he lamented, his voice heavy with self-recrimination.

As he wiped away his tears with a trembling arm, a voice cut through the silence, shattering his self-pity. "I never knew a monster could cry. What a chump," the voice mocked, its tone dripping with disdain. Turning, Omni was met with the sight of Keem engulfed in blue flames, his body illuminated by the fiery glow.

Confusion and disbelief warred within Omni as he watched Keem rise to his feet, seemingly unscathed by the flames that licked at his skin. "Who the hell are you calling a chump?

Wait... How the hell are you not burning? Keem, what is going on?" Omni stammered, his mind struggling to comprehend the surreal scene unfolding before him.

Keem's expression was unreadable as he gazed upon his own form, bathed in the brilliant light of the flames. "I can feel the energy surging within me. I can even feel the control of it," he mused to himself, his voice tinged with wonder and awe. And then, to Omni's astonishment, Keem began to levitate, defying the laws of gravity with apparent ease, leaving Omni speechless, his mouth hanging open in disbelief.

"It's Whitey's doing," a mature female voice echoed from the darkness, breaking the tense silence. Omni remained still, his senses alert, while Keem absorbed the fire and turned his attention to the woman emerging from the shadows. Clad in a dark robe adorned with bright yellow eyes, she introduced herself as Pi.

Omni's body trembled with apprehension as he blurted out, "That name is close to Fie!" Keem shook his head at Omni's realization, muttering to himself, "Duh, dummy." Gathering his composure, Keem stepped closer to Pi, his curiosity piqued.

"What is going on, and what do you know about Fie?" he asked, his voice steady despite the turmoil within.

Pi met their gaze with an unwavering stare. "You have inherited the soul of the dragon, and Fie is my twin brother," she revealed, her words hanging heavy in the air. Omni's mind raced with questions, his fear mingling with a newfound sense of purpose.

Pi continued, recounting her recent encounter with the dark energy and Fie's relentless pursuit of power. "I felt the energy three days ago when Whitey and I went out to seek it," she explained. "Once I realized it wasn't who I was looking for, I returned here."

Omni's voice was barely a whisper as he asked, "What do you want with me?"

Pi's response was solemn yet tinged with longing. "Nothing. I was looking for my loved one that Fie took from me years ago. I was hoping to see those brown eyes again," she confessed, her voice filled with sorrow.

Returning from the darkness, Pi presented them with a dragon egg, a relic of Whitey's legacy. "This is Whitey's last egg, and she would like for you to have it. Protect this egg with your life, and it will protect you forever," Pi declared, her words carrying the weight of a solemn oath. As they prepared to leave the mountain, Keem accepted the egg, placing it carefully in his backpack. As they descended from Pi's mountain, her words lingered in Keem's mind, filling him with newfound determination. "Now fly like a dragon in the wind," she had said, and Keem embraced the feeling of freedom as he carried Omni with him through the air.

"How do I get rid of the darkness? It's not like I decided to be dark. Hell, I almost broke down when I thought you died," Omni confessed to Keem as they neared the ground.

"I am alright," Keem reassured him, his voice steady despite the weight of their conversation.

Once they landed, Omni and Keem made their way back to the training ground in silence, each lost in their own thoughts. The setting sun painted the sky with hues of orange and pink as they finally arrived.

"So, what did you find out about Fie?" Nakh asked, breaking the silence as Omni grew a cannabinoid plant from the ground. "And what's up with that egg?" Nakh added, eyeing the dragon egg that Keem carried.

Omni, distracted by the weight of their recent encounters, absentmindedly reached for his lighter to ignite the rolled plant. However, before he could do so, Keem focused his intent on the tip of the plant, and it burst into flame with a vibrant blue hue, stunning everyone present. The group stood in a state of astonishment, their eyes fixed on Keem's display of his newfound power.

"Wow!" Hutch exclaimed, breaking the silence as murmurs of amazement rippled through the group.

As they began discussing their evolving abilities, Omni silently passed the plant, his mind preoccupied with unspoken worries.

"Where are you going?" Nakh's voice rang out, punctuating the air with concern.

"I've smoked enough for the night. I'm going to bed," Omni replied tersely, his demeanor distant as he retreated to the sleeping area, his hands buried in his pockets, and his footsteps heavy with unresolved thoughts.

The following morning, Nakh awoke to find Omni in his room, the scent of the cannabinoid plant wafting through the air. Concern etched on his face, Nakh approached his friend, ready to delve into the unspoken concerns that weighed heavily on Omni's mind.

"What time is it?" Nakh asked, breaking the silence of the morning.

Omni, lost in contemplation, glanced at the dimly lit room. "I don't know. But can you tell me more about the pineal thing you brought up a few days ago?" he inquired, seeking knowledge to distract himself from his inner turmoil.

Nakh, ever patient, sat up in bed, ready to share his wisdom. "The pineal gland is known as the third eye, and it serves as your conduit to spiritual energy. Positioned as the sixth chakra out of seven, it governs the flow of your energy," he explained calmly, reaching for the plant and taking a puff before passing it back to Omni.

As the smoke swirled around them, Nakh continued, "Meditation is the key to unlocking and harnessing this energy. I'll guide you through some techniques later today."

Omni remained seated, the weight of his thoughts evident in his furrowed brow. Sensing his friend's need for company, Nakh tossed aside his bedcovers and swung his legs over the edge of the bed. "Okay, okay, okay. Let's go!" he declared, offering a reassuring smile to Omni, ready to support him through whatever challenges lay ahead.

Hutch, Keem, Dallas, Nakh, and Omni gathered together on the training ground, ready for another day of honing their skills. "We came up with a group name last night. We are now

The Root," announced Hutch, his voice filled with determination. However, Omni remained silent, his mind preoccupied with his own inner struggles.

They formed a circle, crossing their legs as they prepared to focus their energies. Hutch, Dallas, and Nakh closed their eyes, clasping their hands together in front of them, while Omni observed, intrigued. Around Hutch, a powerful stream of water began to flow, encircling him with its fluid energy. Dallas, on the other hand, was enveloped in ice, the chill emanating from it palpable even from a distance.

Omni, ever curious, leaned toward Nakh, noticing a peculiar absence of visible energy. "Where's Nakh's energy?" he questioned, extending his hand forward in an attempt to understand. However, as his hand approached Nakh, he encountered an invisible barrier—a vibrational field surrounding Nakh that prevented Omni from passing through.

The three stopped meditating, and Hutch began to explain, "Okay, that was meditating. It's been enough time for the distilled water to soften your pineal gland and open your third eye. You have to connect the chakras in your hands together to intertwine your energy. Once you connect your chakras, you will feel your energy pulse at your fingertips. Clear your mind from all of your thoughts and allow the energy to flow."

Omni, though skeptical, nodded and joined the circle. He closed his eyes and tried to follow Hutch's instructions. As he concentrated, he felt a faint warmth beginning to build in his hands. Slowly, it spread, becoming a gentle pulse that resonated through his fingertips.

Following Hutch's instructions, Keem and Omni closed their eyes, joined their hands, and began to meditate. Keem's meditation started off low and windy, his energy swirling around him like a gentle breeze. Sensing the movement of energy, Omni cautiously opened one eye, feeling the wind from Keem's energy.

As Omni stood up and backed away with Nakh, Dallas, and Hutch, Nakh shouted, "Get back!" anticipating something unusual. Suddenly, Keem's energy intensified, and fire joined in with the flow. The three companions jumped back even further, their eyes widening in astonishment as a dragon began to form out of Keem's energy, its majestic form taking shape before them.

Taki's urgent call interrupted the meditation session, and Keem's energy lowered as he emerged from his meditative state.

"We saved a few of our citizens from the kingdom, and our soldiers are back. Come to the shore!" she exclaimed, her voice filled with urgency.

Rushing to the shore, the group witnessed a scene of chaos as small boats arrived, carrying injured people. Omni immediately ran to assist a citizen with a missing arm, his heart heavy with concern. "What happened?" he asked, his voice tinged with empathy.

"The King is mad. He captured us and forced us to be slaves. We are worked and drained of our energy until we can barely lift our eyelids. Many have died working, and he impregnates the women to create more workers. He is mad. He even kills his own men for the smallest reasons," the citizen explained, his words painting a grim picture of the kingdom's brutality.

With a solemn nod, Omni helped carry the injured citizen into the medical tent, his mind reeling with the horrors of the kingdom's tyranny.

Dallas pointed out to the sea, his finger tracing the silhouette of a ship on the horizon. "There's the ship, Marius!" he exclaimed to Hutch, his voice carrying a note of urgency.

General Rock, accompanied by some of his soldiers, approached the Root group. Taki stepped forward to address them. "These men have been with us for a few days and were given a hard decision from the elders. The kingdom has been planning on attacking us, but we do not know when. Helping us would be the decision and their choice to choose from," she explained, her words weighted with the gravity of their situation.

General Rock scrutinized the members of Root, his gaze lingering on each of them. His men exchanged murmurs among themselves, contemplating the implications of their decision. Finally, General Rock spoke, his voice firm and resolute. "I have men and a ship as well. I'm down for the cause, and so are my men. What do you say, Dallas?" he inquired, turning to face Dallas directly.

Hutch turned to Dallas, anticipation evident in his expression. *This is my dream. But I've never been to war before. And we would be on enemy territory. But I am stronger than before,* Keem thought to himself, his confidence bolstering his resolve.

"I'm all in!" Keem declared, throwing his arm up in a gesture of determination.

General Rock chuckled heartily at Nakh's words. "The choice was always yours. I cannot turn down the words of the elders. Plus, we could use the help. We lost many men on our last trip to bring back captured citizens," he admitted, his tone carrying a hint of resignation.

"Why should we wait for them to attack? We should go after them before they can strategize a plan. The element of surprise has always been the best element," Nakh proposed confidently, extending his hand toward General Rock in a gesture of camaraderie.

General Rock regarded Nakh with a nod of agreement, his expression reflecting a sense of shared purpose. "Agreed. Let's make our move," he declared, firmly grasping Nakh's hand in a handshake of alliance.

In the medical tent, Omni's concern for the wounded drove him to seek answers from the attending doctor. After assisting a wounded man onto a bed, he approached the doctor with a series of questions weighing on his mind.

"How do you manage to heal these people, considering the severity of their injuries?" Omni inquired, his voice reflecting a mix of compassion and curiosity. "Many of them have lost limbs, and others appear malnourished. How do you plan to restore their strength and vitality?"

The doctor, accustomed to the grim realities of their situation, responded calmly but with a hint of weariness in his tone. "Our approach involves halting blood circulation to the severed limbs and administering herbal remedies for pain relief. As for nutrition, fresh foods are crucial, but our supplies are insufficient given the overwhelming number of patients requiring care."

Omni's brow furrowed in thought as he contemplated the doctor's words. "What resources do you lack?" he inquired, eager to assist in any way he could. In response, the doctor retrieved a medical book on natural healing and handed it to Omni. "We're running low on coca leaves for pain management, and our food stores are depleted. Many of the injured have lost their appetite, making it challenging to replenish their strength. Do you have a plan to acquire these supplies?" the doctor queried, retreating to the rear of the tent.

As the ship finally arrived, Hutch, Dallas, and Keem hurried to greet it, eager to see what aid or allies it might bring. Meanwhile, Nakh made his way to the medical tent, intending to find Omni and join him in assisting the wounded.

Upon entering the tent, Nakh noticed the bustling activity and inquired about Omni's whereabouts, receiving gestures pointing toward the rear. Following the direction indicated, Nakh found Omni amidst a field of herbs, fruits, and vegetables meticulously tended to.

Curious, Nakh queried, "What's all this for?"

"I've cultivated every plant mentioned in this book," Omni explained, gesturing toward the comprehensive tome. "And I've even synthesized them into a regenerative pill—a potent blend of energy-producing plants in concentrated form. I'm aiding the wounded and the doctors, but I have a pressing question," he added, his expression serious.

"What's on your mind?" Nakh inquired as they strolled back through the tent.

"Are we going to take down that tyrant king?" Omni asked, his voice tinged with anger as he extracted a rolled cannabinoid plant and lighter from his pocket.

Nakh's response was resolute. "Absolutely. Hopefully, first thing in the morning. They won't be expecting visitors," he declared with a hint of amusement, envisioning the element of surprise they could wield. With a determined nod, Omni sparked the plant, taking a puff before raising his voice in a defiant proclamation. "WE ARE ROOT, AND WE WILL SAVE YOUR PEOPLE!" His words ignited a wave of cheers and renewed hope among the islanders, echoing the resilience and determination of their small but resolute band.

Freedom Fighters

As the boats set sail under the cover of night, anticipation for the impending confrontation hung heavy in the air. Root and the soldiers prepared themselves for battle, equipping themselves with weapons, armor, and medical supplies. Hutch's boat was to carry Root and General Rock while the soldiers rode alongside in smaller vessels.

Omni meticulously distributed regen pills and food supplies to the soldiers, ensuring they were as prepared as possible for the impending conflict. With the battle plan in place, Root and General Rock were ready to embark on their mission.

As the last to board the ship, Omni and Nakh exchanged a solemn moment. "Are you ready?" Nakh inquired, concern evident in his voice. Omni's response carried a mix of determination and uncertainty. "I can't fathom what drives a man to such depths of cruelty—kidnapping, enslaving, even murder. Fie's darkness pales in comparison. But I'm resolved to put an end to it," he stated, rolling a cannabinoid plant as they walked toward the meeting cabin.

Inside, the rest of the group awaited, eager to learn more about their adversary. "Tell us about the King," Keem urged

General Rock, the faint glow of Omni's ignited plant illuminating the tense atmosphere.

General Rock's words painted a grim picture of the king's atrocities. "He strikes deals with outsiders, trading technology for gold," he began, his voice heavy with disdain. "And he imports slaves, many of whom are unable to control their abilities."

The group listened intently, horrified by the revelation. "These slaves are kept imprisoned in cells within the kingdom's largest building," General Rock continued, his tone growing more somber. "But perhaps his most heinous act is the coliseum—his prized possession. He erects a force field around the battle zone and forces the slaves to fight for his entertainment."

Omni's voice cut through the silence, filled with both anger and disbelief. "What kind of experiments?" he demanded, passing the ignited plant to General Rock.

"He seeks to strip the slaves of their god-like abilities," General Rock explained grimly. "Yet, his endeavors have yielded no success. Every slave subjected to his experiments has perished. The King believes that wealth is the only true power, and since the slaves possess no riches, he deems them unworthy of their abilities."

General Rock's revelation sparked a fire within the group. "I've never faced the King himself," he admitted, his voice tinged with determination. "But my men and I have clashed with his soldiers on numerous occasions."

He continued, his tone becoming more resolute. "The soldiers don steel suits for protection against swords, a testament to the King's paranoia. However, within his castle, he maintains only five guards to carry out his commands. But be warned, he also has two formidable royal guards—figures we must be wary of."

The group exchanged glances, steeling themselves for the upcoming confrontation with the King and his forces. General Rock's description of the two royal guards sent a shiver down the group's spines. "Meet Mechanic and Ooze," he announced gravely. "Ooze is a master of close-range combat. His staff can transform into any weapon he desires, making him a deadly adversary up close. What's more, he possesses a lethal poison that courses through his chakras, capable of incapacitating with just a touch."

As the group absorbed this information, General Rock continued, his tone growing darker. "Mechanic, on the other hand, is a fusion of man and machine. His cybernetic limbs and facial features belie a dark history of experimentation. He excels in long-range combat, with his mechanical arms capable of transforming into devastating weapons. However, his vulnerability lies in his human half—any contact with bare skin could prove fatal."

The gravity of the situation weighed heavily on the group as they contemplated the formidable foes they would soon face. As Nakh outlined the plan, Keem's mind raced with possibilities. "Could the outsiders the kingdom trades with be the city?" he pondered silently, the pieces of the puzzle slowly falling into place.

"First, Keem and I will infiltrate the kingdom quietly," Nakh began, his voice steady and determined. "We'll free the slaves in the coliseum, inciting them to rebel against their oppressors. Once they're liberated, we'll demolish the coliseum to ensure it can never be used for such atrocities again."

Nakh's instructions continued, each step carefully calculated to maximize their chances of success. "Omni, you'll lead a team to free the remaining slaves, while Hutch and Dallas target the enemy's pier, disrupting their supply lines. Meanwhile, General Rock will coordinate a full-scale assault on the kingdom, drawing the attention of the King and his elite guards."

With the plan laid out and the flames of the plant extinguished, Nakh urged his comrades to prepare for the coming battle. "Be ready by morning, everyone," he concluded, his voice resonating with determination as they dispersed to their cabins. In the quiet of his own room, Keem tenderly placed the dragon egg in its makeshift bed, whispering a promise to protect it as he settled in for the night.

As the first light of dawn painted the sky, Root began their preparations for the impending battle. Each member engaged in a light meditation, focusing their minds and honing their energies for the challenges ahead. On the deck of the ship, Nakh approached Omni, who sat in meditation, the smoke of the cannabinoid plant swirling around him.

"It's time. Are you ready?" Nakh inquired, his tone carrying a mix of urgency and resolve.

Omni paused for a moment, contemplating the weight of the upcoming conflict. "I'm not sure. Everyone has grown and become much stronger. But I believe in your plan, and I believe in you. Together, we will put an end to this tyranny," he affirmed as they left the cabin, heading toward the bow of the ship.

Omni distributed regen pills to his comrades as they gathered at the front of the ship, their faces set in determined expressions. Nakh outlined the plan, dividing them into two groups and assigning specific tasks to each.

"Hutch and Dallas, you'll take one boat and head to the shipyard. Await the signal before taking action," Nakh instructed, his voice firm and commanding. "Keem, Omni, and I will take another boat to the kingdom. Once ashore, Keem and I will proceed to the coliseum by air. When the slaves are safely evacuated, Keem will launch a fireball into the sky. Hutch, Dallas, that will be your cue. Meet us at the king's throne."

With a resolute laugh, Nakh leaped from the ship onto a smaller boat, his confidence bolstered by the unwavering determination of his comrades.

As Nakh's boat glided toward the shore, Omni and the soldiers leaped out, swiftly making their way toward the slave encampment, guided by a soldier familiar with the layout of the kingdom. Meanwhile, Keem took to the skies, bearing Nakh aloft as they blended seamlessly with the early light of dawn.

The kingdom sprawled before them, its structures gleaming in the gentle glow of the rising sun, casting long shadows across the landscape. Navigating the air currents, Keem and Nakh scanned the horizon, searching for their target.

"Do you see the biggest building?" Keem called out to Nakh, his voice carried on the breeze.

Nakh squinted, his eyes scanning the cityscape below. "No, but I see the castle. It seems to blend seamlessly with the rest of the city," he remarked, a hint of confusion in his tone.

Suddenly, Keem's keen eyes caught sight of their destination. "There! It's right there!" he exclaimed, his voice filled with determination as he began to descend toward the looming structure, the first rays of sunlight painting its towering walls in hues of gold and amber.

Omni and the soldiers crept closer to the slaveholding, their movements masked by the cover of bushes. The structure loomed before them, resembling a prison with its lack of towering walls.

"Once we free the slaves, I want you to lead me to the King's castle," Omni instructed the soldier who had guided them before, turning to address another soldier. "And you, lead the weaker slaves back to the ship and inform General Rock to prepare for the attack on the castle," he commanded, his voice firm with resolve.

As they observed the entrance, guarded by two sword-wielding sentinels, Omni's keen eyes scanned the perimeter, noting the peculiar lack of defenses. His brow furrowed in contemplation, his mind racing to unravel the mystery. "With only two guards, why don't they fight back?" he murmured to himself, his voice barely audible amidst the tension of the moment. "Are these slaves so utterly broken, their will to survive extinguished, that they willingly participate in their own demise?"

A sense of unease settled over him as he pondered the possibilities, the weight of the situation pressing down on his shoulders. The air crackled with anticipation, each passing second stretching into eternity as Omni wrestled with the implications of what lay ahead.

"They'd be outnumbered," he reasoned, his voice tinged with determination as he steeled himself for the imminent confrontation. Gripping the hilt of his weapon with firm resolve, he exchanged a silent nod with his companions, signaling their readiness to take action.

Manipulating the vines that sprouted from the earth, he swiftly ensnared the guards, immobilizing them. Seizing the opportunity, the soldiers swiftly subdued the guards, rendering them incapacitated. With the path cleared, Omni and the soldiers moved forward to pry open the heavy door, anticipation coursing through their veins as they prepared to confront the challenges that lay beyond.

Hutch and Dallas finally located the shipyard, their boat skimming silently through the water as they discussed their strategy.

"We'll combine our attack for our first move, then get up close and personal like usual," Hutch relayed to Dallas, their voices low as they huddled on the deck, appearing as inconspicuous as possible from a distance.

Meanwhile, Keem and Nakh descended into the heart of the coliseum, surrounded by a swarm of guards. With a determined glare, Keem's eyes blazed with fiery intensity as he extended his hand, conjuring a massive ring of flames around them. Simultaneously, Nakh manipulated the air around them, forming a swirling vortex of wind just inside the perimeter of the fire.

With a forceful push, Keem directed the gusts of wind to merge with the flames, creating a powerful conflagration that sent the guards hurtling backward. Seizing the moment, Nakh drew his tuning sword, its resonant vibrations rippling through the air as he brought it down upon the ground with precision, shattering the force field that imprisoned the slaves.

Together, Keem and Nakh sprinted forward, their movements fueled by determination, as they worked swiftly to unlock the doors and liberate the captives from their chains, their actions marking the beginning of the long-awaited rebellion against the oppressive rule of the Kingdom.

As Omni swung open the door, the dim light revealed a harrowing sight: a multitude of weary and battered souls, their eyes reflecting years of suffering and oppression. The air was heavy with despair, each breath filled with the collective anguish of the enslaved.

Without hesitation, the soldiers surged forward, their movements fueled by a shared commitment to liberation. They worked tirelessly, freeing the captives from their chains and guiding them toward the path of freedom.

Witnessing the dire state of the slaves, Omni's heart swelled with empathy and determination. Drawing from his reserves, he conjured a supply of regen pills and cast them into the midst of the crowd. "Take these," his voice cut through the despair, ringing with urgency and compassion. "Reclaim your strength and your will to fight!"

Though the darkness of their plight weighed heavily upon them, Omni's gesture offered a glimmer of hope amidst the shadows. With renewed resolve, the slaves began to reach out for the pills, their spirits bolstered by the promise of newfound energy and resilience.

The slave's words struck Omni like a heavy blow, his heart sinking with the weight of their despair. He watched as the slave, worn and weary, approached him with a mixture of defiance and resignation.

"What makes you think you can change what's going on here?" the slave's voice was filled with bitterness and skepticism. "If we are free now, we would be slaves again tomorrow. Who would feed us? Where would we stay? You cannot change the system without money."

Omni listened in silence, the gravity of the slave's words weighing heavily upon him. The reality of their situation was stark and unforgiving. It wasn't just about breaking their physical chains; it was about dismantling the oppressive system that held them captive, a system woven with threads of poverty and exploitation.

The slave's voice trembled with a mixture of anger and resignation as he continued, "We will work until we die. If it is not for the king, then we would be slaving for some other ruler. Did you bring us all money?"

Omni's gaze softened with empathy as he met the slave's eyes. He understood their despair, their fear of exchanging one form of servitude for another. Yet, in that moment, he also saw a spark of defiance, a flicker of hope amidst the darkness.

"I brought no money, sir," Omni reiterated, his voice firm but tinged with sadness. "I just came with my faith in freedom, and I believe we can end this cycle."

But the slave's response was curt and final, his resolve hardened by years of hardship and oppression. "If you cannot buy my freedom, then you cannot save me," he declared, his words heavy with the weight of bitter experience.

Omni watched as the slaves returned to the fold of defiant souls, their spirits battered but unbroken, their resilience a testament to the indomitable human spirit. In that moment, Omni realized that their liberation would require more than just physical freedom; it would demand a revolution of hearts and minds, a collective uprising against the tyranny of injustice.

Omni's voice, filled with passion and conviction, cut through the heavy atmosphere of despair that hung over the chamber. As he spoke, his words carried a spark of hope, igniting a flame of defiance within the hearts of the downtrodden slaves.

"I may not be able to buy everyone's freedom," Omni began, his tone resolute, "but if any one of you believes in freedom and is willing to fight for it, then we can make a change now."

His words resonated with a profound truth, stirring something deep within the souls of those who listened. Slowly, heads lifted, eyes met, and a shared sense of determination began to take root.

"My life has no price on it, and neither does yours," Omni continued, his voice growing stronger with each word. "So join me. Let me help you liberate yourselves from this tyrant!"

With his head held high and his fist raised in defiance, Omni stood as a beacon of hope amidst the darkness. In that moment, he became more than just a liberator; he became a symbol of courage, inspiring those around him to rise up and reclaim their freedom.

As the echoes of his words faded into the silence, a sense of resolve settled over the chamber. The slaves, once resigned to their fate, now stood united in their determination to fight for a better tomorrow. With Omni leading the way, they knew that anything was possible.

As the chaos unfolded and the slaves poured out of the coliseum, their pent-up fury exploding into a frenzy of destruction, Keem's expression darkened with anger. He moved with purpose, intent on quelling the violence before it spiraled out of control. But before he could intervene, Nakh's voice cut through the tumult, halting him in his tracks.

"Nakh, they're destroying everything!" Keem protested, his eyes blazing with a mix of frustration and concern.

Nakh placed a reassuring hand on Keem's shoulder, his gaze steady and calm amidst the chaos. "I know, but sometimes, the only way to break free is to let the fire burn itself out."

Keem's brow furrowed in uncertainty, torn between his desire to protect the innocent and his trust in Nakh's wisdom.

Yet, as he looked around at the devastation wrought by generations of oppression, he knew that Nakh was right.

Reluctantly, Keem nodded, his fiery aura flickering as he suppressed his urge to intervene. With a deep breath, he steadied himself, channeling his energy toward a different purpose – not to quench the flames, but to ensure that they burned brightly enough to illuminate the path to freedom.

Together, Keem and Nakh stood amidst the chaos, their resolve unyielding as they watched the city burn. For in the crucible of destruction, they knew that the seeds of revolution were being sown, paving the way for a new dawn of liberation.

As Nakh's words settled over the scene, Keem's conflicted emotions churned within him. Anger and frustration warred with a sense of duty and trust in Nakh's guidance. With a deep breath, Keem made his decision.

His eyes ablaze with a fiery mix of red and blue, Keem strode purposefully toward the towering wall of the coliseum. Each step crackled with energy, the air pulsating with the raw power emanating from him.

Reaching the wall, Keem paused, the flames dancing around him in a mesmerizing display of power. With a focused intensity, he directed his energy, channeling it into his hands as if forging a weapon from the very essence of fire itself.

A surge of power erupted from Keem's palms, a searing torrent of flames engulfing the wall with ferocious intensity. The once-imposing barrier crumbled before his might, reduced to nothing more than smoldering debris.

In the wake of destruction, Keem stood, a lone figure amidst the chaos, his actions signaling the beginning of a revolution. Though the path ahead was uncertain, his resolve burned brighter than ever, a beacon of hope for those who dared to challenge the chains of oppression. As the flames consumed the wall of the coliseum, chaos erupted within the city. The crackling of fire intertwined with the shouts of the enslaved and the clatter of crumbling structures, creating a symphony of destruction that echoed through the streets.

Keem's fiery display served as a beacon of defiance, a signal to his comrades Hutch and Dallas, urging them to join the fray. With a determined expression, Keem raised his hands skyward, summoning forth a massive fireball that soared high into the air.

The blazing orb arced gracefully against the backdrop of the awakening dawn, casting a fiery glow over the city. Its ascent was a clarion call, a declaration of rebellion that reverberated throughout the kingdom, igniting the spirit of resistance in those who had long suffered under the king's tyranny.

As the flames licked the sky and the city erupted in chaos, Root's resolve solidified. The battle for freedom had begun, and there was no turning back.

The King's Fall

As the fireball hung in the sky like a burning sun, its message was clear: the time for liberation had come, and Root would stop at nothing to ensure that freedom prevailed.

The fiery blaze erupted in the distance, catching the attention of Dallas and Hutch. A silent understanding passed between them.

"There it is," Dallas remarked, his gaze fixed on the distant spectacle.

Hutch, rising to his feet, followed Dallas's gaze. "I see it," he acknowledged with urgency. "Keem's signal. Let's get to work."

With swift determination, they redirected their focus toward their next objective. Hutch channeled his energy toward the water, conjuring waves that surged toward the shipyard. Initially gentle, the waves gained strength, causing the boats to sway and shift. With each passing moment, Hutch's concentration intensified, fueling the waves until they rose high above the ships, crashing against the pier with formidable force. Dallas, meanwhile, focused his intent on the colossal tidal wave racing toward the shipyard, its towering form threatening to engulf everything in its path.

As the wave surged forward, sucking up boats and ships in its wake, Dallas extended his arms outward, his power coalescing around him. With a mighty effort, he froze the tidal wave and all the water, trapping the vessels within a frozen prison. Hutch and Dallas leaped off the boat, their feet pounding against the ice as they sprinted toward the towering frozen wave looming over the shipyard.

The soldier guided Omni toward the imposing castle, their footsteps echoing through the deserted streets of the Kingdom. Meanwhile, the other soldier led the majority of the liberated slaves back to the safety of the ship. In the chaotic wake of their liberation, the remaining slaves scattered through the Kingdom, unleashing havoc and disorder wherever they tread.

A substantial contingent of the king's guards converged upon the coliseum, their presence marked by the clatter of armored footsteps and the gleam of polished weapons. Hovering above the scene, Mechanic commanded attention with his jet boosters roaring to life beneath his feet.

"I got him!" Keem declared, soaring upward toward Mechanic with determination etched into his features, even as the guards closed in on Nakh from all sides.

Nakh charged forward, swiftly closing the distance between himself and the guards. With a powerful leap, he vaulted into their midst, swinging his sword with precision and ferocity. As the blade connected with the guards, a rippling wave of vibrational energy emanated from the point of impact, sending shockwaves surging through their ranks and knocking most of them back with force.

Mechanic raised his arms, and his hands transformed into missile launchers. With a swift motion, he fired two missiles downward, aiming for Keem. Reacting quickly, Keem dodged the missiles, narrowly avoiding the explosive impact as they steamed behind him but toward Nakh. As the missiles hurtled toward Nakh, he reacted swiftly, seizing one of the guards and hurling him upwards into the path of the incoming projectile. The missile struck the unfortunate guard, causing a violent explosion that engulfed him in flames. Nakh deftly evaded the second missile, swiftly dodging out of harm's way as it exploded, taking out two other guards in its fiery blast.

Keem reached Mechanic and swung at him two times with his fists covered in flames. Mechanic managed to dodge one punch but took the other squarely to the face as he simultaneously shot missiles out and flew back to create distance. Mechanic's robotic face began to melt as he transformed one of his hands into a frost gun, aiming it directly at Keem.

Back at the shipyard, Hutch and Dallas confronted a group of guards, ready to defend their mission. As they braced themselves for battle, Hutch's gaze locked onto their adversaries, while Dallas conjured an ice sword, ready to strike. With a silent nod exchanged between them, they moved seamlessly into action, their movements fluid and synchronized as they stood back-to-back, prepared to face whatever challenges came their way.

As Ooze charged toward Hutch with a tomahawk in hand, his imposing figure cast a shadow over the shipyard. His muscular frame exuded power, and his eyes gleamed with fierce determination. With each step, the ground seemed to tremble beneath him, emphasizing his formidable presence. As he raised his weapon, the glint of the blade caught the sunlight, adding an ominous edge to his menacing aura.

Hutch swiftly reacts, his body liquefying as if made of water, allowing him to avoid Ooze's attack effortlessly. Dripping onto the floor, Hutch's liquid form slithers behind Ooze as he launches his attack. Dallas swiftly reacts, spinning around to block Ooze's incoming strike with his ice sword. With Dallas engaged in defense, Hutch seizes the opportunity. Solidifying back into his body, he maneuvers behind Ooze, ready to launch a counterattack.

"We got him!" Dallas declared triumphantly to Hutch, their coordinated efforts proving effective as they gained the upper hand in the intense battle.

"Watch out, Dallas!" Hutch's warning came just in time as a guard rushed behind Dallas, poised to strike. Reacting swiftly, Dallas leaped out of harm's way, narrowly evading both the guard's attack and Ooze's deadly tomahawk.

However, as the guard lunged forward, the momentum of his charge carried him directly into Ooze's path. With a swift and decisive motion, Ooze thrust his tomahawk forward, piercing through the guard's defense and embedding it deep into his body, effectively neutralizing the guard.

"Almost had me there," Ooze remarked casually as he retrieved his weapon from the fallen guard's body, his tone laced with a hint of amusement.

Hutch turned to confront the oncoming guards, engaging them in combat as Dallas swiftly transformed his body into pure ice, crafting another sword to aid in the fight.

Meanwhile, Ooze adjusted his tomahawk, transforming it into a double-ended sword, all while removing his gloves with menacing intent.

With a determined glint in his eyes, Dallas faced Ooze and the guards, his ice sword poised for battle. "Let's dance," he said, his voice steady and resolute.

Omni strode into the castle, determination etched into his expression as he confronted the chamber where the King was guarded by five formidable warriors. The soldier accompanying him braced for the imminent clash, the tension palpable in the air. As they entered the hall, the five guards sprang into action, brandishing their spears and forming a defensive line to protect their sovereign.

"I knew someone would come, but I was expecting a slave. Get them out of my sight!" The King's command echoed through the hall as he reclined on his throne, taking a swig of his alcohol. With a dismissive wave, he signaled his guards to dispose of the intruders.

Without hesitation, the guards lunged forward in unison, their spears aimed at Omni and the soldier, their intent clear: to eliminate the perceived threat to their ruler. Omni swiftly reacted, conjuring two vines from his hands that snaked around the legs of two guards, hurling them into the nearest wall with a forceful impact. Meanwhile, one guard lunged at the soldier with his spear, but the soldier skillfully parried the attack, deflecting the thrust with his weapon.

With a swift motion, Omni raised his left arm and effortlessly snapped the spear in half, rendering the guard's weapon useless. At the same time, he conjured a brick wall spiked with menacing protrusions, effectively barricading himself and the soldier from the remaining two guards' advances, forcing them to halt their attacks momentarily. The soldier delivered a powerful punch, striking the guard squarely and sending him staggering backward until he fell to the ground with a thud, collapsing near the King's throne.

"STOP! This is pitiful," the King declared with disdain, his voice echoing through the hall as he approached the fallen soldier. Gripping the soldier's arm firmly, he hoisted him up, his gaze shifting to Omni. "What is your reason for coming here?" he demanded, his tone a mixture of curiosity and contempt, as he flung his own guard through the wall of the castle with casual ease.

"We come to stop you from walking over people," Omni declared firmly, his voice resolute as he confronted the King. As the King approached, his hand outstretched toward the soldier's sword, a palpable tension filled the air, anticipation hanging heavy in the moment.

"I would not be able to walk over people if they had wealth. Wealth is the power to purchase people and treat them like material or even entertainment," the King retorted, his words laden with a chilling sense of authority.

As the soldier's sword left his hand and found its place in the King's grip, the monarch wasted no time in demonstrating his ruthless dominance, impaling one of his guards through their steel suit. Omni felt a shiver of fear creep through him, realizing the extent of the King's callousness and power. The guard's suit began to shake uncontrollably as the King extended his hand in Omni's direction. In a startling turn of events, the guard was pulled toward the King with a forceful magnetism, the front of his suit adhering to the monarch's hand as if drawn by an invisible tether.

"Why do you kill your own men?" Omni demanded, his voice edged with both disbelief and outrage.

As the King forced the back of the guard's suit to connect with the front, merging them into one solid metal plate, effectively crushing the guard in the middle, Omni's question hung heavy in the air, filled with accusation and a desperate search for understanding.

"These men," the King began, stretching his arms out toward his guards against the wall, "work for me. They have no wealth. So they have no power. They are no more than money to me, and I can burn my money if I want." With a cruel gesture, he made the two guards collide, a chilling display of his absolute dominance over their lives, reducing them to mere pawns in his twisted game of power and control.

As the clash in the coliseum reached its peak, Nakh emerged victorious, having swiftly dispatched the guards that stood in his way. With his path now clear, he prepared to lend his strength to Keem in the fight against Mechanic. As Mechanic's frost gun threatened to overwhelm Keem's fiery attacks, Nakh saw an opportunity for a strategic maneuver. He signaled Keem to draw closer, urging him to trust in their plan.

"Let him get close and then try to grab him," Nakh yelled as he flew by. Keem hesitated, but Nakh interrupted him, emphasizing the importance of trust and proximity.

"Trust me and stay close," Nakh insisted, leaping from stone to stone to reach the top of the coliseum.

As Keem and Mechanic engaged in their aerial duel, darting and weaving through the air, Nakh's presence loomed from above. Having ascended the towering structure of the coliseum, Nakh stood at its peak, his figure silhouetted against the morning sky.

From this vantage point, Nakh observed the intense battle unfolding below, his eyes tracking the movements of Keem and Mechanic with unwavering focus. Despite the dizzying heights and the swirling clash of elements, Nakh's keen perception kept him attuned to every twist and turn of the confrontation.

Amidst the fray, Keem conjured a towering wall of flames, obscuring Mechanic's vision and momentarily distracting him from the impending threat. Mechanic, undeterred, swiftly transformed his frost gun into a powerful water hose, aiming it at the heart of the fiery barrier.

The rush of water surged forth, slicing through the flames with relentless force, creating a gaping hole in the wall of fire. Seizing the opportunity presented by Mechanic's diversion, Nakh's voice cut through the roar of the inferno. "Drop low!" he commanded, his directive guiding Keem's movements as he descended toward his robotic adversary.

Meanwhile, Nakh's sword, gleaming in the morning light, descended with lethal precision, its trajectory hidden within the billowing flames until the last possible moment. With expert timing, the blade hurtled toward Mechanic, its trajectory carefully calculated to intercept the mechanical menace when his attention was diverted. As Keem swiftly descended, he lunged forward and seized Mechanic by his metallic legs, anchoring himself firmly to his robotic foe. At the same time, Nakh's sword, guided by his expert hand, sliced through the air with deadly accuracy, aiming for Mechanic's arms as he attempted to fend off the impending strike.

The blade met its mark with a resounding clash, the vibrations emanating from its impact reverberating through Mechanic's metal frame. The force of the blow sent shockwaves rippling through his body, causing his upper torso to recoil backward in a futile attempt to evade the relentless assault.

Seizing the opportune moment created by Nakh's strike, Keem unleashed his own formidable strength, tearing at Mechanic's lower body with relentless determination. With a powerful wrenching motion, Keem succeeded in ripping Mechanic's lower half away from his torso, severing the robotic menace at its weakest point.

The mechanical monstrosity, now incapacitated and rendered powerless, faltered in the face of Keem and Nakh's combined might. As the dust settled and the echoes of battle faded, the once-formidable Mechanic lay defeated, a testament to the indomitable spirit of those who fought for freedom.

With a swift and practiced motion, Keem relinquished his grip on Mechanic's severed legs and deftly caught Nakh's sword as it arced through the air. Without missing a beat, he soared toward Nakh, bridging the distance between them in an instant.

As Keem approached, he extended the sword toward Nakh, offering it back to its rightful owner with a determined gaze. "Let's head to the throne," he declared, his voice ringing with resolve as he prepared to carry Nakh away to their next destination.

Nakh accepted the sword with a nod of gratitude, his determination mirrored in his eyes as he prepared to face their ultimate challenge. With Keem's support, he braced himself for the trials ahead, ready to confront the tyrant king and bring an end to his reign of oppression once and for all.

As the battle on the ice reached its climax, Hutch found himself locked in a deadly dance with Ooze. With lightning-fast movements, Ooze lunged forward, his poisonous hands poised to strike at Hutch. Reacting swiftly, Hutch summoned all his strength and determination, channeling it into a powerful kick that shattered the ice beneath him. With a resounding crack, he plunged into the freezing waters below, narrowly evading Ooze's deadly grasp.

With fierce determination, Dallas swung his ice sword at Ooze's lower body, aiming to disrupt his balance and buy himself some time. As Ooze recoiled from his failed attempt to reach Hutch, Dallas seized the opportunity to strike. But Ooze was quick to recover, leaping into the air and transforming his double-edged sword into a massive sledgehammer-like weapon. With a thunderous crash, the hammer collided with Dallas's ice sword, shattering it into countless icy fragments.

Dallas, now defenseless, braced himself for the inevitable impact, his eyes narrowing with resolve as he prepared to face Ooze's relentless assault head-on. As Hutch emerged from the freezing water with a mighty splash, droplets flew through the air, landing on Ooze's hand just as he swung his final, potentially devastating blow at Dallas. With keen awareness, Dallas seized upon the opportunity, honing his concentration on Ooze's wet hands as they began to transform into solid ice. Caught off guard by the sudden change, Ooze lost his grip on his weapon, which clattered to the ground. Meanwhile, Hutch, leveraging his mastery over water, manipulated the liquid from the hole he emerged from, shaping it into restraints that encased Ooze's body, effectively immobilizing him.

"This ends now!" Dallas declared, his voice resolute as he exerted his control over the water, freezing everything around Ooze except for his head.

Seizing the opportunity, Hutch swiftly grabbed Ooze's massive hammer, hoisting it high above his head with a powerful swing that brought it crashing down onto Ooze's head, driving it into his shoulder with a sickening crunch.

With the threat neutralized, Hutch wasted no time, gesturing to Dallas to follow as they hurriedly made their way onward, leaving behind the scene of their victory.

In the solemn grandeur of the throne room, Omni stood firm, his gaze locked with that of the King. The air crackled with tension as they faced each other, two opposing forces on the brink of collision. Behind Omni, the soldier stood ready, a silent sentinel in this high-stakes confrontation.

The King, seated upon his ornate throne, exuded an aura of authority and arrogance, his gaze piercing as he surveyed his adversaries. Despite the gravity of the situation, a haughty smirk played upon his lips, a testament to his unwavering confidence in his power.

Omni's jaw clenched, his fists tightening at his sides as he braced himself for the exchange to come. He knew that challenging the King would not be without risk, but the plight of the enslaved and oppressed fueled his resolve. As tension mounted and the confrontation reached its zenith, Omni and the King stood locked in a battle of wills, each determined to emerge victorious in their struggle for freedom and justice.

"How much is your life worth?" the King's question echoed through the hall, dripping with contempt.

"You cannot buy me. My life is worth more than money, and wealth does not determine my power," Omni declared firmly.

The King turned toward Omni's soldier, his gaze filled with calculated interest. "How much will you want to kill your partner? You can be my right hand," he offered with twisted confidence.

The soldier, gripping the shattered spear with determination, retorted, "I will never work for a man like you," before lunging at the King.

In a swift and merciless response, the King seized the soldier by the throat, his grip tightening with each passing moment. His attention shifted back to Omni as he continued his taunts.

"You are probably not even worthy to fight in the coliseum against the slaves. No one has ever seen a winner after he wins a battle in the coliseum. I kill the winner myself so no one in the Kingdom will ever think they know what power feels like. Why do you think the whole Kingdom is metal? Because I control metal, so I control the Kingdom and everyone in it," he spat out with aggressive certainty, his dominance looming over the room.

In an act of defiance, Omni's arm began to transform, taking on a rocky texture as he launched himself toward the King, his resolve unyielding. Omni's fist connected with the King's face with a resounding thud. However, the King remained unfazed, swiftly seizing Omni's arm in a vice-like grip.

Just then, Keem and Nakh swooped in from the ceiling, shattering through the glass window in a dramatic entrance.

"If I cannot buy you, it means you are nothing. You're less than a slave," the King sneered, his voice dripping with disdain. "I hang people like you in the courtyard to show everyone that wealth is the only true power."

With a forceful kick to Omni's stomach, the King sent him crashing to the ground, the impact reverberating through the room. As Hutch and Dallas burst into the hall, they witnessed the King callously placing his foot on Omni's head, exerting pressure with evident contempt.

"These fools come to help you? They help you, you help the slaves. I do not need any help," the King declared, his voice dripping with arrogance. "People without wealth always use help as a false sense of hope. People take advantage of those who are in need of help. And they use their need to only complete their own goals."

The weight of the King's foot bore down on Omni's head, his words a cruel reminder of the power dynamics at play in the Kingdom.

With an elemental symphony of ice and wind, Dallas and Keem orchestrated a furious assault upon the tyrant king. Ice clones, born from Dallas's frosty command, swarmed the monarch, their frozen fists striking with relentless determination. At the same time, Keem unleashed a tempest of gusting winds, a force of nature aimed at toppling the oppressive ruler from his lofty perch.

As the King stumbled backward under the onslaught, his grip on Omni faltered, allowing Hutch to swoop in and snatch his comrade from harm's way. With fierce determination, Hutch carried Omni to safety, retreating alongside Dallas as they regrouped to face their formidable foe once more. But even as they retreated, the King's dark laughter echoed through the hall, a chilling reminder of the power he wielded and the battle that lay ahead.

As the King crushed the last ice clone with disdain, his words reverberated through the hall like a thunderclap. "You three are dressed like the people from the city. How dare they betray me," he seethed, his voice dripping with contempt.

Keem stepped forward defiantly, his gaze meeting the King's with unwavering resolve. "We are from the city, but we are not with them. How do you have the technology from the city anyway? Do you do business with the city?" he challenged.

The King looked down upon Keem, a twisted smile playing on his lips. "The city believes in what I believe in. Wealth is the only true power. I gave them the gold to make them powerful, and they give me the technology to keep control of my Kingdom. They are just now learning how to control their people. That's why they send us the people who cannot control their power," he explained, his words laced with arrogance.

In a swift and calculated move, the King lunged at Nakh, his actions swift and precise. Nakh reacted instinctively, swinging his sword as Dallas leaped to his aid. The clash of steel echoed through the chamber as Nakh's blade met the King's hand, drawing blood but failing to halt his advance. The force of the impact pushed the King back only slightly, a testament to his overwhelming strength. As Dallas launched his attack, his movements swift and determined, the King intercepted him effortlessly, delivering a single blow that sent Dallas crashing into the wall with bone-shattering force. Nakh, too, felt the King's wrath as a powerful kick sent him hurtling backward, leaving a deep dent in the unforgiving stone.

Undeterred by the overwhelming odds, Keem soared toward the King, his determination unyielding. But before he could reach his target, the King seized him mid-air, his grip like iron around Keem's neck. Yet, as the flames of defiance ignited within Keem, his eyes blazed with a fierce intensity, and his body became engulfed in swirling blue flames.

The heat emanating from Keem's fiery form grew ever more intense, forcing the King to release his hold, his hands recoiling from the searing heat. Keem landed on his feet, his resolve unbroken, ready to face the tyrant who dared to challenge their quest for freedom.

As Omni lay in pain, his thoughts echoed loudly within the confines of his mind. Despite the agony coursing through his body, his spirit remained unbroken, fueled by an unwavering belief in the power of friendship and the possibility of change.

"He's wrong," Omni whispered to himself, his voice a defiant murmur amidst the chaos of battle. "I have faith in my friends, and their unwavering support is giving me hope—hope in change. He must see that his way is wrong."

With each heartbeat, Omni's resolve grew stronger, his conviction a beacon of light in the darkness of oppression. Though battered and bruised, he remained steadfast in his belief that together, they could overcome any obstacle and forge a brighter future.

Keem and Nakh, their determination burning brightly in their eyes, combined their powers, unleashing a torrent of energy aimed squarely at the King. In a synchronized effort, they drove him back, step by step.

The King stumbled upon the icy surface beneath him, losing his footing and crashing to the ground. His regal demeanor shattered, and the impact echoed through the chamber, symbolizing the collapse of his tyrannical reign.

With fierce determination, Dallas raised his arm, channeling his power through the ice beneath the fallen monarch. Sharp ice stalactites shot up from the ground, encasing the King in a frozen prison. Each icy spike seemed to pierce not just his flesh, but the very essence of his authority, rendering him powerless and immobile.

As Omni inched closer to the fallen King, his mind raced with a daring plan. "In the natural healing book, I've read about DMT," he mused silently, his determination unyielding despite the pain coursing through his body. "A high dosage should take over a man's mind."

With each labored movement, Omni drew nearer to the tyrant, his fingers grazing the ground as he crawled forward. "I'd rather him hallucinate and live in this false world that he believes in," he contemplated, his resolve steeling with every passing moment, "rather than him enforcing it on the people."

As he reached the prone figure of the King, a sense of purpose filled Omni's heart, driving him forward with unwavering determination. It was time to put his plan into action and bring an end to the King's reign of tyranny once and for all.

The King extended his arms, intending to unleash his formidable power and wreak chaos and destruction upon the entire Kingdom, sparing none in his path, not even Root itself.

With a malevolent gleam in his eyes, he envisioned the complete annihilation of everything within his domain. The tremors that shook the buildings were but a prelude to the cataclysm he intended to unleash. Every structure, every home, and every landmark would be razed to the ground, reduced to nothing but rubble and dust.

As the metals of the Kingdom levitated around him, the King wielded them with wrathful intent, ready to rain down a storm of destruction upon his subjects. His twisted vision left no room for mercy or compassion. He sought to crush any semblance of resistance, leaving behind only a barren wasteland devoid of hope or defiance. Even Root, the very heart of the Kingdom, would not be spared from his fury.

Each passing moment tightened the King's grip on the elements, his determination unyielding as he prepared to unleash devastation upon the Kingdom and all its inhabitants.

Amidst the looming threat, a palpable sense of fear gripped Root. Their faces were etched with worry and uncertainty. Unlike Omni, who bore the burden of knowing the King's true capabilities and harbored a daring plan, the rest stood bewildered and apprehensive, their minds clouded by the magnitude of the impending catastrophe.

Omni's courageous advance toward the King, driven by a resolve that seemed to transcend mortal fears, left Root with a mix of admiration and confusion. They couldn't discern Omni's plan amidst the chaos, watching in anxious anticipation, hoping that his actions would lead them to salvation.

The King's display of power deepened Root's dread, each tremor a grim reminder of the impending danger. Nervous glances were exchanged, hearts heavy with uncertainty as they braced themselves for whatever might come next.

In the face of such overwhelming peril, Root found themselves grappling with a sense of helplessness, unsure of how to confront a foe whose power seemed boundless. Yet, even in their fear and confusion, a glimmer of hope flickered within them, fueled by Omni's unwavering courage and the faint promise of a plan hidden beneath their uncertainty.

"The end is upon us!" the King's voice thundered through the chamber, a chilling declaration of his intent to unleash chaos upon Root.

With a malevolent gleam in his eye, he readied every metal object, his hands poised to unleash destruction upon them all. In a swift movement, Omni seized the King's hand, his fingers tightening around it with determination. The King's eyes, once filled with malice, now rolled back in his head as Omni swiftly administered the DMT directly into his bloodstream through the wound on his hand.

The DMT, like a whisper of change, surged through the King's veins, swiftly making its way to his brain. There, amidst the intricate network of neurons and synapses, it began its work, unfurling its hallucinogenic effects with relentless intensity. Colors danced and shapes shifted, reality itself bending and contorting under the weight of the psychedelic onslaught. As the drug took effect, the metallic objects suspended in the air began to plummet to the ground, a cascade of impending destruction halted by Omni's intervention.

In that crucial moment, Nakh, driven by the desire to end the King's tyranny, leaped forward, his blade poised for the final blow. "NOOOOO!" Omni's voice pierced the air, halting Nakh's advance in mid-air.

As Omni spoke, his voice trembled with exhaustion, yet there was a note of triumph in his words. "I injected him with a large portion of DMT," he explained, his breaths labored as he released the King's hand and rolled onto his back. Dallas and Nakh exchanged puzzled glances, their expressions a mix of concern and curiosity.

"What is that?" Dallas asked, his voice tinged with uncertainty.

"It is a psychedelic compound," Omni replied, his tone carrying a hint of solemnity. "Let's say a spiritual journey. One so strong that his consciousness will never find his body again." A weary smile played across Omni's lips before he finally succumbed to exhaustion, slipping into unconsciousness.

With a mixture of urgency and gentleness, Nakh cradled Omni's unconscious form in his arms, mindful of every movement to avoid causing him further harm. The weight of their friend's limp body served as a somber reminder of the trials they had faced and the sacrifices made along the way.

98

Root, their faces etched with a complex array of emotions—
relief at having survived the ordeal, apprehension about what
lay ahead, and a glimmer of hope for a better future—trailed
behind Nakh, their steps heavy with exhaustion but fueled by
determination.

Exiting the grandiose halls of the castle, they emerged into
the open air, greeted by a scene of utter devastation. The once-
majestic kingdom now lay in ruins, a testament to the
destructive power unleashed by the King in his final, desperate
moments. Amidst the aftermath of destruction, the toll of the
fierce battle was starkly evident. The once-vibrant streets now
lay strewn with the remnants of fallen debris and the echoes of
lives lost in the struggle for freedom. The people of the land,
though liberated from the oppressive shackles of slavery and
the tyrannical rule of the King, mourned the loss of those who
had sacrificed everything in the fight for a better tomorrow.

The once-mighty kingdom, now reduced to rubble and ruin,
stood as a solemn testament to the price of power unchecked
and the consequences of greed and tyranny. Yet amidst the
devastation, there remained a glimmer of hope—a sense of
newfound freedom and the promise of a brighter future for those
who had endured the darkest of days.

Nakh stood amidst the devastation, his mind reeling from the display of power they had just witnessed. Despite unleashing his most formidable attacks, the King had barely flinched, leaving Nakh in awe of the sheer strength possessed by their adversary.

As they made their way toward the ship, Keem's voice rang out with unwavering confidence, a beacon of hope amidst the destruction. His words lifted their spirits, reminding them of their collective determination to prevail against all odds.

Battered and bruised, they reached the awaiting vessel, where General Rock and his men greeted them with relief and admiration. Their triumphant return bore testament to their courage and resilience in the face of tyranny.

With Dallas safely escorted to shore, General Rock's words resonated with a sense of victory and anticipation. Their mission had exceeded their wildest expectations, and they were eager to return home, bearing the fruits of their hard-won liberation.

But amidst the celebration, Nakh's thoughts lingered on the destruction left behind and the questions that still remained unanswered. The King's power had been formidable, a reminder of the challenges that lay ahead in rebuilding their shattered world.

As General Rock took the helm, guiding the ship back to the island of knowledge, the other boats trailed behind in a solemn yet determined procession. Root, weary from the arduous battle, retreated to their cabins to recuperate, their bodies and spirits in need of rest after the tumultuous events of the day.

As the sun dipped below the horizon, casting a radiant glow across the tranquil waters, the sky transformed into a canvas of vibrant hues. Shades of purple intermingled with the remaining traces of daylight, painting a breathtaking spectacle that served as a poignant reminder of the beauty that endured despite the turmoil they had faced.

In the silence of the night, Nakh found himself consumed by the enigmatic words echoing in his mind's eye. "Your knowledge will rise in the same place as the sun," the voice had proclaimed, leaving Nakh to ponder its elusive meaning. With furrowed brows and a heart heavy with curiosity, he wrestled with the riddle, seeking to unravel its secrets. Jotting down the words, he hoped for clarity with the dawn, where the sun might shed light on the mysteries that whispered in the night.

A Bright New World

As they approached the medical tent, Taki and her team sprang into action, swiftly assessing Omni's condition and preparing to administer the necessary care. Nakh hovered nearby, his concern for Omni evident in his every gesture.

Inside the tent, the atmosphere was a blend of hurried efficiency and quiet determination. The medical team worked tirelessly, their hands moving with practiced precision as they tended to the wounded and offered comfort to those in pain. Taki, her face etched with a blend of exhaustion and resolve, directed the efforts with a steady hand, her presence a calming influence amidst the chaos.

Omni winced as the healers began their work, the pain of his injuries mingling with the weight of the recent battle. Nakh's mind, however, remained fixated on the cryptic message, its meaning eluding him despite his best efforts to decipher it.

As the night deepened, a sense of calm began to settle over the island. The wounded received the care they needed, and the once-weary crew found solace in the promise of rest. Keem, his thoughts still lingering on the dragon egg, joined Nakh outside the medical tent.

"How's Omni?" Keem asked, his voice low but filled with concern.

"He'll recover," Nakh replied, his gaze distant as he pondered the message. "But there's something I need to figure out."

Keem nodded, understanding the weight of Nakh's thoughts. "We'll face whatever comes next together," he said, his words a promise of solidarity.

As the night wore on, the island of knowledge offered a respite from the hardships they had endured. The crew of Root found comfort in each other's presence, their bonds strengthened by the trials they had overcome. As the first light of dawn began to break, Nakh felt a renewed sense of determination, ready to face the challenges that lay ahead with unwavering resolve.

Meanwhile, the remaining members of Root followed General Rock and Taki toward the captain's quarters, their hearts filled with gratitude for the assistance they had received. As they walked, Taki expressed their deep appreciation for the help provided by the crew.

"Thank you for your invaluable assistance in saving our people," Taki began, their words resonating with sincerity. "Your actions have given us more than hope; they have instilled within us a belief in our collective strength. Together, we can overcome any challenge that comes our way."

Before Taki could finish, General Rock interjected, his voice filled with a sense of camaraderie and respect.

"Let them have time to make decisions for themselves without your suggestions, Taki," General Rock intervened, his tone firm but understanding. "They have been through a lot, and I'm sure they want to rest. So what are your plans, Root? What is next for you all?"

"I would love to stay. I mean, if we have nothing ahead of us," Dallas said, flashing a warm smile at Taki.

"We could stay and help this land become stronger," Keem chimed in, eliciting a reciprocal smile from Taki.

"We that Settl...." Hutch began, but his words were cut off as Nakh stormed in, a note clutched tightly in his hand.

"I had a vision. Well, not a vision, but you all get it!" Nakh burst in, excitement evident in his voice as he slapped the paper on the table.

"Your knowledge will rise in the same place as the sun," the paper read. Nakh pulled out his map and unrolled it on the table, inviting the others to gather around.

"If we are here," Keem said, pointing to the island of knowledge on the map.

"And the sun rises over here," Nakh added, indicating the eastern direction on the map.

"Then what is here?" Hutch asked, pointing to the furthest east zone on the map.

Nakh's finger traced the map, highlighting the furthest east zone marked with a mysterious symbol. "Here lies the Eastern Kingdom," he declared, his voice tinged with curiosity. "It's a place shrouded in legend and mystery, said to hold ancient secrets and untold wisdom. If the message is correct, our next journey must take us there."

General Rock responded, "That is what the elders believe to be the Land of Gods. But you cannot just pass through to the Land of Gods. You must go around the nomad's land and enter the two other zones. The next zone is just a short sail away into the snowy mountains."

"So be it. We leave at noon," Hutch said decisively before exiting the tent, followed by Keem, Nakh, and General Rock.

With a shared understanding, Root accepted the challenge that lay before them. They would chart a course through unknown territories, driven by a thirst for knowledge and a desire to uncover the secrets of the world beyond. As they left the tent, their footsteps echoed with purpose, each step bringing them closer to their destiny.

Outside, the sun cast long shadows across the island, painting the landscape in hues of gold and amber. The air was alive with anticipation, the promise of adventure beckoning them forward. With a final glance back at the tent, Root set off on their journey, their hearts ablaze with the fire of determination and the promise of new horizons.

As Dallas stirred from sleep, the soft light filtering through the curtains cast a gentle glow over the room, illuminating Taki's peaceful face as she lay beside him. With a sense of determination and affection, he turned to her, offering words of reassurance. "I will come back for you," he murmured, his voice filled with conviction.

Taki's eyes fluttered open, her gaze meeting his as she listened intently. "I believe in you," she replied, her tone soft and comforting. "You showed real strength protecting us the way you did. I'm sure no one can stop you from returning to me." Her words carried a sense of trust and faith in his abilities.

Dallas felt a surge of warmth at her encouragement, a flicker of resolve igniting within him. Despite the challenges ahead, her unwavering support fueled his determination. "The thought of leaving you now is harder than fighting the King," he confessed softly, his voice barely above a whisper.

"Why think so far into the future when we can continue to live in the present?" Taki's words hung in the air, a gentle reminder to cherish the moments they shared together, to find solace in the present amidst the uncertainty of the future.

With a tender gesture, Dallas reached out to Taki, his touch conveying a sense of affection and longing. As he pulled her close, their connection deepened, the worries of the outside world fading into the background. In that fleeting moment, they found solace in each other's embrace, finding strength in their bond to face whatever challenges lay ahead.

Keem sat in quiet contemplation, the dragon egg cradled gently in his lap. With closed eyes, he entered a state of light meditation, focusing on the connection between himself and the mysterious creature within the egg.

"We are one. We are one body. We are one mind. Together, we are forever," Keem whispered softly, his words carrying a sense of reverence and unity.

Suddenly, he felt a surge of energy emanating from the egg, a powerful resonance that seemed to echo his own thoughts and emotions. Opening his eyes, Keem placed his hands on the smooth surface of the egg, channeling his intent and vitality into its core.

"I never did name you," Keem mused aloud, his gaze fixed on the enigmatic shell. "Hmmm. What about Hwedo? I think that will fit you perfectly."

As if in response to his words, the egg began to wiggle, a subtle movement that filled Keem's heart with joy. "I knew you would like it," he chuckled, gently placing the egg into his backpack with a sense of anticipation and companionship.

Hutch and Nakh entered the medical tent, their footsteps muffled by the soft ground beneath their feet. As Omni stirred awake, they greeted him with warm smiles, their concern evident in their eyes.

"Am I the only one hurt?" Omni quipped, his voice laced with a hint of amusement despite the pain evident on his face.

"Yes, you are. And the freed civilians, obviously," Hutch replied, a chuckle escaping his lips as he glanced at Nakh.

"Next time, wait for the rest of us, but you did well. How are you feeling? You've been out for at least a day," Nakh inquired, his tone filled with genuine concern as he examined Omni's condition.

"I'm getting better. Luckily enough, I made that field of herbs before we left for battle. What's next for us?" Omni replied, wincing slightly as he shifted position, the discomfort evident in his movements.

"We're headed south, around Nomads' Land, and toward the Zone of Gods," Hutch explained, his tone serious as he rolled a cannabinoid plant while reclining.

As Omni listened to Hutch's words, he couldn't help but feel a sense of anticipation mingled with apprehension. The prospect of venturing into unknown territory filled him with excitement, yet the thought of facing the challenges ahead also brought a twinge of anxiety.

"We will seek knowledge and the truths there," Nakh added, his eyes reflecting the flickering light of the lantern as he passed it to Omni.

Omni accepted the lantern gratefully, its warm glow casting shadows across the interior of the tent. As he glanced around, he noticed a pile of clothing neatly folded in one corner, a stark contrast to the rugged surroundings of their makeshift shelter.

"What's this?" Omni asked, gesturing toward the pile of garments with a curious expression.

Hutch grinned, a mischievous glint in his eyes. "General Rock has provided us with warm clothes for the cold," he explained, his tone laced with excitement.

Omni's eyes widened in surprise as he examined the clothing laid out before him. They were unlike anything he had ever seen, a blend of their usual streetwear attire and the practical clothing needed for the harsh conditions ahead. Thick fur-lined coats, sturdy leather boots, and woolen scarves lay atop the pile, their urban style infused with elements of warmth and durability.

"We'll need these to brave the harsh conditions ahead," Nakh remarked, his voice tinged with determination as he inspected the garments with a critical eye.

Omni nodded in agreement, a sense of gratitude washing over him as he realized the thoughtfulness behind General

Rock's gesture. With renewed resolve, he began to don the warm clothing, the anticipation of their journey outweighing any lingering apprehension. As he fastened the fur-lined coat around his frame, he couldn't help but feel a sense of camaraderie with his companions, united in their quest for knowledge and truth amidst the unforgiving wilderness of Nomads' Land.

Navigating through the bustling medical tent, Nakh finally spotted Omni nestled in the back near the field of healing herbs. With a sense of relief, he made his way over to his friend, eager to reunite with him before their departure.

"He's in the back," the doctor informed Nakh, prompting him to navigate through the maze of beds and equipment until he reached Omni's side.

"So you're out here again," Nakh remarked with a playful grin as he approached Omni, a mixture of concern and amusement evident in his expression.

Omni nodded, his features drawn with weariness as he held up a small ball of fruit and vegetable extract. "I can regenerate my energy with this pill, but I can't restore my health," he explained, his voice tinged with frustration as he took a hesitant bite of the concoction.

As Omni grimaced at the taste, Nakh couldn't help but chuckle at his friend's reaction. "What's wrong with you?" he teased, a hint of laughter in his tone as they made their way back through the tent.

"It tastes like death itself!" Omni exclaimed, his face contorted in disgust as he struggled to swallow the remainder of the bitter pill. "Can you take me back to the bed? I'll just die there," he joked, his words laced with playful exaggeration.

With a shake of his head, Nakh helped Omni back to his bed, exchanging amused glances with his friend as they navigated through the crowded tent.

Emerging onto the deck of the ship, Omni and Nakh were greeted by the sight of Keem and Hutch, who were busy preparing for their journey. As they approached, Dallas appeared with Taki by his side, the two sharing a tender moment before parting ways.

"I'll be waiting," Taki said softly, her voice filled with warmth as she kissed Dallas goodbye and watched him board the ship.

"Smooth operator!" Omni remarked with a grin as he observed Dallas's joyful expression, a sense of camaraderie and anticipation filling the air as they prepared to set sail once more.

As the ship cut through the azure waves, a sense of triumph filled the air. Dolphins frolicked playfully in the ship's wake, a joyful escort on their journey. With the oppressive rule of the Kingdom behind them, the crew's spirits soared, buoyed by the promise of freedom and adventure that lay ahead.

Yet, amidst the exuberance, an air of uncertainty lingered. The crew, united in purpose, gazed toward the horizon with determined resolve. Ahead lay the unknown expanse of the snowy mountains, a realm shrouded in mystery and peril. Though their destination was still distant, the weight of anticipation hung heavy in the air.

Gathered at the bow of the ship, Root engaged in earnest discussion, mapping out their path forward. Each member contributed their thoughts and insights, their voices blending in a symphony of determination and resolve. As the sun began its descent, casting a golden hue upon the vast expanse of sea, they stood united, ready to face whatever challenges awaited them in the days to come.

"Here, Keem. Take a hit of this. Omni left it for us before heading to his cabin," Nakh suggested, offering Keem a rolled cannabinoid plant.

Keem accepted it with a nod of thanks, sparking it up before posing a question. "Does anyone know what's waiting for us in the next zone?"

Hutch took a drag before responding, "Dallas and I heard it's the domain of beasts. Not your typical creatures."

"Dragons, perhaps?" Keem wondered aloud, eyeing his dragon egg thoughtfully.

Hutch nodded gravely. "Expect the unexpected. That's the best approach. Omni should be feeling better by tomorrow, and we'll reach our destination before dawn. But remember, no one leaves the ship until sunrise. We can't afford any surprises."

With a collective understanding, they shared the plant, finding solace in each other's company. As the night deepened, they bid one another goodnight and retired to their cabins, bracing themselves for what lay ahead.

The ship's arrival at the prehistoric zone coincided with the onset of a deep, foreboding slumber that enveloped Omni's consciousness. In the depths of his subconscious, he found himself plunged into a realm of darkness and despair, a twisted reflection of his inner fears and doubts.

Lying prone amidst the ruins of a desolate cityscape, Omni felt the weight of defeat pressing down upon him like a suffocating shroud. His companions, once stalwart allies in their quest for freedom, now lay scattered around him, their bodies broken and lifeless, silent witnesses to the carnage wrought by their relentless adversary.

Above them, the figure of the King loomed like a specter of doom, his gaze cold and merciless as he reveled in his triumph over the fallen heroes. With each step he took, the ground trembled beneath his feet, a testament to the sheer force of his malevolent power.

Omni's heart clenched with anguish as he beheld the devastation wrought upon his friends. "But I defeated you," he protested, his voice echoing hollowly in the desolate landscape.

The King's laughter cut through the air like a blade, his words dripping with venomous scorn. "Victory is fleeting, and your feeble attempts to defy me have only led to your downfall. You are nothing but a weakling, unworthy of the power you seek to wield."

With a cruel gesture, the King delivered a final, fatal blow, crushing Dallas beneath his heel with a sickening crunch. The sight sent shockwaves of horror coursing through Omni's veins, his soul recoiling from the stark reality of his failure.

Yet, even in the face of such despair, a flicker of determination ignited within Omni's spirit. "Yes, I may be weak," he admitted, his voice trembling with newfound resolve. "But I draw strength from the bonds of friendship that unite us. With their faith as my guiding light, I will rise again, stronger and more resolute than ever before."

As he spoke these words, a radiant light began to pierce the darkness, suffusing the landscape with a luminous glow. In its brilliance, Omni glimpsed a path forward, a beacon of hope amid the shadows of despair.

With a renewed sense of purpose burning within him, Omni awoke from his troubled slumber, his mind clear and his resolve unshakable. Though the challenges ahead loomed daunting and unknown, he faced them with courage and determination, ready to confront whatever trials fate may have in store.

Omni awoke to the stillness of the night, the darkness enveloping the ship like a heavy shroud. With a silent sigh, he rose from his slumber, his mind clouded with a sense of restlessness that refused to be ignored. As he dressed himself in the dim light of the lantern, his movements slow and deliberate, he couldn't shake the feeling of unease that gnawed at the edges of his consciousness.

With the lantern in hand, casting a feeble glow over the deck of the ship, Omni made his way toward the exit, his footsteps echoing softly against the wooden planks beneath him. The air was heavy with anticipation, the silence broken only by the gentle lapping of waves against the hull and the distant cry of nocturnal creatures in the darkness beyond.

As he stepped out onto the deck, the cold night air washed over him like a tangible presence, sending a shiver down his spine. The stars twinkled overhead, their distant light offering a faint glimmer of solace amidst the enveloping darkness. With each breath he took, Omni felt a sense of clarity begin to settle over him, his thoughts drifting toward the unknown horizon that lay ahead.

Despite the uncertainty of their journey, there was a quiet determination in Omni's gaze, a steadfast resolve that burned brightly in the depths of his soul. With a sense of purpose driving him forward, he set off into the night, his lantern casting a steady beam of light to guide his way. Whatever trials awaited him beyond the safety of the ship, he was ready to face them head-on, his spirit unyielding in the face of adversity.

"I have never seen snow before," Omni murmured to himself as he cautiously stepped onto the pristine white expanse that stretched out before him. The cold air bit at his cheeks, sending tendrils of frosty breath spiraling into the night. Holding the lantern aloft, he cast a soft glow over the untouched snow, illuminating its crystalline surface with a warm, golden light.

With each step he took, the snow crunched softly beneath his boots, the sound echoing in the stillness of the night. He couldn't help but marvel at the purity of the snow, its softness and serenity a stark contrast to the chaos and turmoil of the world he had left behind.

As he walked, sparks flew from the tip of the cannabinoid plant he held, its faint glow casting eerie shadows on the snow-covered ground. The air was heavy with the scent of pine and frost, a potent reminder of the untamed wilderness that surrounded him.

Despite the chill that seeped into his bones, Omni felt a sense of exhilaration coursing through his veins. This was a world unlike any he had ever known, a land of mystery and wonder waiting to be explored. With each passing moment, he felt his spirits lift, his curiosity driving him ever onward into the unknown.

"What the hell?" Omni's voice cut through the icy air as he stumbled upon a colossal creature, unlike anything he had ever seen before. Before him stood a woolly mammoth, its massive form shrouded in thick, fur-like hair that seemed to insulate it from the biting cold.

With wide eyes, Omni approached the mammoth cautiously, his curiosity overriding any sense of fear or apprehension. He couldn't tear his gaze away from the majestic creature, marveling at its sheer size and prehistoric appearance.

"I've never seen hairy elephants before either," he muttered to himself, the words hanging in the frigid air like frost. The mammoth regarded him with a mixture of curiosity and wariness, its ancient eyes gleaming in the dim light of the lantern.

Omni couldn't shake the feeling of unease that settled over him as he stood in the presence of this ancient behemoth. Everything about this place seemed to defy logic and reason, leaving him questioning the very fabric of reality.

"What is up with this place?" he wondered aloud, his voice barely a whisper in the vast expanse of the snowy wilderness. Little did he know, his encounter with the mammoth was just the beginning of a journey that would take him to the very edge of his understanding.

The ground trembled beneath Omni's feet as the mammoth's bellow reverberated through the icy air. With a surge of primal instinct, the colossal creature charged forward, its massive tusks gleaming in the faint moonlight.

Before Omni could even process the looming threat, his attention was seized by the sudden appearance of two sleek forms materializing from the shadows. With lethal grace, the saber-toothed tigers bounded into view, their lithe bodies poised for the kill as they encircled Omni with silent precision.

Trapped between the thundering advance of the mammoth and the stealthy approach of the tigers, Omni found himself at the mercy of these ancient predators. The air hung heavy with the tension of imminent danger, each heartbeat echoing in his ears as he assessed his dire situation.

As the tiger's menacing growls reverberated through the frosty air, Omni dropped his lantern, the light flickering out as it hit the ground. With a swift motion, he focused his intent, drawing upon his earth powers to erect a circular wall of wood around him, a barrier between him and the advancing creatures. As the wall materialized, the animals hesitated, sensing an unseen force at work.

Inside his makeshift fortress, Omni remained unaware of the unfolding events beyond the wooden barrier. He reached into his pocket, retrieving one of his regen pills, knowing he would need the extra energy to confront the creatures. With a quick swallow, he felt a surge of vitality course through him, preparing him for the imminent clash.

Outside the enclosure, the mammoth let out another roar, though its once powerful cry now sounded weakened. To Omni's surprise, both the mammoth and one of the tigers began to bow, their movements deferential. In a sudden transformation, the second tiger morphed into the form of a person, standing upright before Omni's wooden fortress.

"You have the green thumb. You must follow us back to the village. Our people have been waiting for you," the man declared with an air of authority. Omni, perplexed by the sudden turn of events, cautiously dismantled the wooden barrier he had erected, his guard still up.

"Where is the other tiger?" Omni's tone was laced with suspicion as he scanned the surroundings, searching for any sign of the missing creature. Despite the man's seemingly innocuous request, Omni remained on high alert, his instincts warning him of potential danger.

Omni quickened his pace as he approached the ship, eager to reunite with his friends and seek refuge from the unsettling encounter in the wilderness. However, before he could even reach the boarding ramp, Hutch's men rushed past him, weapons drawn and expressions tense with readiness for a confrontation.

"Wait, wait, wait!" Omni called out, his voice echoing across the deck as he hurried to catch up with them. He could feel the tension in the air thickening with each passing moment, knowing that any sudden movements could escalate the situation further.

As he reached the boarding ramp, Omni held up a hand, signaling for his companions to halt their advance. "They are with me. Well, he is," he explained, gesturing toward Lowell, who followed closely behind.

Omni chuckled nervously as he watched the mammoth's imposing figure, his laughter echoing through the snowy landscape. With a wave of his hand, he effortlessly conjured another cannabinoid plant from the ground, the green leaves poking through the pristine white snow.

"The other two of my friends are animals. The rest of us can morph into any animal we imagine and even talk with the animals," Lowell explained, his voice calm as he stroked the mammoth's massive tusk with a sense of familiarity.

Just as Omni was about to respond, Hutch's voice broke through the conversation. "Omni! We were just looking for you. It's time to smoke," he called out, Root emerging from the boat behind him.

"They want us to come to their village. The tiger—I mean, Lowell—said his chief is waiting on me," Omni explained, passing the newly grown plant to Hutch.

Keem's brows furrowed in confusion. "What do they want with you?" he questioned.

"My ability," Omni replied simply, his tone betraying no hint of uncertainty.

With Hutch and the others in tow, Omni followed Lowell toward the village, the conversation flowing freely as they smoked and walked. "The village is ahead, just past the last of this snow," Lowell informed them, leading the way.

As they trekked through the snow-covered landscape, Nakh seized the opportunity to inquire about the village. "Could you tell us about your village?" he asked Lowell.

Meanwhile, Omni couldn't contain his excitement. "Can I ride the mammoth?" he blurted out, his eyes gleaming with childlike wonder.

Lowell's response to Nakh's question drew Omni's attention back to the conversation. "We have been waiting for him since we were visited by the light," Lowell explained, his words carrying a weight of reverence. "They taught us how to become one with the land. Through stillness and deep meditation, we have learned to speak with the animals, the land, and even our bodies."

Intrigued by Lowell's mention of the light, Omni pressed for more information. "What do you mean about the light? Are you saying the sun?" he asked, his curiosity piqued.

"I'm not sure. That's what the legend tells us. But the sun is the greatest source of energy," Lowell replied, his voice tinged with a sense of awe. "We sun gaze, allowing the sun's ray's energy to empower the third eye. The sun will grow your pineal gland and expand your power."

As they ventured deeper into the village, they discovered a remarkable harmony between nature and civilization. The homes, crafted from sturdy branches and woven vines, blended seamlessly with the lush foliage of the surrounding forest.

Colorful flowers cascaded from rooftop gardens, their petals dancing in the gentle breeze, while winding paths meandered between the trees, inviting exploration.

Vivid murals adorned the walls of the treehouses, depicting scenes of nature, animals, and the village's rich history. Each mural told a story, capturing the essence of the villager's deep connection to the land and their reverence for the natural world.

In the central square, a majestic tree towered over the village, its branches reaching toward the sky like outstretched arms. Beneath its sprawling canopy, villagers gathered to share meals, stories, and laughter, their voices mingling with the rustle of leaves and the songs of birds.

Throughout the village, the air was alive with the sounds of life: the chirping of crickets, the chatter of squirrels, and the gentle rustle of leaves in the breeze. It was a place of serenity and peace, where time seemed to slow, and the worries of the outside world melted away.

As they stood outside the towering tree, its roots stretching deep into the earth, they beheld a scene of solemn reverence. At the base of the tree, bathed in the dappled light filtering through the branches, sat the village chief, flanked by two spiritual leaders. The trio sat in silent meditation, their faces serene and their bodies perfectly still.

Around them, the air thrummed with palpable energy, as if the very essence of the earth itself flowed through the roots of the ancient tree. The villagers, gathered in a respectful circle, watched with hushed reverence, their eyes alight with quiet awe.

The chief, a figure of wisdom and authority, exuded a sense of tranquility and inner strength. His weathered face bore the marks of years spent in communion with nature, and his eyes sparkled with otherworldly wisdom.

Beside him, the two spiritual leaders emanated an aura of quiet power, their presence commanding respect and reverence. Clad in flowing robes of earthy hues, they seemed to blend seamlessly with the natural world around them, their connection to the land evident in every gesture and movement.

As the group approached, the chief and his spiritual advisors opened their eyes, their gaze falling upon Omni and his companions with a serene intensity. It was clear that they were not just inhabitants of this village but guardians of its ancient wisdom and traditions.

As Omni stepped forward, a solemn hush fell over the gathering. With measured steps, he approached the ancient tree, its gnarled roots forming a natural threshold to the sacred space within. With a glance back at his companions, Omni took a deep breath and crossed the threshold, disappearing into the cool shadows of the tree's interior.

Inside, the atmosphere was suffused with a gentle, golden light filtering through the canopy above. The air was thick with the scent of earth and moss, carrying with it a sense of timeless wisdom and reverence.

In the heart of the chamber, seated upon a bed of soft moss, the village chief awaited Omni's arrival. His eyes, bright with an inner light, met Omni's with a silent understanding as the young man approached.

Without a word spoken, Omni took his place before the chief, mirroring the elder's posture of calm dignity. In the stillness of the chamber, surrounded by the ancient wisdom of the tree and the silent reverence of the assembled villagers, Omni awaited the chief's guidance with a sense of quiet anticipation.

"Welcome to the Tree of Life," the chief's voice resonated within the sacred chamber, carrying an air of reverence and wisdom. "This is our center of growth, wisdom, protection, and redemption."

With a knowing gaze, the chief continued, "We sensed your aura arrive on our shores, guided by the light that foretold your coming. It instructed us to await your presence here, promising that we would teach you everything the light has bestowed upon us."

Stepping forward, the chief's expression softened with a sense of purpose. "We will impart upon you the ancient arts of geokinesis and chlorokinesis, enabling you to harness the power of earth and plants to their fullest potential. Through this mastery, the light promised that you would liberate us from our fears."

Drawing closer, the chief extended a small seed toward Omni, its significance clear in the solemnity of the moment. "Eat this seed," he instructed, his voice imbued with the weight of generations past. "It will serve as the catalyst for your transformation, allowing us to recreate your abilities and guide you on your path toward enlightenment."

The chief emerged from the depths of the sacred tree, his presence commanding respect and reverence. With a gentle yet authoritative tone, he addressed Root, his words carrying the weight of ancient wisdom.

"You all are not my guests," the chief declared, his voice resonating with sincerity. "You all are my equals, which makes you more than family."

Turning to his villagers, the chief's eyes softened with warmth as he extended his arms in a welcoming gesture. "Welcome them in," he instructed, his voice filled with kindness and acceptance. "Embrace them as if they were your own children."

With those words, the villagers welcomed Root with open arms, enveloping them in a sense of belonging and kinship that transcended mere hospitality. Together, they stood united beneath the canopy of the Tree of Life, bound by the bonds of shared purpose and mutual respect.

"What are your names?" the chief inquired, extending a hand to Keem in a gesture of camaraderie.

One by one, each member of Root introduced themselves, their voices resonating with a sense of pride and unity. Even the soldiers, typically reserved and stoic, spoke up, eager to be acknowledged and welcomed into the fold. It was a moment of shared humanity, where names became more than mere labels but symbols of identity and connection within the embrace of the village community.

"Lowell, take them to meet the Mother, and she will take care of their food and shelter. I will escort Omni," the chief instructed, his voice carrying the weight of authority and respect. As the others were led away by Lowell, Omni remained with the chief, his curiosity piqued by the mysterious seed he had been given.

"What is this seed?" Omni inquired, casting a glance at the small, unassuming object cupped in his hand.

"It is the seed of life," the chief explained, his tone reverent. "A universal symbol of creation. It shall blossom within you, unlocking your true power and allowing you to connect with nature."

With these enigmatic words lingering in the air, the chief and Omni continued their journey, ascending a steep hill that led away from the village.

"Keep your eyes focused on the sun," the chief instructed, settling beside Omni. "We will meditate until your seed sprouts and you receive its power."

Omni nodded, turning his gaze toward the radiant orb in the sky. With the chief by his side, he entered a state of deep

130

meditation, allowing his mind to quiet and his senses to attune to the energy of the sun. Time seemed to stretch as they sat atop the hill, enveloped in the warmth and tranquility of the moment, waiting for the seed of life to awaken within Omni.

As the rest of Root packed their belongings in the shelters, Lowell engaged in conversation with the mother of the village. Their voices mingled with the gentle rustle of leaves and the distant chatter of animals, creating a soothing backdrop to their exchange. They spoke of matters both trivial and profound, sharing stories of their respective journeys and experiences. Meanwhile, the villagers bustled about, attending to their daily tasks with practiced efficiency, their sense of community evident in every gesture and interaction.

"I feel power with this group. Where did they come from, young one?" the mother asked Lowell, her eyes fixed on Root.

"They are with the chosen one. The chief took him to grow," Lowell replied, his gaze drifting momentarily toward the hill where Omni and the chief sat in meditation.

"Why didn't he show them anything? He knows that no one is strong alone. You four. What are your names?" the mother inquired, her attention now fully on Root.

"We go as Root, but I'm Keem. This is Dallas, Hutch, and Nakh," Keem replied, gesturing to each member of their group in turn.

"I'm the mother of these lands. I protect these lands with nature itself. If you are here to help your friend, then follow me to show you how to protect them all," the mother declared, her voice carrying an air of authority as she led Root out of the village, their path winding through the lush foliage of the surrounding forest.

As they reached an open clearing, the mother gestured for Root to sit in a circle around her. "I want to see your powers through meditation. What I show you today will not be learned instantly. It will take focus and control," she instructed, her voice carrying a serene authority.

With a collective nod, Root settled into a comfortable position, their minds and bodies ready for the meditation ahead. The mother closed her eyes, leading them through a series of deep breaths, guiding them to center their thoughts and tap into the wellspring of energy within.

As they delved deeper into the meditation, each member of Root began to sense a connection to the earth beneath them, feeling the subtle vibrations of life coursing through the soil.

With the mother's guidance, they focused on channeling this energy, harnessing it to manifest their individual abilities.

Keem felt a surge of strength and resilience wash over him, his muscles tingling with newfound power. Dallas experienced a heightened awareness of his surroundings, his senses sharpening as he attuned himself to the subtlest of movements in the environment. Hutch found himself enveloped in a cocoon of soothing energy, his anxieties melting away as he basked in a sense of inner peace. Nakh, ever attuned to the rhythms of nature, felt a deep connection to the flora and fauna surrounding them, his empathy extending to all living beings.

With their energies swirling and pulsating around them, Root embraced the mother's guidance, focusing their thoughts on joy. Each member of the group summoned memories of happiness and contentment, allowing those feelings to suffuse their beings and radiate outwards.

As they concentrated on their collective joy, a subtle transformation began to take place in the world around them. The air seemed to shimmer with a newfound vibrancy, infused with the essence of their positive emotions. Flowers bloomed in riotous colors, their petals unfurling with an exuberant flourish.

Birds soared overhead, their songs echoing with a melodic harmony that resonated through the clearing.

The mother watched with a serene smile, her eyes alight with pride at the sight of Root's collective power. "Your happiness has the power to bring life and vitality to the world around you," she observed. "Remember this, for it is a testament to the strength of your bond and the potential within each of you."

As Root collectively focused on thoughts of their beloved family and friends, a sense of warmth and unity enveloped them. Their minds intertwined, weaving a tapestry of memories and emotions that stretched across the expanse of their shared consciousness.

In response to their heartfelt reflections, the sky above began to shift and churn, as if stirred by unseen hands. Dark clouds parted, revealing a radiant spectrum of colors that arced gracefully across the heavens. A brilliant rainbow unfurled itself, its vibrant hues painting the sky with a dazzling display of light and color.

Root watched in awe as the rainbow stretched across the horizon, a breathtaking symbol of hope and connection. Each color seemed to pulse with its own unique energy, resonating with the collective love and bond shared between them. It was as if the very essence of their family and friends had manifested in the sky above, a tangible reminder of the strength and beauty of their relationships.

As Dallas immersed himself in thoughts of Taki, a gentle flurry of snow began to descend from the heavens above. Each delicate snowflake drifted gracefully down from the sky, shimmering like tiny crystals in the air. The landscape around them was soon transformed into a winter wonderland, blanketed in a soft layer of pristine white snow.

The mother observed the snowfall with keen interest, her wise eyes sparkling with understanding. She extended her hand, allowing a few snowflakes to land gently upon her palm. Each snowflake was a masterpiece in its own right, intricate and unique, a testament to the joy and happiness that Dallas's thoughts had invoked.

"Someone is very happy," the mother remarked, her voice carrying a sense of warmth and wisdom.

She regarded Dallas with a knowing smile, acknowledging the depth of emotion reflected in his expression. In that moment, amidst the falling snow and the beauty of nature surrounding them, Dallas felt a profound sense of peace and contentment wash over him.

As the day gradually waned and the golden hues of sunset painted the sky, the chief and Omni remained steadfast atop the hill, immersed in deep meditation. Time seemed to stretch endlessly, hours passing by unnoticed as they sought communion with the natural world around them.

Throughout their meditation, the sun cast its warm rays upon them, infusing them with its radiant energy. Omni's mind was a whirlwind of thoughts and emotions, his senses heightened by the tranquil surroundings. With each passing moment, he delved deeper into his own consciousness, seeking to unlock the latent power that lay dormant within him.

As the sun dipped below the horizon, painting the sky in hues of orange and pink, Omni finally felt a sense of calm wash over him. With a deep breath, he closed his eyes, allowing himself to surrender to the stillness of the moment. In that serene silence, he felt a connection to the earth beneath him, to the very essence of life itself.

At long last, as the day drew to a close and darkness descended upon the land, Omni found himself at peace. With a sense of clarity and purpose, he opened his eyes, ready to embrace the journey that lay ahead.

As the wind whispered through the landscape, Omni felt the gentle caress of its invisible fingers tugging at his dreadlocks, as though urging him to listen. In that moment, he sensed a profound connection with the elements, an ancient bond that transcended time and space.

"We must become one," he whispered softly to himself, his words carried away by the wind. He closed his eyes, surrendering to the unseen forces that surrounded him.

With each breath, he felt the essence of the earth coursing through his veins, intertwining with his very being.

As the wind continued to swirl around him, Omni felt a deep sense of unity with his body. It was no longer just a vessel for his consciousness but a sacred temple, housing the essence of his soul. In that realization, he understood the true power of his existence.

"We can contain anything possible," he thought, his mind reaching out to embrace the infinite possibilities that lay before him. He knew that with his companions by his side, they would be unstoppable. Their strength would complement each other, forging a bond that could withstand any challenge.

"I need you as my companions," he murmured, his voice carried away by the wind. With each word, he felt a surge of energy coursing through him, filling him with a newfound sense of purpose. Together, they would navigate the trials that lay ahead, their spirits intertwined in a dance of light and shadow.

The energy of the earth swirled around Omni in a mesmerizing dance, its ethereal tendrils weaving through the air like ribbons of light. With each passing moment, the aura surrounding him intensified, pulsating with a vibrant energy that seemed to emanate from the very core of the earth itself.

As the surge of energy enveloped him, Omni felt his senses heighten, his awareness expanding to encompass the world around him. The earth beneath his feet thrummed with life, sending waves of power coursing through his body. With each breath, he drew in the essence of the earth, allowing it to infuse him with its boundless strength.

His dreadlocks, caught in the swirling currents of energy, billowed around him like a wild mane, a testament to the raw power surging through his veins. With each movement, they danced in the wind, a living embodiment of his connection to the earth.

In that moment, Omni felt truly alive, his spirit soaring on the wings of the earth's energy. With a sense of awe and reverence, he raised his arms to the sky, embracing the power that flowed through him. He was no longer just a man but a conduit for the elemental forces of nature, a guardian of the earth and all its wonders.

As the night waned and the first light of dawn painted the sky with hues of gold and pink, Root returned with the mother, their journey through the night filled with revelations and newfound understanding. The rest of the soldiers, exhausted from their adventures, lay sound asleep, their dreams filled with echoes of the day's events.

"You are in love," the mother remarked softly, her words carrying the wisdom of ages. "The change in nature proves that. I can control all of weather because I have a deep love for every being on this earth. I believe every being in this world has love in their heart, even if they have a hurt soul. Revenge may be a sign of pain, but it also shows your love for your lost one. Love conquers all."

With those profound words, the mother left Root to rest, her presence lingering like a gentle breeze in the quiet stillness of the night. As they drifted off to sleep, Root felt a sense of peace settle over them, knowing that love was indeed the most powerful force in the world, capable of healing even the deepest wounds.

As Dallas thought of his beloved Taki, his heart swelled with warmth, suffused with the energy of love. In that moment, surrounded by the tranquil beauty of nature and the gentle embrace of the mother's teachings, he felt a profound connection to his emotions. Love, pure and unyielding, flowed through him like a river, filling him with a sense of peace and contentment. With each breath, he embraced the certainty that their bond was unbreakable, a beacon of light guiding him through the darkness of uncertainty.

As dawn broke over the horizon, casting its golden hues across the sky, Omni remained immersed in deep meditation, the potent energy still swirling around him like a protective aura. Meanwhile, Root stirred from their restful slumber, greeted by the gentle murmur of the awakening village. Villagers bustled about, bearing trays of nourishing food and refreshing rainwater, offering sustenance to revitalize their weary bodies for the day ahead. With each sip and morsel, Root felt invigorated, their spirits lifted by the warmth of the villagers' hospitality and the promise of a new day filled with possibilities.

As the group gathered, their minds filled with curiosity and anticipation, Keem voiced their collective thoughts, eager to delve deeper into the wisdom the mother possessed. "Where's the mother? We need to learn more from her; she knows more than she perceives. We can get stronger from what she knows, and I'm sure Omni is being enlightened," he mused aloud, his tone reflecting a blend of determination and reverence for the elder's insights.

Nakh's concern mirrored his own, his brow furrowing as he scanned their surroundings. "Wait, where is Omni, as a matter of fact?" he interjected, his gaze darting around the room in search of their absent companion.

Just then, Lowell appeared, his presence providing a semblance of reassurance amidst the uncertainty. His expression held a mix of solemnity and resolve as he addressed their inquiries.

"He is still meditating on the highest hill," Lowell replied, his words carrying a weight of solemnity.

With a nod of understanding, Nakh swiftly departed to check on their friend, his footsteps resolute as he made his way toward the hill where Omni remained in deep meditation.

Meanwhile, Keem's thirst for knowledge remained unquenched, his focus shifting toward their shared goal of harnessing their newfound abilities.

"Can you teach us anything?" Keem's inquiry cut through the air, filled with a palpable eagerness for knowledge.

"Yeah, the mother taught me a few things too. She's big on sharing, so she always teaches her learnings," Lowell responded, his tone carrying the weight of experience and wisdom.

With a nod of agreement, Lowell gestured for Keem, Dallas, and Hutch to follow him as they embarked on a journey back to where they had trained the day before.

"Let us go to where you trained yesterday and work on a few things," Lowell suggested, his voice brimming with determination and purpose as they set off along the familiar trail.

As Nakh ventured through the village, his gaze swept over the bustling activity, searching for any sign of Omni's whereabouts. His quest led him to a clearing where he unexpectedly encountered the chief, a figure of authority and reverence among the villagers.

"Chief," Nakh greeted respectfully, acknowledging the presence of the esteemed leader.

142

The chief turned toward Nakh, his expression calm yet knowing, as if he had anticipated Nakh's arrival. "Nakh," he acknowledged in return, his voice carrying a hint of solemnity.

Nakh's curiosity piqued, sensing that the chief held insights that could aid him in his search for Omni.

"Is Omni okay? We haven't seen him since we split up," Nakh inquired, his tone tinged with concern as he addressed the chief.

In response, the chief's gaze shifted toward the hill where Omni remained in deep meditation. "He's progressing fast," the chief remarked, a sense of admiration evident in his voice. "I've witnessed people spend years in similar pursuits before even beginning to tap into the energies as he has. It took me a week just to attain oneness with my body."

Nakh absorbed the chief's words, a mixture of wonder and reassurance filling him as he observed Omni's silhouette against the horizon. Despite his initial worries, the chief's explanation instilled a newfound confidence in Omni's journey and abilities. With a silent nod of gratitude, Nakh resolved to stand by Omni's side, offering support and encouragement on the path ahead.

"So when will we know if he is finished?" Nakh asked the chief, a trace of apprehension coloring his voice.

"We will not know, but we will sense it once he has completed his newfound communion," the chief replied solemnly. "He must greet himself to every plant, salt, stone, crystal, gem, and all things made from the earth before he can exit his meditation. The energy of every living thing wants to be heard, but you cannot listen to what they are saying; you must feel them. Let us wait."

Nakh nodded in understanding, accepting the chief's wisdom with a silent reverence. Settling beside the chief, they shared a cup of tea, the gentle warmth of the beverage soothing their spirits as they awaited the culmination of Omni's transformative journey. In the quietude of the hilltop, amidst the whispers of nature, Nakh found solace, knowing that Omni's communion with the earth would herald a profound awakening.

As the rest of Root headed toward the training area, a shadow lurked amidst the dense foliage of the trees, its presence cloaked in darkness. Silently observing their movements, the shadow remained concealed, its intent shrouded in mystery as it watched with an eerie stillness.

"So, what did she show you yesterday?" Lowell asked Root, his curiosity evident in his tone.

Dallas, still chuckling softly to himself, responded, "She showed us that with our love inside, we can tap into the Earth's natural abilities and even perform natural disasters." His laughter underscored his words, reflecting the joy he associated with love.

As Dallas's laughter filled the air, Lowell began to speak again, his voice carrying a note of contemplation, "What's so funny? Did she mention appreciation?" However, before he could finish his sentence, they were interrupted by the sudden appearance of two sets of ninja twins, their presence unexpected and their intentions unclear.

"We found them. I knew we could, brothers and sisters," Ani declared with a triumphant gleam in her eyes. She stepped forward confidently, gesturing to her siblings one by one. "I'm Ani. This is Ina, Om, and Mo. Together, we're Stats, and you are on the GOLDRUSH!"

Her words rang out with conviction, each syllable laced with determination. However, as Ani directed her finger toward Hutch, a sudden realization dawned upon her. With a subtle shift in her expression, she quickly corrected herself, redirecting her finger toward Dallas instead.

"I'm getting my gold, Dallas!" Ani proclaimed, her tone echoing with both determination and a touch of embarrassment. Meanwhile, the other members of Stats lowered their heads slightly in response to Ani's initial mistake, a brief moment of chagrin passing over their features before they regained their composure.

"What is the Goldrush?" Keem inquired, his curiosity piqued by the mention of the unfamiliar term.

Hutch, taking a moment to explain, responded with a hint of resignation in his voice. "It's a wanted list," he began, his tone betraying a sense of familiarity with the subject. "They take criminals in exchange for money. Not like the money in the city, but for gold. It's the only currency in this world."

A pause followed Hutch's explanation, during which the implications of his words sank in among the group. Keem furrowed his brow slightly, pondering the significance of this new information, while the others exchanged concerned glances, realizing the potential ramifications of encountering members of the Goldrush.

"But I didn't think the Goldrush stretched this far," Hutch added, his tone tinged with surprise at the unexpected encounter with Ani and her siblings.

Ani's voice cut through the conversation sharply, commanding attention as she addressed the group. "Hey! Shut up, we are talking here. Not you," she asserted, her words carrying a hint of hostility as she strode purposefully toward them.

Her abrupt interruption caused a moment of tense silence among Keem, Hutch, and the others, their expressions reflecting a mixture of surprise and apprehension at Ani's brash demeanor. With her approach imminent, they braced themselves for whatever confrontation may follow.

Reacting swiftly to Ani's aggressive advance, Root instinctively stepped forward, positioning themselves between Ani and Lowell. Their movements were decisive, their stance firm and unwavering as they formed a protective barrier around Lowell, shielding him from Ani's approach.

With a calm yet assertive demeanor, Root met Ani's gaze head-on, their eyes conveying a silent message of readiness and resolve. Their determination to defend Lowell was palpable, their intent to maintain order in the face of Ani's aggression clear to all who witness the unfolding confrontation.

As Ani charged toward the group, Keem swiftly moved to intercept her, aiming to neutralize the threat. However, just as he closed in, he realized that the Ani he targeted was merely a holographic clone, a distraction created by the real Ani.

With the group's attention diverted by the holographic clone, the real Ani took advantage of the chaos, sneaking behind them with lethal intent. Without warning, she unsheathed her sword and thrust it into Lowell's back, catching him off guard and causing him to stagger from the sudden assault.

As Ina rushed after the group, Ani seized the opportunity to use Lowell as a shield, pushing the sword deeper into his back as she charged from behind. The sudden, brutal attack caught everyone off guard, heightening the sense of urgency and danger in the unfolding confrontation.

Reacting swiftly to the chaos, Dallas and Hutch leaped in opposite directions, seeking to evade Ani's deadly assault. Meanwhile, Keem ascended into the air, his body enveloped in flames as he hurled a searing fireball toward Ina, aiming to disrupt her pursuit and provide cover for his companions. As the fireball hurtled toward Ina, it passed through her form with no effect, revealing her as a mere holographic clone conjured by Ani's cunning. Undeterred by the illusion, Keem maintained his focus, prepared to counter any further deception.

A throwing knife whistled through the air, aimed directly at Hutch, who barely managed to sidestep the deadly projectile. Hutch's evasion was swift, but as the knife split into three, his efforts proved futile. Despite his attempt to dodge, one of the blades found its mark, slicing across his arm. With a grunt of pain, Hutch staggered back, clutching his wounded limb.

With a sudden flurry of motion, Mo emerged from the shadows, brandishing hook swords and sporting menacing mantis wings. He swooped down upon Keem from his blind side, launching a swift and unexpected assault. His kick connected with force, sending Keem tumbling to the ground, momentarily stunned by the unexpected attack from above.

Meanwhile, Om, the twin brother of Mo, manipulated the bugs in the area to crawl up the legs of Dallas. Dallas concentrated deeply, tapping into his powers over ice. As the bugs crawled up his legs, he channeled his energy, transforming his body into ice. With a sudden chill, the bugs froze upon contact, falling to the ground lifeless. With his ice sword in hand, Dallas charged toward Om, who swiftly drew his own blade in response. The clash of their weapons filled the air as they engaged in a fierce duel amidst the chaos of battle.

Keem, determined despite his injuries, rose to his feet and confronted Mo head-on. However, Mo's expertise in praying mantis-style kung fu proved formidable, countering Keem's every move with swift and precise strikes. Despite his best efforts, Keem found himself struggling to keep up with Mo's skillful maneuvers.

As the battle intensified, Ani conjured more holographic clones of herself, adding to the chaos of the skirmish. Meanwhile, Ina emerged from the bushes, seamlessly blending in with the illusions created by the clones. With her surroundings obscured by the multitude of Ani's doppelgangers, Ina moved with stealth and agility, ready to strike when least expected. Ani, Ina, and the horde of clones darted around the battlefield in a dizzying display, their movements creating a whirlwind of confusion. Hutch found himself disoriented, unable to discern the real girls amidst the flurry of illusions. With each passing moment, the visual cacophony grew, leaving Hutch struggling to keep track of his adversaries amid the chaos.

Ina hurled a lone ninja star in Hutch's direction, but as it hurtled through the air, she concentrated her intent upon it, causing it to multiply into a flurry of deadly projectiles. The stars streaked toward Hutch from all angles, their razor-sharp edges glinted ominously in the sunlight as they closed in on their target. Hutch swiftly transformed into a liquid state, his form flowed effortlessly to the ground, evading the onslaught of ninja stars unscathed.

As the lethal projectiles whizzed past him harmlessly, Hutch reformed his solid shape, ready to retaliate against his assailants.

Dallas engaged in a fierce swordfight with Om, their blades clashed in a symphony of steel. With each clash, sparks flew, illuminating the battleground with brief bursts of light. They exchanged blows with precision and skill, their movements were fluid and calculated. Locked in combat, they seemed evenly matched, each testing the other's strength and resolve. As they continued their duel, their swords seemed to sing, the rhythm of their fight echoed through the air.

"There was no stopping me," Dallas declared confidently, his ice sword emanated a chilling aura that began to encase Om's blade in frost. As the freezing effect spread, Om's movements became sluggish, his sword weighed down by the icy grip of Dallas's power. With each passing moment, the ice crept closer, threatening to immobilize Om's weapon entirely.

With a swift and calculated move, Dallas shattered Om's sword with a powerful strike, sending ice shards flying through the air. Seizing the opportunity, he whirled around and extended his leg, sweeping it in a low arc to trip Om off his feet. As Om lost his balance, he crashed to the ground with a resounding thud, struggling to regain his footing.

With a decisive thrust, Dallas plunged his ice sword deep into Om's chest, the blade pierced through his heart with chilling precision. As the sword penetrated Om's body, a wave of icy energy radiated outwards, freezing the ground and air around the fatal wound. Om's eyes widened in shock and agony as the cold spread rapidly through his veins, immobilizing him in a frozen grip of death.

As the chilling scene unfolded, Hutch channeled his power over the elements, conjured a dense fog that billowed outwards, shrouding the area in a thick mist. The fog rolled in swiftly, obscuring the sight of everyone present, enveloped them in a veil of impenetrable white. Through the swirling haze, the lifeless form of Om lay motionless on the ground, his body now an icy monument to the ferocity of the battle that had transpired.

Amidst the eerie silence and swirling mist, Stats looked on in stunned silence, their expressions a mixture of shock and disbelief at the sudden turn of events. With their emotions in turmoil, Stats stood frozen in place, their minds reeled from the shock of witnessing the demise of their brother. The once confident and composed siblings now found themselves gripped by a profound sense of loss and vulnerability. As they gazed upon the lifeless body of Om, a heaviness settled over them, weighing down their spirits with the crushing reality of his passing.

Ani, Ina, and Mo, the remaining members of the shattered quartet, stood together in somber silence, their usual bravado replaced by a quiet sorrow. The bond that once united them now felt fragile and fractured, their sense of unity shattered by the cruel hand of fate. In the midst of the swirling fog, their figures appeared hunched and forlorn, the weight of grief etched upon their faces.

In this moment of profound loss, Stats found themselves adrift in a sea of uncertainty, grappling with the painful truth of mortality and the fragility of life. The once invincible aura that had surrounded them was shattered, leaving behind a sense of vulnerability and doubt. As they confronted the harsh reality of their brother's death, they pondered the uncertain road that lay ahead, unsure of what the future may hold for them.

As Mo cried out in anguish, Keem's strike found its mark, sending him crashing to the ground with a pained grunt. The force of the blow left Mo reeling, his body trembled with the impact as he struggled to regain his footing. Beside him, Ani and Ina watched in horror, their hearts heavy with sorrow at the sight of their fallen comrade.

"Mo!" Ani's voice trembled with emotion as she rushed to her brother's side, her eyes filled with tears of anguish. Ina followed close behind, her expression mirroring the grief etched upon Ani's face. Together, they knelt beside Mo, offering him comfort and support in his moment of need.

As Keem stood over them, his features twisted with determination, a palpable tension filled the air. The once fierce adversaries now found themselves united in grief, their animosity was overshadowed by the shared sorrow of loss. In this moment of vulnerability, they were reminded of the fragile nature of life and the bonds that connected them as fellow travelers on this tumultuous journey.

As Ina charged at Keem with her dual swords, Keem readied a fireball to counter her attack. Suddenly, emerging from the thick fog, Hutch intervened swiftly, launching a powerful kick that sent Ina tumbling to the ground beside Mo. As the shadow emerged from the trees with startling swiftness, it swooped in to intercept Keem's incoming fireball. The sudden appearance of the shadow added a new layer of complexity to the already chaotic scene, cast an aura of mystery and danger over the unfolding conflict. Ina and the shadow crashed to the ground, their collision sent shockwaves through the battlefield, momentarily halting the clash between the combatants.

As the dust settled from the collision, both sides found themselves momentarily stunned, their attention drawn to the figure rising amidst the chaos. It was an unexpected sight—a mere 11-year-old boy brushing off the debris and adjusting his glasses with an air of nonchalance. Root and the others watched in bewilderment as the boy approached, his presence commanding an unexpected sense of authority despite his youth.

The boy's voice pierced the tense atmosphere, his words echoing with a haunting clarity that demanded attention. As he rose from the ground, dusting off his glasses with deliberate care, his gaze bore into the assembled group with a mixture of sorrow and unwavering resolve.

"You have taken the life of my brother," he began, his voice steady despite the turmoil swirling within him. "Though we may not have shared blood in our past lifetime, he was my kin, my comrade, my ally in this lifetime. His loss cuts deep, a wound that bleeds with the pain of a bond forged in battle and camaraderie."

Root and the others stood in stunned silence, their eyes locked on the boy as he spoke. His words carried the weight of a soul burdened by tragedy yet fueled by a fierce determination to seek justice for his fallen kin.

"But know this," the boy continued, his tone firm and resolute. "Though death may claim us, it cannot extinguish the fire that burns within. I have walked the path of darkness and emerged unscathed, reborn into a world of shadows and secrets."

As he spoke, a palpable tension filled the air, the gravity of his words hanging heavy over the battlefield. Each syllable seemed to carry the weight of a lifetime of hardship and sacrifice, a testament to the boy's resilience in the face of adversity.

"I was but a child when I first took up the blade, thrust into a world of violence and deceit," he confessed, his voice tinged with a hint of bitterness. "But with each passing day, I grew stronger, honing my skills in the crucible of combat until I emerged as a force to be reckoned with."

Root and the others listened intently, captivated by the boy's tale of survival and redemption. Despite his youth, there was a wisdom in his words, a depth of experience that belied his tender age.

"And now," the boy declared, his voice ringing out with quiet authority, "I stand before you as a guardian of justice. My brother's death will not go unanswered."

With that, the boy straightened his posture, his gaze steely and unwavering as he prepared to face his adversaries. In that moment, he embodied the spirit of a warrior, his resolve unshakeable and his determination unyielding in the face of adversity. Ina nodded solemnly, her expression reflecting a mix of gratitude and determination as she stepped back, placing her trust in Otto's capable hands. With a swift, fluid motion, Otto drew his twin swords, the gleaming blades catching the light as they arced through the air with deadly grace.

Root and the others watched in awe as Otto assumed a poised stance, his movements betraying a lifetime of training and discipline. Despite his young age, there was an air of seasoned confidence about him, a testament to his skill and prowess as a warrior.

As the tension thickened, Otto's gaze hardened, his focus narrowing on the adversaries before him. With a silent nod to Ina, he advanced with purpose, his swords poised to strike with lethal precision.

In that moment, Otto was more than just a boy seeking retribution for his fallen brother—he was a force of nature, a whirlwind of steel and determination, ready to face whatever challenges lay ahead with unwavering resolve.

Otto's steps were deliberate as he advanced toward Dallas, his gaze unwavering and his determination palpable. With a swift, practiced motion, he pointed his sword at Dallas, the glint of steel reflecting the intensity of his resolve.

"You will be first," Otto declared, his voice resonating with a solemnity that belied his youthful appearance. "I don't care for the gold. I care for the hunt."

The weight of his words hung heavy in the air, carrying with them a sense of purpose that brooked no argument. In that moment, it was clear that Otto was driven not by material gain, but by the thrill of the chase, the adrenaline-fueled pursuit of his quarry.

Dallas met Otto's gaze with a steady calmness, his own resolve matching that of his adversary. Though the threat of conflict loomed large between them, Dallas remained composed, his focus unwavering as he prepared to meet Otto's challenge head-on.

The atmosphere crackled with tension, both combatants locked in a silent exchange of determination and intent. Each step they took toward one another echoed with the promise of a fierce and unforgiving battle.

As they stood locked in a silent standoff, the tension between them crackled like electricity, the air thick with anticipation. In the heart of the forest, amidst the whispering of leaves and the rustle of underbrush, two warriors faced off in a clash of wills, each determined to emerge victorious in the test of strength and skill that lay ahead.

With a fluid motion, Dallas conjured a second sword, his movements swift and decisive. The glimmer of the newly formed blade danced in the dappled light filtering through the canopy, a testament to his mastery over the elements.

"This will not be easy prey," Dallas declared, his voice a steely resolve cutting through the tension that hung heavy in the air. With determination etched into every line of his face, he charged forward, his feet carrying him swiftly toward Otto.

As Keem surged forward with determination, Mo intercepted him mid-stride, his sword raised in a defensive stance. With a fierce cry, Mo leaped at Keem, his attack swift and relentless.

Caught off guard by Mo's sudden assault, Keem reacted instinctively, bringing up his arms to defend against the onslaught. The clash of their weapons reverberated through the air, each blow ringing out like a thunderous echo in the midst of the chaotic battle.

Keem fought with all the skill and prowess he possessed, his movements fluid and precise as he sought to gain the upper hand against his opponent. Despite Mo's relentless assault, Keem held his ground, his determination unyielding as he met each strike with unwavering resolve.

In the midst of the chaos, the forest echoed with the sounds of their struggle, the clash of steel and the grunts of exertion filling the air. Each combatant fought with all the ferocity of a cornered beast, their every movement a testament to their dedication to the fight.

With lightning speed, Otto darted past Dallas, his movements so swift that Root could scarcely follow them with their eyes. In a blur of motion, Otto closed the distance between himself and Hutch, his swords flashing as he launched a ferocious assault.

Hutch barely had time to react as Otto's blade sliced through the air, cutting a deep gash along the side of his arm. The force of the blow sent Hutch staggering backward, pain flaring through him as he fought to maintain his balance.

As Hutch leaped backward, clutching his wounded arm, Otto's laughter echoed through the clearing, a taunting sound that sent a chill down Root's spine. With a sinister grin, the boy circled Hutch like a predator stalking its prey, his eyes gleaming with malice.

Otto's words sent a shiver down Root's spine, the casual demeanor belying the danger that lurked within. With a swift motion, he sheathed his swords, the metallic clang echoing through the clearing as he cleaned his glasses with deliberate care.

Root watched warily as Otto's gaze swept over the battlefield, his eyes gleaming with a predatory intensity. There was a cold calculation in his movements, a sense of purpose that sent a chill down Root's spine. In the face of such ruthless determination, Root knew that they would need to remain vigilant if they were to stand any chance against their adversary.

As Otto adjusted his glasses, a wicked grin spread across his face, the glint of malice in his eyes unmistakable. "I like everything in twos," he declared, his voice dripping with ominous intent. It was a simple statement, but in that moment, it carried with it a weight of foreboding, a harbinger of the trials that lay ahead.

Hutch winced as the burning sensation intensified, his arms throbbing with pain. The precision of the cuts sent a shiver down his spine, as if a ghostly hand had traced the same path twice, leaving behind a searing reminder of vulnerability. He glanced at the mirrored wounds, a chilling realization settling in as he saw the symmetry of his injuries.

"What... What's happening?" Hutch muttered, his voice strained with disbelief.

Otto watched with a sinister grin, his gaze fixed on Hutch's mirrored wounds. "Twos, twos, twos," he chanted softly, a mocking tone underlying his words.

"My blades epitomize duality," Otto boasted with a chilling calmness. "A single slash from me delivers dual devastation—the mirror image of the cut, perfectly mirrored. Should I aim for your eye, both would be gouged with a single stroke."

With a deft motion, Otto withdrew his swords, the glint of steel reflecting his sinister intent. The air grew tense as Root prepared themselves for the next wave of attacks, knowing that Otto's skill with his dual blades made him a formidable and deadly opponent.

Hutch's eyes widened in horror at Otto's explanation, the implications sinking in with a sickening weight. The boy's proficiency with his blades, coupled with the unnerving precision of his strikes, painted a grim picture of the danger they face.

"That's... that's impossible," Hutch stammered, his voice trembling with a mixture of fear and disbelief. "How... How can you do that?"

Otto's grin widened, the gleam in his eyes betraying a twisted pleasure in his ability to sow terror. "The perfect cut is a dance of twos," he replied cryptically, his words dripping with eerie confidence. "But fear not. Your suffering will be over soon."

Hutch launched himself forward, aiming to retaliate, but Otto darted away with lightning speed, leaving Hutch to fend off his frustration. Instead, Otto rushed to aid Mo in his skirmish against Keem. Keem swiftly raised his guard to defend against Otto's attack, but Otto's blade managed to slice across the back of Keem's hand, drawing blood. Keem reacted quickly, summoning flames that erupted on the ground, creating a barrier that pushed Otto and Mo backward. Taking advantage of the distraction, he retreated to stand beside Hutch, readying himself for the next onslaught.

Ina hurled a barrage of ninja stars at Dallas, prompting him to dodge aside swiftly. However, as Dallas evaded the projectiles, Otto streaked toward him with lightning speed, slicing at the back of his knees with precision. Otto swiftly delivered a powerful kick, sending Dallas tumbling to the ground in a flurry of motion. Dallas landed with a thud near Om's lifeless body, his form crumpling against the earth in a jarring impact.

"I hope you are born at the same time as my brother so he can get his revenge personally," Otto taunted, his voice laced with cold determination. Dallas reached out, attempting to freeze Otto's legs with his hand. With a swift and brutal stroke, Otto swung his sword downward, severing Dallas's hand. As Dallas reeled from the shock and pain, his other hand fell off, leaving him defenseless and vulnerable before Otto's relentless onslaught.

"You may have fought well, but your bag of tricks is empty now. This game is over," Otto declared, sheathing his swords and calmly cleaning his glasses, his demeanor radiating confidence and finality.

Hutch, in a desperate attempt to save Dallas, began to liquefy and swiftly move toward him, his form shifting fluidly to reach his fallen comrade. Meanwhile, Keem channeled an intense surge of energy, gathering it within himself to unleash a powerful blast aimed at Mo, intending to send him flying away. Dallas concentrated his intent inward, channeling his power to envelop his entire body in a layer of ice, shielding himself from further harm and fortifying his defenses.

"Oh, no, you don't," Otto exclaimed, swiftly adjusting his glasses and unsheathing his swords.

Just as Hutch lunged to Dallas's aid and the ice threatened to envelop him entirely, Otto struck with lightning speed. His blade descended, slicing into Dallas's body with deadly precision, leaving four gaping wounds in its wake. As Hutch propelled himself out of the water toward Otto, the agile assailant moved with teleporting speed, dodging Hutch's advance. In a swift motion, Otto darted toward Keem, delivering a powerful kick that sent him sprawling to the ground. The force of the impact disrupted Keem's concentration, causing his blast of flames to erupt skyward instead of toward their intended target.

"What the hell was that?" Nakh exclaimed, his voice laden with bewilderment, as he set his cup down in front of him, eyes wide with surprise. He had been engrossed in conversation with the chief, discussing the intricacies of nature's balance, when a sudden disturbance caught his attention. From a distance, he could see an ominous blaze erupting into the sky, casting a fiery glow against the horizon.

His instincts instantly went on high alert, recognizing the unmistakable sign of danger. With a quick glance toward the source of the commotion, Nakh's gaze narrowed, his mind racing to comprehend the unexpected turn of events. As he rose from his seat, a sense of urgency gripped him, compelling him to investigate the disturbance and ensure the safety of his companions.

With a determined nod, Nakh agreed with the chief's assessment. "I'm not sure what's happening, but we must move quickly," he concurred, his voice echoing the urgency of the situation. As they hastily departed from their meeting place, the chief's words reverberated in their minds, urging them to swift action.

The urgency of the situation propelled them forward, their steps quickening as they made their way toward the site of the disturbance. With each passing moment, the sense of unease grew, fueling their resolve to uncover the truth behind the mysterious attack.

Meanwhile, back at the scene of the confrontation, Otto's words hung in the air like a silent challenge, daring Hutch to defy him. The gravity of the situation was palpable, each participant keenly aware of the stakes involved.

With Dallas's fate uncertain and tensions running high, the stage was set for a showdown that would test the resolve of all involved. As Otto and his siblings stood poised for action, Hutch braced himself for the inevitable clash, his determination unwavering in the face of adversity.

Otto approached Hutch, his demeanor composed yet filled with an air of confidence. He glanced at Dallas's prone form, then fixed his gaze on Hutch, who cradled Dallas's head with a mixture of concern and determination.

"One for one. Want to go again and make it three for one? As long as we keep it even," Otto said cockily, turning toward Keem as the clouds began to thicken from the intense heat generated by their battle.

Otto's cocky demeanor hung in the air, a stark contrast to the gravity of the situation. His words dripped with arrogance, a challenge issued with a hint of mockery as he turned his attention toward Keem. Around them, the atmosphere crackled with tension, the heaviness of the impending storm mirrored in the weight of their confrontation.

As Otto spoke, the clouds above began to swell and darken, heavy with the heat of the ongoing battle. The air grew thick with anticipation, each passing moment fraught with the promise of further conflict. Yet, despite the mounting pressure, there was an undeniable thrill in the air, a sense of exhilaration that coursed through the combatants as they prepared for the next exchange.

Keem met Otto's challenge with a steely resolve, his gaze unwavering as he squared off against his opponent. Though outnumbered and facing daunting odds, there was a fire in Keem's eyes, a determination to stand firm in the face of adversity.

As Keem's fury surged, Otto's demeanor remained remarkably composed, almost detached. His response carried a weight of indifference, as if the outcome of their confrontation was inconsequential in the grand scheme of things.

"You will pay for this!" Keem's voice reverberated with anger, his words laced with fierce determination.

In contrast, Otto's tone was calm, almost dismissive, as he countered, "I thought I told you already once. It's not about the money; it's about the sport." His words hung in the air, carrying a subtle implication that their clash transcended mere monetary gain.

The atmosphere crackled with tension as Otto's gaze locked onto Keem's, his expression betraying a hint of apathy toward the materialistic motivations that often fueled such conflicts.

"I think my sisters and brothers care less about the money now that our brother has passed," Otto added, his voice devoid of sentimentality, as if the loss of their sibling had reshaped their priorities in unforeseen ways.

As Nakh and the villagers set out toward the escalating confrontation, Hutch knelt beside Dallas, a sense of urgency in his movements. With a solemn expression, he leaned in closer, his voice low but filled with resolve.

The rain began to fall, a gentle rhythm echoing the somber mood that enveloped them. Hutch's words hung heavy in the air, laden with regret and sorrow, as he poured out his heart to his fallen comrade.

"We've been through so much together, Dallas," Hutch murmured, his voice choked with emotion. "Side by side, we faced every challenge, every obstacle. You were more than just a friend—you were family. And I let you down."

Tears mingled with the raindrops, tracing silent paths down Hutch's cheeks as he grappled with the weight of his words. In that moment, amidst the downpour, he felt the full extent of his loss, the absence of his steadfast companion cutting deep into his soul.

"I should have trusted you more," Hutch whispered, his voice barely audible over the drumming of the rain. "You had the strength, the courage...everything it took to lead us. I'm sorry I didn't see it sooner."

As the rain continued to fall, a poignant reminder of their shared grief, Hutch bowed his head in silent reverence, offering a final farewell to his fallen brother.

"I may have been too stubborn to take the lead," Dallas uttered between labored breaths, a trickle of blood staining his lips as he managed a weak chuckle. "But change is inevitable. Let me share with you the love that Taki bestowed upon me."

With a trembling hand, Dallas extended his palm toward Hutch, a gesture laden with the weight of their shared experiences and the depth of their camaraderie. Despite the pain and uncertainty of their circumstances, there was a flicker of serenity in Dallas's eyes, a silent reassurance that their bond would endure beyond the trials they faced.

"Through all the challenges, Hutch, we've stood together," Dallas continued, his voice tinged with both sadness and resolve. "And even as I depart, know that our journey together has left an indelible mark upon my soul. Take my hand, my friend, and let our memories guide you through the storms that lie ahead."

As Hutch reached out to grasp Dallas's hand, a sense of bittersweet acceptance settled over them, a poignant acknowledgment of the inevitable passage of time and the enduring strength found in their shared connection. And in that fleeting moment, amidst the turmoil of battle, they found solace in each other's presence, drawing comfort from the unspoken bond that bound them together.

As their hands intertwined, an ethereal energy pulsed between them, bridging the gap between their souls. Dallas's gaze softened, his eyes reflecting the depth of his gratitude and the tranquility that enveloped his being.

"She showed me that true fulfillment stems from the heart," Dallas murmured, his voice infused with serene wisdom born of his newfound understanding. "Despite the pain of my wounds, my heart brims with contentment. In her presence, I found the peace that had long eluded me."

Hutch listened intently, his heart heavy with sorrow yet uplifted by the profound bond they shared. He felt the warmth of Dallas's essence enveloping him, a comforting embrace that transcended the physical realm.

"You've been more than a brother to me," Dallas continued, his words imbued with a quiet strength. "And though my time in this world may be drawing to a close, know that my spirit will always be by your side."

As Dallas's final breath escaped him, Hutch felt a surge of icy tears welling in his eyes, freezing upon his cheeks as a poignant tribute to their enduring friendship. In that solemn moment, amidst the echoes of battle and the whispers of the wind, Hutch vowed to carry Dallas's memory in his heart, drawing strength from the indelible imprint of their shared journey.

As the deluge intensified, each raindrop seemed to carry with it a potent energy, permeating the air with a sense of renewal and vitality. Omni, deep in his meditative state atop the hill, felt a subtle shift within him, as if the very essence of nature was stirring within his being.

With each droplet that cascaded down from the heavens, the seed nestled within Omni's stomach began to awaken from its dormant state. A gentle warmth suffused Omni's abdomen, accompanied by a faint pulsing sensation that synchronized with the rhythm of the falling rain.

As the moisture seeped into the soil below, nourishing the earth with its life-giving properties, a profound connection blossomed between Omni and the natural world. The seed, imbued with the essence of creation, responded to the elemental forces swirling around it, unfurling tendrils of growth that extended outward with newfound vigor.

Omni's senses became attuned to the subtle symphony of life unfolding around him—the rhythmic patter of raindrops, the rustle of leaves in the wind, the steady thrum of his own heartbeat echoing in harmony with the pulse of the earth.

In this moment of communion with nature, Omni felt a surge of boundless potential coursing through him, as if he were a conduit for the very essence of existence itself. With each passing moment, the seed within him flourished, its roots anchoring him to the earth while its branches reached upward toward the heavens.

As the rain continued to pour down, nourishing both the land and Omni's burgeoning connection with the natural world, a sense of profound transformation began to unfold. In this sacred union of earth and sky, Omni sensed that he was on the brink of a profound awakening—a rebirth of body, mind, and spirit that would forever alter the course of his journey.

As the energy within Omni surged and pulsed with newfound intensity, the very ground beneath him began to tremble and quake in response. The earth itself seemed to resonate with Omni's burgeoning power, amplifying the energy coursing through his veins.

With each heartbeat, waves of raw energy radiated outward from Omni's core, sending shockwaves rippling through the surrounding terrain. The air crackled with electricity, charged with the potent force of Omni's awakening abilities.

As Omni's connection to the earth deepened, he felt an overwhelming sense of empowerment coursing through him, as if he were tapping into a wellspring of primal energy that had lain dormant within him all along. The very elements seemed to bend to his will, responding to the call of his burgeoning power.

Amidst the tumultuous upheaval, Omni remained rooted in his meditation, his focus unyielding as he embraced the transformative energy surging through his body. With each passing moment, he felt himself becoming more attuned to the natural rhythms of the earth, his senses sharpening as he forged a deeper connection with the world around him.

As the ground continued to quake and tremble, Omni's resolve remained unwavering. He knew that this moment marked the beginning of a profound transformation—a journey of self-discovery and empowerment that would unlock the full extent of his abilities and reshape the very fabric of his existence.

With each surge of energy coursing through him, Omni embraced the power within, allowing it to flow through him like a mighty river, guiding him on his path toward enlightenment and unlocking the true depths of his potential.

As Otto turned his gaze toward the source of the powerful energy, his eyes widened with curiosity and intrigue. Despite the onslaught of attacks from Keem, his attention was momentarily diverted by the overwhelming force emanating from Omni's direction.

The intensity of the energy pulsating from Omni's location was palpable, radiating outwards in powerful waves that seemed to ripple through the very fabric of reality. Otto could sense the sheer magnitude of Omni's awakening, the raw potential surging within him like a tempest waiting to be unleashed.

Despite the chaos of the battle raging around him, Otto found himself drawn to the enigmatic figure of Omni, intrigued by the profound transformation unfolding before his eyes. There was a primal energy to Omni's presence, a raw power that seemed to transcend the physical realm and tap into something far greater.

Even as Keem's relentless assault continued unabated, Otto couldn't help but feel a sense of awe and reverence toward Omni's burgeoning abilities. It was as if he was witnessing the birth of a new era, a paradigm shift that would forever alter the course of their world.

With a newfound sense of purpose, Otto refocused his attention on the battle at hand, steeling himself against Keem's relentless attacks. But deep within, he couldn't shake the feeling that the true challenge lay not in the skirmish before him, but in understanding the unfathomable power that Omni now wielded.

As Keem began to engulf himself in flames, preparing to defend against Otto's impending attack, Otto swiftly closed the distance between them with remarkable agility. With a lightning-fast slide, he maneuvered underneath Keem's fiery defense, his movements fueled by instinct and precision.

Before Keem could fully manifest his flame body, Otto's boot connected with a solid impact, striking Keem squarely and disrupting his concentration. The force of the kick sent Keem staggering backward, momentarily throwing him off balance.

As flames flickered around him, Keem struggled to regain his footing, his fiery aura wavering under the unexpected assault. Despite his best efforts to maintain control, Otto's swift and decisive maneuver had caught him off guard, leaving him vulnerable to further attacks.

With steely determination, Otto pressed his advantage, ready to capitalize on any opening presented by Keem's momentary lapse in defense. As the battle raged on, the clash between their opposing forces intensified, each combatant pushing themselves to the limits in pursuit of victory.

With a defiant glare, Hutch rose to his feet, his resolve unshaken despite the overwhelming odds stacked against him. As Otto approached with calculated precision, Hutch's focus sharpened, honing in on the imminent confrontation that lay ahead.

"You do not know real speed," Hutch declared, his voice ringing out with determination. "I'll show you the true essence of speed right before I kill you."

With each word, Hutch's confidence surged, fueled by a fierce determination to confront his adversary head-on. As Otto continued his approach, Hutch braced himself, channeling his inner strength in preparation for the imminent clash.

Meanwhile, Otto remained undeterred, his movements steady and deliberate as he closed the distance between them. With a casual sweep, he cleared his foggy glasses, his expression betraying a hint of amusement at Hutch's bold proclamation.

As the tension mounted, the air crackled with anticipation, signaling the impending clash between two formidable opponents. In the heart of the storm, Hutch stood resolute, ready to face whatever challenges lay ahead in his relentless pursuit of justice.

With lightning speed, Otto drew his swords, ready to unleash a devastating assault upon Hutch. But before he could execute his attack, Hutch vanished into thin air, leaving Otto momentarily disoriented by the sudden disappearance of his adversary.

For a fleeting moment, there was silence, broken only by the sound of rain cascading down around them. Otto scanned the area, his senses on high alert as he searched for any sign of Hutch's presence.

But Hutch remained elusive, his whereabouts shrouded in mystery as he expertly evaded Otto's pursuit. With each passing second, the tension between them intensified, heightening the anticipation of their inevitable confrontation.

As the rain continued to pour, the stage was set for a battle of wits and skill between two formidable adversaries, each determined to emerge victorious in the face of overwhelming odds.

With the agility of a shadow, Hutch moved swiftly, his form barely discernible amidst the cascading droplets. Otto found himself besieged by a flurry of attacks seemingly emanating from all directions, yet unable to discern their origin.

Each strike landed with precision and force, leaving Otto struggling to defend himself against the onslaught. Hutch's movements were a blur, his attacks executed with such speed and finesse that Otto could scarcely react in time.

Despite his formidable skills, Otto found himself outmatched by Hutch's uncanny agility and stealth. Try as he might, he could not anticipate Hutch's next move, leaving himself vulnerable to each successive strike.

As the rain continued to fall, Hutch's assault intensified, his movements blending seamlessly with the cascading droplets around them. With each attack, he pressed his advantage, his determination unyielding as he sought to overcome his adversary with relentless precision.

In the midst of his teleportation, Hutch conjured an ice sword with a flick of his wrist, its crystalline blade gleaming in the dim light. With swift and precise movements, he unleashed a barrage of slashes upon Otto, each strike propelled by the force of his momentum.

The ice sword cut through the air with a sharp whistle, its frozen edge biting into Otto's flesh with chilling intensity. Hutch's attacks were relentless, his movements fluid and seamless as he danced around his opponent, exploiting every opportunity to strike.

Despite Otto's best efforts to defend himself, he found little respite from Hutch's onslaught. The ice sword carved through his defenses with ease, leaving him battered and bloodied in its wake.

With each successive strike, Hutch pressed his advantage, his determination unwavering as he sought to overwhelm Otto with the sheer ferocity of his assault. In the swirling mist and driving rain, the two adversaries clashed with a primal intensity, locked in a deadly dance of ice and steel.

Hutch, regaining his footing, knelt beside Dallas, his gaze fixed upon Otto with unwavering resolve. With a subtle gesture, he channeled his intent into the raindrops swirling around Otto, manipulating their molecular structure with practiced precision.

In an instant, the raindrops transformed into razor-sharp icicles, gleaming ominously in the dim light. With a swift and decisive motion, they hurtled toward Otto, driven by the force of Hutch's will.

The icy projectiles found their mark, piercing through Otto's defenses with lethal accuracy. One by one, the icicles struck true, embedding themselves in Otto's flesh with chilling finality.

As the last of the icicles found its mark, Hutch rose to his feet, his expression impassive as he surveyed the scene before him. "Your mission has failed," he declared, his voice laced with quiet determination.

With Otto incapacitated by the barrage of ice, Hutch turned his attention back to Dallas, offering a silent prayer for his fallen comrade. Though victory had come at a heavy cost, he remained steadfast in his resolve, prepared to face whatever trials lay ahead.

As Omni gradually emerged from his deep meditation, a sense of foreboding gripped his senses. The tranquility of his inner sanctuary gave way to a growing awareness of the turmoil unfolding in the village below.

With heightened intuition, he could feel the palpable tension in the air, the echoes of conflict reverberating through the earth itself. Each tremor and disturbance spoke volumes, painting a vivid picture of the chaos and strife besieging his surroundings.

As he opened his eyes and surveyed the landscape, a sense of urgency washed over him. Without hesitation, he rose to his feet, his movements imbued with purpose and determination. Though he had yet to fully comprehend the extent of the danger, one thing was clear: his village was in peril, and he could not stand idly by.

With agile grace, Omni leaped from the hill, his movements fluid and purposeful. As he descended, his connection to the earth manifested in a stunning display of verdant energy.

With a mere thought, he willed the growth of towering trees beneath him, their sturdy branches extending outward like welcoming arms. With practiced ease, he grasped onto the nearest branches, swinging from them with the agility of a woodland sprite.

Each leap carried him closer to the village, the rush of wind through his hair and the rustle of leaves beneath his feet fueling his determination. With each swing, he felt the pulse of the earth beneath him, a reassuring reminder of his connection to the land and its inhabitants.

With unwavering focus, Omni propelled himself forward, navigating the dense foliage with the skill of a seasoned acrobat. As he soared through the air, his senses heightened, attuned to the slightest shift in the environment around him.

With each passing moment, he drew closer to the heart of the village, his resolve unwavering in the face of adversity. With the strength of the earth at his side and the determination of a protector, he pressed onward, ready to confront whatever challenges awaited him.

As the villagers closed in on the site of the confrontation, Otto's group watched in shock, their expressions a mix of disbelief and resignation. Despite the gravity of the situation, Otto managed a defiant smile, his words carrying a chilling finality.

"I will come back and kill you," Otto vowed, his voice laced with a grim determination even as he lay dying on the ground.

The weight of his words hung in the air, a stark reminder of the cycle of violence that had unfolded.

With his last breath, Otto's defiance echoed through the clearing, a testament to the fierce loyalty he held for his comrades. Though his life had come to an end, the impact of his actions reverberated through the hearts of those who had known him, leaving an indelible mark on the unfolding events.

As the villagers arrived at the scene, the Stats, gripped by fear and panic, made a desperate attempt to escape amidst the chaos. With a swift motion, one of them hurled a smoke bomb into the air, engulfing the surroundings in a thick veil of smoke.

Amidst the swirling mist, their figures blurred and indistinct, the Stats sought to vanish into the cover of darkness, driven by a primal instinct to evade the looming threat posed by Hutch. Their actions, born out of fear and desperation, betrayed the underlying tension that simmered beneath the surface.

As the smoke billowed and swirled, obscuring their movements, the Stats seized the opportunity to slip away, their footsteps echoing faintly against the damp earth. With each hurried stride, they sought to put distance between themselves and the looming specter of retribution that hung in the air.

Yet even as they vanished into the shroud of smoke, their flight was tinged with an unmistakable sense of apprehension, for they knew that their actions had not gone unnoticed. In the aftermath of the confrontation, the repercussions of their choices would ripple through the fabric of their lives, shaping the course of their uncertain futures.

Sensing the telltale energy signatures of the fleeing Stats, Omni wasted no time in springing into action, his resolve steeled by a sense of duty and determination. With a swift leap, he bounded forward, his movements fluid and purposeful as he pursued the fleeing figures through the dense undergrowth.

Meanwhile, the villagers, undeterred by the sudden chaos, quickly mobilized their resources in a bid to apprehend the fleeing Stats. Riding atop agile raptors, they surged forward with speed and precision, their eyes trained on the elusive figures ahead.

As the chase unfolded, a tense race against time ensued, with Omni and the villagers alike striving to close the gap and bring the fleeing Stats to justice. Through the dense foliage and winding trails, their pursuit continued unabated, fueled by a relentless determination to see justice served.

With each passing moment, the tension mounted, the air thick with anticipation as the pursuit reached its climax. As the gap between pursuers and pursued narrowed, the fate of the fleeing Stats hung in the balance, their desperate flight set against the backdrop of a world poised on the brink of change.

Caught between the relentless pursuit of Omni and the villagers, the fleeing Stats faced a critical decision: to stay together or scatter in a desperate bid to evade capture. Sensing the imminent threat posed by Omni and the oncoming raptors, they quickly weighed their options and chose to split up, hoping to outmaneuver their pursuers through cunning and agility.

With a shared glance of determination, the Stats divided, each member veering off in a different direction. Like shadows melting into the surrounding landscape, they vanished into the dense foliage, their paths diverging as they sought to evade capture.

For Omni and the villagers, the sudden dispersal presented a new challenge: tracking and intercepting multiple targets scattered across the terrain. Undeterred, they pressed on, their determination unwavering as they pursued the elusive Stats with resolve.

Amidst the tangled undergrowth and winding trails, the chase intensified, with each member of the fleeing group fighting to outmaneuver their pursuers and reach safety. Every twist and turn of the terrain heightened the stakes of their daring escape.

As the pursuit continued, the raptors, swift and agile, split into smaller groups to cover more ground. Despite their speed, they found themselves outmatched by the cunning maneuvers of Mo and Ina, who expertly navigated the dense foliage and rugged terrain, staying a step ahead.

With keen senses and intimate knowledge of the land, Mo and Ina evaded the raptors' pursuit, utilizing stealth and agility to slip through the forest unnoticed. Darting through the undergrowth and leaping over fallen logs, they maintained a relentless pace, driven by the urgency of their escape.

Despite the raptor's best efforts, Mo and Ina remained elusive, their movements fluid and unpredictable as they zigzagged through the wilderness. Ducking behind rocks and darting through narrow ravines, they used every available advantage to stay ahead, their determination unyielding in the face of danger.

As the chase continued, the gap between the hunters and the hunted narrowed, tension mounting with each passing moment. With the raptors hot on their trail, Mo and Ina knew that their only chance of survival lay in outmaneuvering their relentless pursuers and finding sanctuary beyond the reach of their enemies.

Ani, in a desperate attempt to shake off her pursuer, multiplied herself, creating a dizzying array of clones. The forest echoed with the phantom images, but Omni remained undeterred by the illusion. He relied not on sight alone but on a deeper connection with the natural world around him.

With each step, Omni felt the subtle vibrations of the forest, attuned to the slightest disturbances and the faintest whispers of movement. Ani's clones attempted to obscure her true presence, but Omni's connection to the earth allowed him to discern the genuine from the illusory.

Moving through the dense undergrowth, Omni honed in on the true essence of Ani's energy, disregarding the distractions of her decoys. With focused determination, he followed the thread of her presence, his senses sharpened by his bond with nature.

Despite Ani's attempts to confound him, Omni remained steadfast, his intuition guiding him unerringly through the labyrinth of the forest. With each passing moment, he closed the distance between them, his resolve unwavering in the face of deception.

Finally, as the echoes of Ani's clones faded into the shadows, Omni emerged victorious, having pierced through the veil of illusion to confront the true source of her presence. With a swift and decisive movement, he closed in on Ani, ready to bring an end to her flight and ensure justice prevailed in the heart of the wilderness.

Perched high in the branches of a nearby tree, Omni surveyed the forest below, his connection to the natural world granting him command over the elements themselves. With focused intent, he reached out to the environment around Ani, bending the very fabric of the forest to his will.

As Ani darted through the undergrowth, her illusions flickering around her like shadows in the moonlight, Omni remained poised and vigilant, his senses attuned to her every movement. With a subtle gesture, he manipulated the earth beneath her feet, causing the ground to shift and buckle beneath her weight.

Caught off guard by the sudden disturbance, Ani stumbled, her footing faltering as she tumbled to the forest floor with a startled cry. As she struggled to regain her balance, Omni watched from his perch above, his expression unreadable as he observed the consequences of his manipulation.

With Ani momentarily incapacitated, Omni descended from the tree, his movements fluid and deliberate as he approached her prone form. Though she attempted to scramble to her feet, he remained a silent and imposing figure, his presence a testament to his mastery over the natural world.

As Ani gazed up at him with a mixture of defiance and trepidation, Omni's gaze bore into her, his eyes alight with an inner fire that spoke of his unwavering determination. With a single gesture, he signaled his intent, his command over the environment a silent but potent reminder of the power he wielded.

With Ani's fate hanging in the balance, Omni stood ready to administer justice, his resolve unshakable as he prepared to confront the consequences of her actions. In the heart of the forest, amidst the whispering leaves and shifting shadows, the struggle between light and darkness raged on, with Omni poised to tip the scales in favor of righteousness.

With a swift motion, Ani drew her sword, its gleaming edge slicing through the thick vine that ensnared her. As the blade cleaved through the tangled foliage, she freed herself from the grip of Omni's earthbound trap, her movements quick and decisive.

With a determined expression, Ani leaped to her feet, her sword held at the ready as she faced her adversary. Despite the setback, her resolve remained unbroken, her gaze locked onto Omni with unwavering intensity.

As she squared off against him, the tension in the air crackled with the promise of conflict, each combatant poised to unleash their full arsenal of skills and abilities. With her sword gripped tightly in her hand, Ani prepared to defend herself against whatever challenges lay ahead, her determination burning bright amidst the shadows of the forest.

As Ani's hand tightened around the hilt of her sword, a sudden movement from the forest floor caught her off guard. With lightning speed, a thick vine shot forth, snaking its way through the undergrowth until it coiled around her sword hand with a vice-like grip.

Caught off balance, Ani grappled with the vine, struggling to free her hand from its constricting hold. The tendrils of the plant seemed to pulse with a life of their own, their strength matching her own in a contest of wills.

Desperation fueled her efforts as she attempted to wrench her hand free, but the vine held fast, its grip unyielding against her struggles. With her sword hand immobilized, Ani found herself vulnerable, her options dwindling as she faced the unexpected challenge from the forest itself.

As Ani's struggles intensified, the surrounding vines responded with a primal instinct, their sinewy forms entwining around her with increasing ferocity. With each thrash and twist, more tendrils emerged from the forest floor, snaring her limbs and coiling around her body like serpents constricting their prey.

Ani's movements grew more frantic as the vines ensnared her, their grip unyielding and relentless. She fought against the encroaching vegetation, but her efforts proved futile as she found herself bound tightly, immobilized within a web of verdant tendrils.

Surrounded by the dense foliage, Ani's form became obscured beneath the layers of foliage, her struggles gradually subsiding as she was enveloped by the embrace of the forest itself. With each passing moment, she found herself sinking deeper into the earth, her fate sealed within the natural confines of the wilderness.

With Ani secured to his back, Omni returned to the group, his expression solemn as he took in the scene of mourning that greeted him. He gently lowered Ani to the ground, her bound form resting among the fallen leaves and underbrush.

The villagers and Root members gathered around, their faces etched with sorrow and contemplation. Some bowed their heads in silent reverence, while others whispered words of solace and remembrance for those lost in the tumultuous clash.

Omni's presence brought a sense of solemnity to the gathering, his quiet demeanor a testament to the weight of the recent events. As he looked upon his companions, he felt the gravity of their shared loss, a somber reminder of the fleeting nature of life and the trials they faced together.

With a heavy heart, Omni joined the circle of mourners, offering his silent support and solidarity in their time of grief. Though words may fail to ease the pain, the presence of companionship and unity provided a glimmer of solace amidst the darkness that enveloped them.

Nakh approached Omni with a heavy heart, his expression reflecting the weight of the news he carried. As he drew near, he began to recount the events that had transpired, his voice tinged with sorrow.

"Omni," Nakh began, his tone solemn, "a group of assassins, likely hired to collect the bounty on Dallas and Hutch, descended upon us. In the ensuing confrontation, Lowell and Dallas fell victim to their blades. However, Hutch managed to strike back, taking down their leader in a valiant effort."

The weight of loss hung heavily in the air as Nakh spoke, the somber reality of their fallen comrades casting a pall over the group. "The toll of this battle has been steep," he continued, his voice thick with emotion. "We mourn the loss of those who fought alongside us, their absence leaving a void that cannot easily be filled."

With a heavy sigh, Nakh turned his attention to Hutch, offering silent support in the face of their shared grief. Together, they stood amidst the shadows of loss, finding solace in each other's presence as they grappled with the harsh realities of war and sacrifice.

As Nakh reached Hutch's side, he gently placed a comforting hand on his shoulder, offering silent solidarity in their shared sorrow. Hutch's tears flowed freely, carrying with them the weight of loss and grief that gripped the entire group. The bond they shared, strengthened by their trials, provided a fragile but vital support system as they faced the long road ahead.

In the midst of Hutch's anguish, his tears seemed to take on a life of their own, spreading like ripples in a pond, touching the hearts of each member of their company. Soon, the air was filled with the sound of collective mourning as tears fell freely from the eyes of those who had stood beside Dallas in battle.

Their cries echoed through the forest, a poignant lament for a fallen comrade, a brother-in-arms who had given his life in the pursuit of their shared cause. In that moment of raw emotion, their bond was forged anew, bound together by the bitter sting of loss and the enduring strength of their unity.

As Omni whispered his question to the chief, the elder's gaze turned solemn, betraying the weight of years of hidden fears. Without a word, the chief gestured for Omni to follow as he began to lead him away from the group, their footsteps echoing softly in the forest.

In a secluded glade, surrounded by the ancient sentinels of the woods, the chief finally spoke, his voice low and measured. He revealed to Omni the dark secret that had haunted their village for a decade, a tale of shadow and death that lurked within the depths of a nearby cave.

"Ten years ago, our village was plagued by a series of mysterious deaths," the chief began, his voice tinged with the weight of sorrow and apprehension. "At first, we believed them to be mere accidents, tragedies born of misfortune. But as time passed, the deaths multiplied, both among our people and the creatures of the forest."

He paused, the silence of the forest seeming to press in around them like a living presence. "Eventually, we discovered the source of our woes—a witch, dwelling within the depths of a nearby cave. Her malevolent power cast a shadow over our village, and we found ourselves powerless to confront her."

The chief's words hung heavy in the air, the truth of their plight weighing heavily upon them both. "Since then, we have lived in fear, avoiding the witch's domain and praying that her anger remains dormant. But the specter of her wrath haunts our every step, a constant reminder of the fragile balance between life and death."

As Omni absorbed the gravity of the chief's revelation, he felt a newfound determination take root within him. Though the task ahead seemed daunting, he knew that he could not turn away from the village's plight. With the chief's guidance, he would face the witch and bring an end to the shadow that had plagued their home for far too long.

With a solemn nod, Omni acknowledged the weight of the chief's words, understanding the magnitude of the task that lay before them. As they stood together in the hushed serenity of the forest, the echo of their shared resolve seemed to linger in the air, a silent promise of courage in the face of darkness.

With a final glance at the village, shrouded in mourning for those lost, Omni and the chief turned their steps toward the looming silhouette of the cave. In the depths of its shadowed recesses awaited the source of their fears, but also the possibility of redemption and liberation from the witch's curse.

Their journey was just beginning, but as they ventured forth into the unknown, they carried with them the hope of their people and the steadfast determination to confront the darkness that threatened to consume them all. With the chief's wisdom as their guide and Omni's newfound strength as their beacon, they embarked on a quest that would test their courage, their resolve, and the very essence of their being.

New Beginnings

As the dawn broke, Omni found himself awake, a plume of smoke swirling lazily around him as he sat outside. He awaited the stirrings of Nakh, his thoughts wandering in the quiet of the early morning.

Meanwhile, inside the medical hut, Keem and Hutch were both in states of rest, their bodies healing from the wounds of the previous day's battle. The air inside was heavy with the scent of medicinal herbs, a comforting reminder of the village's care for its own.

Outside, the world was slowly awakening, the sounds of nature gradually filling the air. Birds chirped in the nearby trees, their melodies a gentle backdrop to the scene unfolding in the village.

Omni took a deep drag from his smoke, exhaling slowly as he contemplated the events that had transpired. The weight of responsibility hung heavy on his shoulders, but he knew he couldn't falter now. There was much to be done, and he would need the support of his comrades to see it through.

As the sun continued its ascent in the sky, casting long shadows across the village, Omni remained vigilant, his gaze fixed on the horizon. With a sense of determination burning in his chest, he knew that whatever lay ahead, he would face it head-on.

As Nakh's eyelids fluttered open, he found himself greeted by the soft light of dawn filtering through the cracks in the hut's walls. Blinking away the remnants of sleep, he shifted slightly, his senses coming alive as he took in his surroundings.

Through the haze of morning grogginess, Nakh's gaze landed on Omni, who sat just outside the hut, his back turned toward him. The faint aroma of smoke lingered in the air, a telltale sign of Omni's presence.

With a quiet rustle, Nakh adjusted himself into a sitting position, his movements careful so as not to disturb the stillness of the moment. He watched Omni for a moment longer, a sense of familiarity settling over him as he took in the sight of his companion.

"The village has a problem," Omni began, his voice carrying a weight of concern. "That group was looking for Hutch and Dallas. That makes it more our problem than just the village's."

Nakh, still groggy from sleep, blinked slowly as he processed Omni's words. Rubbing the sleep from his eyes, he shifted his gaze to meet Omni's, a hint of confusion lingering in his expression.

"There's a witch that they fear inside of a cave," Omni explained to Nakh, his voice low and serious, as he passed him the cannabinoid plant.

Nakh accepted the plant with a nod of understanding, his gaze fixed on Omni as he processed the information.

"But we do not fare well against sorcery," Nakh admitted, a hint of fear flickering in his eyes. "Remember how Fie manipulated us, pitting us against each other?"

Omni nodded, acknowledging the gravity of their situation. "Yes, I remember," he replied, his tone tinged with concern. "But we cannot allow fear to paralyze us. We must find a way to confront this threat head-on, no matter the risks."

"I encountered Fie's sister, and she showed no hostility toward me. The chief aided me, believing I could be of assistance to him in return. Fear not, Nakh. I promise to shield you this time," Omni asserted confidently, accepting the plant back from Nakh.

Nakh quickly dressed, and together, he and Omni made their way to meet with the chief.

Omni and Nakh entered the serene atmosphere of the sacred Tree of Life, where the chief was already seated, his wise eyes scanning the horizon. The ancient tree's branches stretched out like protective arms, casting dappled shadows on the ground. As they approached, the chief gestured for them to sit nearby, inviting them to share in the solemnity of the moment. The air was heavy with anticipation as they settled in, ready to discuss the pressing matters ahead.

The chief's voice echoed softly under the canopy of leaves, carrying with it a sense of gravity that hung in the air. Omni's reassuring touch conveyed solidarity, a silent promise of support that bolstered Nakh's resolve. With a nod of determination, they affirmed their readiness to face whatever challenges lay ahead, united in purpose and fortified by their bond of camaraderie.

"The witch's weaknesses remain a mystery, as does her appearance. None have survived to recount their encounters. But none have ever been like you," the chief's words struck a blow to Nakh's confidence, emphasizing the daunting challenge they faced.

"I will have a villager escort you to the volcano, and may the love in your two hearts guide you through the shadows," the chief's words resonated as Omni and Nakh departed from the Tree of Life, meeting with one of the villagers who would guide them to the volcano.

"I am Spot, and I will take you to the volcano," the villager named Spot announced as they began their journey along the trail.

"Why do they call you Spot?" Nakh inquired.

"Do not laugh, but the first thing I turned into was a little dog," Spot responded with a hint of amusement. Meanwhile, Omni began to grow a cannabinoid plant out of the ground.

Nakh chuckled. "Out of all these animals," he said, glancing at Omni.

As Omni lit up the plant, Nakh noticed a change in his demeanor. "He usually laughs and cracks more jokes than me," Nakh thought to himself as Omni passed him the plant.

Spot's voice quivered slightly as he pointed to the cave entrance. "This is as far as I'm going to go," he said, his words adding to the unease settling in Nakh's heart. "I'll wait here until you two return." His reluctance to venture further underscored the gravity of their mission, filling the air with tension. Nakh exchanged a glance with Omni, his own apprehension mirrored in his companion's eyes. With a nod, they steeled themselves for what lay ahead, knowing they were on their own from this point onward.

Omni's words echoed in the stillness of the cave, his senses attuned to any sign of the witch's presence. Nakh, on the other hand, relied on a more direct approach, drawing his sword with a determined grip. With a swift, controlled motion, he struck the cave wall, the resounding clang reverberating through the darkness.

The vibrations rippled through the air, penetrating the depths of the cavern. As the echoes faded, a tense silence settled over them, broken only by the soft drip of water echoing from the depths. They waited, hearts pounding, senses alert for any response from within the cavern's depths.

As Omni and Nakh approached the mouth of the cave, a palpable sense of foreboding hung heavy in the air. The very atmosphere seemed to thicken, suffused with an eerie darkness that whispered of ancient secrets and malevolent forces.

Each step they took felt like a descent into the abyss, the shadows closing in around them like suffocating tendrils. The jagged walls of the cave loomed ominously overhead, casting long, sinister shadows that danced with the flickering light of their torches.

The air grew colder with each passing moment, chilling them to the bone and sending shivers down their spines. It was as if the very essence of fear itself lingered within the cavern, seeping into their souls and sowing seeds of doubt and dread.

As they neared the cave's entrance, a sense of unease washed over them like a tide of darkness, threatening to engulf them in its icy embrace. Yet, despite the overwhelming sense of danger that permeated the air, they pressed on, steeling themselves for whatever horrors lay in wait within the depths of the cave.

Omni's words echoed in the stillness of the cave, his senses attuned to any sign of the witch's presence. Nakh, on the other hand, relied on a more direct approach, drawing his sword with a determined grip. With a swift, controlled motion, he struck the cave wall, the resounding clang reverberating through the darkness.

The vibrations rippled through the air, penetrating the depths of the cavern. As the echoes faded, a tense silence settled over them, broken only by the soft drip of water echoing from the depths. They waited, hearts pounding, senses alert for any response from within the cavern's depths.

As Nakh's words echoed through the cavern, the air crackled with a sudden surge of energy, and flames ignited along the walls, casting an eerie glow that illuminated the path ahead. The flickering firelight danced and swayed, casting long, twisting shadows that seemed to writhe and twist like specters in the darkness.

The flames seemed to beckon them forward, leading them deeper into the heart of the cave with an almost hypnotic allure. Each step they took brought them closer to the source of the fiery spectacle, the heat washing over them in waves and stoking the flames of their determination.

Yet, even as they followed the trail of fire deeper into the cave, a sense of unease gnawed at the edges of their consciousness. The flames that illuminated their path also cast sinister shadows that danced and flickered with malevolent intent, their movements twisting and contorting in unnatural ways.

As they ventured further into the depths of the cave, the flames grew brighter and more intense, illuminating the chamber ahead with an almost blinding radiance. Amidst the fiery glow, a figure began to take shape, its form wreathed in shadow and flame, a silent sentinel guarding the secrets of the cave.

"I sense a presence," Nakh declared, his voice echoing off the cave walls as flames suddenly erupted around them, casting a fiery illumination that seemed to guide their path forward. As Nakh's words echoed through the cavern, the air crackled with a sudden surge of energy, and flames ignited along the walls, casting an eerie glow that illuminated the path ahead. The flickering firelight danced and swayed, casting long, twisting shadows that seemed to writhe and twist like specters in the darkness.

The flames seemed to beckon them forward, leading them deeper into the heart of the cave with an almost hypnotic allure. Each step they took brought them closer to the source of the fiery spectacle, the heat washing over them in waves and stoking the flames of their determination.

The flames that illuminated their path also cast sinister shadows that danced and flickered with malevolent intent, their movements twisting and contorting in unnatural ways. Omni turned to Nakh, a puzzled expression on his face, to which Nakh responded with a shrug.

"I didn't do that," he insisted, the flames dancing unnaturally around them. They exchanged a glance, and then they both turned to look at Spot, who had taken a hesitant step back from the cave entrance. "That's a first for me," Spot exclaimed, his voice tinged with apprehension.

"We can do this," Omni said with a reassuring smile, nodding at Nakh to encourage him as they walked into the cave.

In the dimly lit cavern, the air grew thick with an eerie silence, broken only by the distant echoes of their footsteps against the rocky floor. The darkness seemed to press in on them from all sides, enveloping them in a sense of foreboding. Nakh's heart raced with each step, his senses on high alert, while Omni remained steadfast, his determination unwavering.

As they delved deeper into the cavern's depths, the temperature dropped noticeably, sending shivers down their spines. The walls of the cave seemed to loom closer, casting menacing shadows that danced and flickered in the faint light. Every sound, every movement, echoed ominously, amplifying the feeling of being watched.

Nakh's grip tightened around his sword, his knuckles turning white with tension. He stole a glance at Omni, who met his gaze with a reassuring nod. Despite the palpable tension, they pressed on, driven by a shared sense of purpose and the need to confront whatever darkness lay ahead.

"Let's experiment," Omni proposed, his tone filled with curiosity. "Do you think if one of us stops walking while the other keeps going, the flames will remain alight?"

"We'll have to take a chance," Omni suggested, scanning the darkened cave ahead. "I'll walk ahead. You stay here. If the flames go out, you'll know it's not safe to proceed alone."

"That's a valid point. We should proceed cautiously," Nakh responded, his voice echoing softly in the cavernous space.

"I'll scout ahead," Omni offered, his voice steady despite the uncertainty looming in the cavern. "We'll cover more ground this way. Stay alert, Nakh." With a nod, Omni forged ahead.

As Omni pressed ahead into the depths of the cave, Nakh held his position, watching intently as the flames continued to illuminate the path behind his companion. With each step Omni took, the flames remained steadfast, casting a comforting glow in the darkness. Nakh felt a surge of confidence as their plan unfolded successfully, knowing that they had found a way to navigate the treacherous cave without losing sight of their path.

As Omni ventured deeper into the cave, a thick haze of smoke began to envelop the space between him and Nakh. The air grew heavy with the acrid scent, obscuring their surroundings and making it difficult to see. Nakh squinted through the smoke, straining to catch a glimpse of Omni's figure ahead. The once clear path now seemed shrouded in uncertainty, and Nakh's heart quickened with unease. Despite the creeping fog, he remained resolute, determined to stay connected with Omni and forge ahead together through the swirling mist.

"Omni!" Nakh's voice echoed through the cavern, cutting through the dense smoke that now surrounded them. Omni's senses heightened at the urgency in Nakh's tone, and he turned swiftly, his heart racing with concern. Before him lay nothing but a thick veil of swirling smoke, obscuring his view of Nakh and the path they had just traversed. In the midst of the haze, Nakh's voice sounded distant yet urgent, urging Omni to find a way back to him through the enveloping fog.

As the smoke began to dissipate, revealing the dimly lit cave once more, a shadowy figure emerged before Nakh, its form obscured by the lingering haze. Nakh's muscles tensed as he prepared himself for whatever threat lay before him, his hand instinctively tightening around the hilt of his sword. He stood his ground, ready to defend himself against whatever adversary had materialized in the smoke-filled chamber.

As the face materialized out of the swirling smoke, its piercing gaze locked onto Nakh's eyes, sending a shiver down his spine. Suddenly, Nakh felt a wave of intense fear wash over him, as if his deepest and darkest fears had been plucked from the depths of his mind and laid bare before him. Paralyzed by the overwhelming terror, Nakh felt his consciousness slipping away, his body going limp as he fell into a coma-like state under the influence of the mysterious figure's sinister power.

As Omni sprinted through the dense smoke, his heart pounding with urgency, he caught sight of a figure standing over Nakh, her hand resting gently on his head. It was the girl they had been seeking, her presence ominous and foreboding in the swirling haze.

With a sinking feeling in his chest, Omni realized what was happening: she was copying Nakh's ability, harnessing his power for her own nefarious purposes. Time seemed to slow as Omni processed the dire situation unfolding before him, his mind racing with thoughts of how to intervene and rescue his comrade from the clutches of the mysterious assailant.

The smoke hung heavy in the air, obscuring Omni's vision and making it difficult to discern the details of the scene before him. Yet, through the haze, he could see the girl's form clearly, her silhouette outlined against the dim light filtering through the cavern. She seemed almost ethereal, a spectral figure emerging from the depths of the cave.

As Omni approached, his footsteps echoing against the stone walls, he could feel the weight of the moment pressing down on him. Every fiber of his being urged him to act, to disrupt whatever dark ritual the girl was performing on Nakh. But uncertainty gnawed at the edges of his resolve. What could he, a mere mortal with earth-based powers, hope to achieve against such a formidable foe?

Still, he couldn't stand idly by. With a determined gritting of his teeth, Omni surged forward, his mind racing with strategies and possibilities. He knew he had to break the girl's concentration, to disrupt the flow of energy coursing between her and Nakh. But how? What could he do to pierce the veil of darkness that had descended upon them?

As he drew closer, Omni felt a surge of energy coursing through his veins, a primal instinct urging him to fight. With a mighty roar, he summoned forth the power of the earth, channeling it into a swirling vortex of energy that coalesced around him like a protective shield. With each step, he drew nearer to the girl, his resolve hardening with every passing moment.

As Omni approached the girl, her form became clearer through the swirling smoke. Dark tendrils of shadow seemed to writhe around her, emanating from her figure like a sinister aura. Her eyes, pools of pure blackness, seemed to pierce through the haze, locking onto Omni with an intensity that sent shivers down his spine.

Her curly hair framed her face like a halo of darkness, adding to her otherworldly appearance. Despite the obscurity of the surroundings, the faint glint of a shiny necklace around her neck caught Omni's eye, a stark contrast to the darkness that enveloped her.

She stood there, a foreboding figure cloaked in mystery and malevolence, her presence casting a pall over the cavern. And yet, there was an undeniable allure to her, a primal magnetism that drew Omni in even as he fought against the fear that threatened to consume him.

As Omni drew nearer to the girl, he could sense her struggle to control the newly copied abilities. The air around them crackled with untamed energy, swirling erratically as if the powers she had absorbed were fighting against her will.

As the girl grappled with the conflicting visions from her two mismatched eyes, her hands instinctively flew to her head, as if trying to contain the chaos within her mind physically. With one eye glimpsing the future and the other rooted in the present, she teetered on the edge of sanity, caught between two divergent realities.

The strain of processing the discordant streams of time was evident on her face, contorted in a mixture of agony and bewilderment. Each moment was a battleground within her consciousness, a relentless onslaught of conflicting images and sensations.

Omni swiftly manipulated the ground beneath Nakh, creating a makeshift conveyor belt that carried him safely out of the cave. Meanwhile, the witch began to grasp the nature of Nakh's abilities.

With her left eye firmly shut, the witch concentrated all her psychic energy on Omni, her right eye glowing with an ominous intensity. As she stared into his eyes, a surge of power radiated from her, reaching deep into his subconscious mind. Omni's worst nightmares were unleashed, amplified by the witch's malevolent influence. He saw his fears materialize before him, twisted and distorted into grotesque forms that tormented his psyche. The echoes of past traumas reverberated through his mind, each vision more haunting than the last.

As Omni advanced, an eerie transformation began to take hold of him. His flesh twisted and contorted, morphing into a grotesque amalgamation of metal and sinew. Half-man, half-monster, he embodied the very essence of his darkest nightmares. With each step, the clanking of metal echoed through the cave, a chilling testament to the depths of his fear.

"I am my deepest fears," Omni declared with grim determination, his voice tinged with a haunting resonance. He raised his monstrous arm, the jagged edges of metal glinting in the dim light. With a primal roar, he lunged forward, his attack aimed squarely at the witch.

With a swift and fluid motion, the witch phased through the wall, reemerging behind Omni in an instant. Before he could react, she seized him with an iron grip, lifting him effortlessly off the ground. With a powerful surge of strength, she hurled him upwards, smashing him against the unforgiving stone ceiling of the cave.

As he plummeted back to the ground, Omni's mind raced, desperately seeking an escape from the witch's relentless assault. With a burst of concentration, he channeled his earth powers, shaping the ground beneath him into a makeshift tunnel. Just before impact, he disappeared into the newly-formed cavity, vanishing from sight in the blink of an eye.

The ground trembled and shifted as Omni burrowed deeper into the earth, his movements guided by instinct and desperation. Above him, the witch searched frantically for any sign of his whereabouts, her eyes darting from one shadowy corner to the next. But Omni remained hidden, his presence obscured by the very earth itself.

In the darkness of his underground refuge, Omni took a moment to gather his thoughts, his heart pounding in his chest as he planned his next move. Though the witch had the advantage above ground, beneath the surface lay a realm where his powers reigned supreme. With newfound determination, he set his sights on confronting his adversary once more, ready to face whatever dangers lie ahead.

One Step Closer

As dawn broke over the territory, the usual morning tranquility was replaced by an unusual stir of activity. The distant sound of marching feet grew louder, heralding the arrival of a significant figure. A large contingent of soldiers, their armor gleaming under the early sunlight, entered the village, their disciplined ranks escorting a figure of notable importance.

At the heart of this procession, Lord Inertia was carried in on an ornate carriage, resplendent and imposing. The carriage itself was a work of art, adorned with intricate carvings that told stories of past victories and the legacy of the realm. It was drawn by four majestic horses, their coats brushed to a shine, their harnesses decorated with the emblems of her house.

As the carriage made its way through the main thoroughfare, the villagers lined up, their faces bright with anticipation and respect. Children hoisted onto the shoulders of their parents, waved small flags, and the air was filled with the scent of freshly strewn flowers meant to welcome the esteemed leader. Lord Inertia, acknowledging her subjects with a gracious nod, radiated a dignified aura that commanded admiration.

As the rhythmic march of soldiers and the murmur of an excited crowd filled the air, the members of the Roots emerged from their shelters. They were greeted by the vibrant spectacle of villagers lining the streets, their hands filled with colorful flowers, which they tossed in the path of the approaching procession. Cheers and jubilant shouts crescendoed as Lord Inertia's carriage drew nearer, turning the event into a vivid celebration of her arrival.

The Roots watched, somewhat taken aback by the fervor with which the community welcomed this towering figure. Each member of the group exchanged curious glances, absorbing the palpable joy that energized the crowd. Children danced along the edges of the road, picking up fallen petals and throwing them into the air like confetti, creating a fluttering cascade of colors that painted the morning with hues of celebration.

From their vantage point, the Roots could see Lord Inertia acknowledging the crowd with regal waves, her face breaking into a rare smile that seemed to light up her stern features. Her presence seemed to embody both the strength and benevolence that had earned her such deep respect from her people.

As Inertia's carriage passed by where the Roots stood, their focus wasn't just on the lord herself but on the reactions of the villagers—each cheer and tossed flower spoke volumes about the loyalty and love the people felt toward her. It was a powerful reminder of the influence and responsibility she wielded, and the Roots felt a renewed sense of the importance of today's forthcoming discussions.

As the procession drew closer, the air thick with the scent of tossed flowers and the sound of jubilation, Nakh leaned toward Hutch with a puzzled expression. "Who is that?" he asked, nodding toward the figure at the center of the celebration.

Hutch watched the procession intently, his eyes narrowing slightly as he pieced together the events of the previous night with the scene unfolding before them.

"I presume that to be Inertia," he responded, his voice carrying a mix of caution and intrigue. "Members of the League came for me last night, but luckily, Keem and Omni were alert and intervened before anything went too far. Their leader,

Misery, came out afterward, proposing to talk terms with us. It seems they do not plan on killing us—at least for now."

As he spoke, Hutch gestured for Nakh to follow, and they began walking toward Lona, who was mingling with other villagers, her eyes were also fixed on the grand arrival. Hutch's demeanor suggested a mix of readiness and skepticism, reflecting the gravity of their situation.

"Looks like we're stepping into a more complicated game," Hutch continued quietly, ensuring only Nakh could hear. "We need to tread carefully and understand their motives fully before making any commitments."

"So, where do we meet?" Hutch asked Lona, his voice low, as they navigated through the crowd that had gathered to celebrate Inertia's arrival.

The importance of their upcoming discussion weighed heavily on him, visible in the set of his jaw and the attentive glance he cast around the village.

Lona, sensing the urgency and the need for a place befitting such a crucial dialogue, responded with a gesture toward the heart of the village. "Next to the sacred temple," she replied, her voice carrying a reverence that matched the solemnity of the location. The temple, revered in their community for its historical and spiritual significance, stood as a symbol of peace and reflection, making it an ideal backdrop for their delicate negotiations.

The history of countless ceremonies and prayers stood stoic amid the verdant growth that draped its walls. The path to the temple was lined with vibrant tapestries and flowers, remnants of past celebrations, adding a layer of tranquility and beauty to their walk. As they approached, the sound of the village festivities faded, replaced by the gentle rustle of leaves and the distant murmur of a waterfall—a serene setting that encouraged thoughtful deliberation and respect.

Lona paused before the temple, allowing the Roots a moment to take in the significance of the place. "This is where paths converge in peace," she said, her eyes reflecting the sacredness of their surroundings. "A fitting place to find common ground."

The Roots arrived at the designated meeting spot, a broad expanse of open land that stretched toward the horizon under the vast canopy of the sky. They expected to find some structure, perhaps even a grand setup befitting a lord, but instead, they were greeted by the simplicity of nature itself—

no buildings, no shelters, just the unadorned earth underfoot and the gentle rustle of grass swaying with the breeze.

As they scanned the area, their confusion was palpable. The openness of the land was disarming, an unusual choice for a meeting of such gravity. Yet there, in the center of the clearing, stood Lord Inertia, alone without her usual entourage of guards. Her presence, unguarded and poised, was a stark contrast to the lavish procession they had witnessed earlier. She seemed a part of the landscape, grounded and formidable yet open and accessible in a way that was unexpectedly reassuring.

Lord Inertia's choice to meet in such a vulnerable setting spoke volumes. It was a deliberate gesture, symbolizing transparency and perhaps a willingness to engage on equal footing, devoid of the usual trappings of power and security. Her solitary figure awaiting the Roots not only underscored her confidence and authority but also seemed to challenge the conventional dynamics of power meetings.

The Roots exchanged wary glances, their initial confusion giving way to a cautious appreciation of the symbolism at play. The open field, the absence of any physical barriers, and the solitary figure of Inertia—it all crafted a setting that was as much about the negotiation of terms as it was about testing trust and intentions.

As they approached, the ground beneath their feet felt more significant with each step, a reminder that they were walking into a meeting that could very well reshape their understanding and strategy moving forward. The air seemed charged with potential; each breath they took filled with the weight of decisions yet to be made and words yet to be spoken.

As they approached the open field where Lord Inertia stood in solitude, Keem leaned in, whispering to Lona with a hint of suspicion, "Where is the temple?" His eyes scanned the horizon, searching for any sign of the revered structure they were led to believe would be the meeting place.

Lona, sensing his unease, replied softly, yet with an assurance that suggested deeper meanings yet to unfold, "Everything will come to light soon." Her gaze remained fixed on Lord Inertia, indicating that the answers Keem sought were tied to the unfolding events.

As the Roots gathered around, forming a semi-circle before Lord Inertia, the air was thick with anticipation. The lord herself, embodying a calm authority, shifted her attention directly to Hutch, who had taken a slight step forward. Her voice, deliberate and resonant, cut through the silence that had settled over the open field.

"Tell me, Hutch. What is your purpose here?" Lord Inertia asked slowly, her eyes piercing into his, searching not just for his spoken intent but for the truth of his character and the motivations of his group. The question, though direct, carried layers of inquiry—about allegiance, intent, and the potential for trust or conflict.

Hutch, feeling the weight of her gaze and the seriousness of the question, took a moment before responding. His comrades watched intently, aware that his answer could set the tone for their relationship with Lord Inertia and potentially influence the strategic alliances within the territory.

Hutch stepped forward, the grass whispering under his feet, and paused to glance around at his fellow Roots. Their expressions were a mix of determination and caution, reflecting the gravity of the moment. As the members of the League of Assassins began to close in, adding a palpable tension to the air, Hutch's voice cut through the growing unease.

"I came here to put an end to Stats before they got to me," he began, his tone steady and imbued with a deep resolve. "But Dallas' last words stick true with me, and I'd rather not live in a world of revenge." His eyes briefly met those of his companions, seeking silent affirmation before continuing. "We come in search of knowledge. Passing your wall to reach the Land of Gods is the path we must take."

His declaration, clear and resolute, echoed across the open field, reaching the ears of friend and foe alike. There was a brief silence as his words settled over the crowd, challenging yet sincere.

Lord Inertia, having listened intently to Hutch's words, subtly shifted her gaze to Misery, who stood discreetly by her side. With a slight nod that carried the weight of command, she passed a folded note to Misery. The contents, unseen by others, hinted at silent communications and decisions being made on the spot. After delegating her message, Lord Inertia slowly sat down on a makeshift seat, her posture relaxed yet commanding, signaling her readiness to listen further and perhaps dictate the terms of their engagement.

The scene was charged with strategic maneuvering and diplomatic subtleties. Each leader, from Hutch to Lord Inertia, played their part in a delicate dance of power and persuasion. As Misery discreetly read the note, her expression unreadable, the future interactions hung in the balance, dependent on the decisions made in these crucial moments.

Misery's response was concise, a simple acknowledgment, "I see," spoken to Lord Inertia as she leaned closer, conveying understanding or perhaps acceptance of the instructions or decisions contained within the note. This brief exchange, though quietly executed, was loaded with implications about the strategic calculus both leaders were engaged in.

As the conversation dwindled, a noticeable change came over Lord Inertia. She leaned back slightly, her demeanor relaxing as her eyelids fluttered closed. It wasn't with the abruptness of fatigue or illness but seemed a deliberate gesture, possibly a signal or a strategic pause in the proceedings.

The Roots, witnessing this unusual behavior, exchanged puzzled glances. The sight of a leader seemingly falling asleep mid-negotiation was unexpected and perplexing. Their gazes swept around the clearing, seeking clues in the faces of the League members or any indication that this was a planned part of the proceedings. The air filled with a subtle tension, each member of the Root group questioning the appropriateness of their next move in such an odd situation.

Misery, aware of the Roots' confused stares, remained unperturbed, her expression betraying nothing of her thoughts or the significance of Inertia's actions. It was clear that those within the inner circle of the League understood the meaning behind what might seem like an abrupt disengagement.

Misery, holding the note she had discreetly received from Lord Inertia, cleared her throat subtly, drawing the attention of all present. The Roots, still somewhat perplexed by Inertia's sudden withdrawal into apparent sleep, refocused their attention as Misery began to speak.

"We, too are in search of knowledge," she began, her voice carrying a mix of solemnity and urgency. "But our quest is threatened. The demigods are looking to advance into our zone." The mention of demigods stirred a murmur among the Roots; the stakes were evidently higher than any had anticipated.

Misery continued, her eyes scanning the note as if to ensure she conveyed every critical detail. "We have hidden the wisdom inside our temple and are preparing to defend ourselves against the demigods." Her statement laid bare the gravity of their situation, explaining perhaps the strategic importance of their location and the unexpected actions of Lord Inertia.

The revelation that vital knowledge was stored within the temple, coupled with the imminent threat that loomed over them, painted a picture of a community on the brink of conflict, one that could have broader implications for the entire region. This context provided the Roots with a clearer understanding of the complex dynamics at play and the potential role they might assume in this larger conflict.

"As Lord Inertia rests, she gathers her strength for the challenges ahead," Misery added, providing a rationale for Inertia's earlier action that might not have been immediately apparent to the onlookers. "We must all prepare for what is coming. We invite you, the Roots, to join us in this defense, to protect the knowledge that could benefit not just us but many beyond our borders."

The proposal struck a chord with the Roots, aligning with their own quest for knowledge and presenting a call to action that resonated with their deeper values. Misery's words, revealing the threats and opportunities, set the stage for a pivotal alliance, one that would require courage, strength, and wisdom to navigate the impending challenges.

Hutch's response was measured, yet laced with skepticism. "So what does that have to do with us?" he asked, his tone revealing both interest and caution. The Roots had their own quests and challenges; aligning with another group, particularly one as entangled in local conflicts as Misery's, was not a decision to be taken lightly.

Misery, understanding the need for clarity and transparency, turned the note around for all to see. The note, penned in an elegant but firm script, articulated a proposal that sought not just assistance but a partnership. "We are in search of the same thing," Misery read aloud, her voice steady and persuasive. "We will teach you our knowledge, and together we will defeat the demigods, allowing everyone safe passage to the Land of Gods."

The field fell silent as the weight of her words hung in the air. Misery's offer was more than a call for aid; it was an invitation to unite under a common cause, promising mutual benefits—the sharing of critical knowledge and a collaborative effort to overcome a formidable threat.

"Can we all agree to these terms?" the note concluded, posing a direct question that now demanded an answer from each member of the Roots.

The proposal struck at the heart of the Roots' mission. Not only did it offer the possibility of accessing new wisdom, but it also aligned with their broader goals of exploration and understanding. Yet, the mention of defeating demigods introduced a scale of conflict that was perhaps more daunting than any they had previously considered.

As Misery awaited a response, the Roots exchanged looks, each contemplating the implications of this alliance. The decision was monumental, requiring a balance between their thirst for knowledge and the risks of entering a conflict possibly beyond their current scope.

Hutch, sensing the gravity of the decision and the need for a collective resolution, nodded slowly. "We need to discuss this among ourselves," he suggested, his voice reflecting both the potential he saw in the offer and his responsibility to ensure his group's safety and interests were not compromised.

Misery nodded in understanding, stepping back to give them space for deliberation. The Roots gathered in a tight circle, their voices low as they weighed the benefits and risks, their decision here poised to set the course for their future endeavors.

Hutch, after a quiet and intense consultation with his fellow Roots, turned back to Misery, his decision clear in his steady gaze. "If these terms will help us on our journey, then we agree," he stated, his voice resonant with the commitment now shared by his group. It was a declaration not just of acceptance but of readiness for whatever challenges lay ahead.

At that moment, Lord Inertia, who had remained a silent observer, seemingly resting, rose to her feet with a fluid grace that belied the deliberations that had just taken place. "I didn't feel like having that talk," she admitted with a slight smile that seemed to soften the stern aura around her. "Thank you, Misery." Her acknowledgment of Misery's role indicated a well-placed trust in her lieutenant to handle the negotiations adeptly.

With the agreement in place, Lord Inertia's demeanor shifted, becoming more commanding, more the leader of her people and protector of their lands. "Now, let us go to the temple and begin the necessary training," she declared, signaling the start of a new phase in their collaboration.

With a purposeful motion, Lord Inertia stomped the ground twice, her action echoing with authority. The earth responded as if attuned to her will; a hole gradually opened, revealing a passageway that spiraled into the darkness below. The Roots watched in awe, the display of power a vivid testament to the knowledge and secrets that Inertia was about to share.

As the entrance to the underground passage fully materialized, the air filled with a sense of anticipation. This was no ordinary path; it was a gateway to ancient wisdom, to strategies and skills that could define the outcome of their impending challenges against the demigods.

Lord Inertia led the way, her figure silhouetted against the dark opening, beckoning the Roots to follow her into the depths where their training—and their transformation—would begin. The passage, while foreboding, promised a journey not just to the heart of the temple but to the core of their own potential.

As they descended into the subterranean depths, the air grew cool and damp, the sounds of the world above fading into a profound silence. The rough-hewn walls of the passage echoed with each step, leading them inexorably toward a realm of ancient power and hidden knowledge. Lord Inertia's voice became the guiding light in the enveloping darkness.

"The temple is ahead," she began, her voice echoing off the stone walls. "It was built with sacred spiritual artifacts that give off pure positive energy, crafted by the ancients and infused with their wisdom." The reverence in her tone spoke of deep respect for the history and power embedded in the structure they approached.

As they walked, Lord Inertia explained the unique conditions of their training ground. "There are no lights in the temple, as we give up the earthbound ability of sight. You will fight in the dark. You will read in the dark. You will train in the dark." Her words laid out a path of initiation that went beyond physical boundaries, pushing into the realms of spiritual and mental endurance.

"This darkness will boost your melatonin and allow you to see the light from within the darkness," she continued, her voice steady and sure. "This will be the only way for you to grow strong enough to compete against the demigods." Each sentence wove a deeper sense of mystery and challenge, framing their upcoming trials as a transformative journey not just of their bodies but of their spirits.

The passage finally opened into a vast, echoing space that felt sacred and ancient. Even in the absence of visible light, there was a palpable sense of energy that vibrated through the air—a raw, powerful presence that seemed to emanate from the very walls themselves.

Lord Inertia paused, allowing the group a moment to acclimate to the profound darkness that enveloped them. "Here, in this sanctum, your true training begins. Here, you will learn to harness the energy of the universe, to find light in the deepest shadow, and to draw strength from the darkness that surrounds you."

As she slowly led the group deeper into the temple, the faint sound of distant chanting could be heard, a reminder of the spiritual legacy that permeated this ancient place. The Roots felt the weight of the challenge ahead, each step forward a deeper commitment to their path, a step closer to facing the formidable powers of the demigods.

Lord Inertia's voice resonated through the vast emptiness of the underground temple. Her tone imbued with a solemn reverence as she addressed the Roots. "Let the darkness lead your path to one of our many monks inside the temple," she instructed, her words floating in the cool, still air. "They will become your guide and teach you what they know."

As she spoke, the darkness seemed to thicken, enveloping the group in a tangible shroud that obscured all vision yet heightened every other sense. The faint echo of their breaths and the subtle shifts of their movements became the only indications of each other's presence. It was as if the darkness itself was alive, an entity that both isolated and connected them in their shared quest for mastery and enlightenment.

The Roots, now fully enveloped by the void, felt an initial surge of disorientation followed by a slowly burgeoning sense of focus. Each member of the group took tentative steps forward; their hands outstretched, their minds alert to any hint or whisper that could lead them to their destined mentors. The promise of meeting a monk, each a keeper of ancient secrets and powerful teachings, spurred them onward, guiding them deeper into the spiritual labyrinth.

Suddenly, from the depths of the shadow, faint lights began to appear like stars in a night sky. These were not lights in the traditional sense but rather emanations of energy, each one representing a monk in deep meditation. The Roots were drawn to these points of light, each finding a path that seemed almost preordained, leading them to a monk whose teachings were meant for them alone.

As they approached their respective guides, the monks opened their eyes, their gazes piercing yet welcoming. The transition from solitude to mentorship was seamless, marked by a silent acknowledgment that each Root had been expected and that their arrival was a pivotal moment in their spiritual and combative development.

Lord Inertia, observing from the periphery, nodded slightly, satisfied with the unfolding process. The training that awaited the Roots would be rigorous and profound, pushing them to the limits of their physical and metaphysical capabilities. Yet, she knew that this was the only way to prepare them for the monumental challenges posed by the demigods. The darkness, once a symbol of the unknown and fear, was now their realm of transformation and insight.

The group moved silently through the cavernous darkness of the temple, the only sounds being the soft padding of their feet on the cold stone floor and the occasional drip of water from the ancient ceiling. The air was thick with a palpable sense of anticipation and the unmistakable energy of a place long dedicated to spiritual and mystical practices.

As they ventured deeper, the darkness seemed to grow even more profound, if possible, swallowing up the faint light that had initially guided them. The subtle energies that had once seemed like guiding stars now faded, or perhaps the group's ability to sense them diminished as the oppressive darkness played tricks on their perceptions. The transition into this deeper darkness was a test in itself, challenging the Roots to trust in their inner strength and the teachings they were about to receive.

One by one, each member of the Roots found themselves drifting away from the others. The sprawling layout of the temple, designed perhaps to encourage solitary reflection and personal discovery, led them unwittingly down separate paths. The darkness, a constant companion, seemed to fold around each individual, isolating them in their own silent bubble of introspection.

Before long, each Root realized they were alone. The absence of voices or footsteps other than their own underscored the profound isolation. The realization was not immediate; the quiet acceptance of their solitude crept in as each step took them further into their own meditative journey.

In this enforced solitude, the Roots were confronted with their own thoughts, fears, and the raw edges of their determination. The temple's design, intentionally or not, had dispersed them to face individual trials or to meet their designated monk mentors without the comfort or interference of their comrades.

This separation, though initially unsettling, became a crucial part of their training. It forced them to rely solely on their senses and skills to confront the temple's challenges without fallbacks. Each silent, solitary step was a step toward self-reliance and deeper understanding, preparing them for the eventual trials that lay ahead in their quest against the demigods.

As they each navigated their separate paths, the temple's purpose became clear: to strip away external dependencies and distractions, focusing each Root on the internal growth necessary to face the formidable powers they would soon challenge.

While the Roots ventured individually into the enveloping darkness of the temple, the members of the League of Assassins, along with Lord Inertia, navigated the labyrinthine corridors with a cohesion born from familiarity and preparation. Unlike the newcomers, they moved as a single unit, their steps confident and synchronized, each turn and passage known to them from previous explorations.

The temple itself was an ancient structure of considerable size, its architecture a complex network of corridors, vast halls, and countless rooms, each designed with a specific purpose in mind. Some rooms were dedicated to meditation and spiritual encounters, while others housed ancient artifacts and scrolls, holding the wisdom accumulated over centuries. The walls were lined with intricate carvings and symbols that told stories of cosmic battles, spiritual enlightenment, and the foundational myths that shaped the beliefs surrounding the temple.

Lord Inertia led her group with a quiet authority, her intimate knowledge of the temple evident as she guided them through hidden doors and secret passages not apparent to the uninitiated eye. The deeper they went, the more the subtle energies of the place seemed to resonate with the group, a hum of power that was almost tangible.

In one expansive chamber, the walls were adorned with murals depicting the celestial hierarchy and the demigods they were preparing to confront. Here, Lord Inertia paused, allowing her team to absorb the sacred lore that these images conveyed. Her familiarity with the temple also meant that she knew where the most potent artifacts were kept—tools that could enhance their abilities and prepare them effectively for forthcoming battles.

As the League of Assassins moved through the temple, their unity and purpose were clear. Each member was acutely aware of the role they played in the larger scheme of Lord Inertia's plans. Their cohesion was a stark contrast to the Roots' solitary wanderings, highlighting different approaches to mastering the temple's challenges based on their knowledge and preparation.

This dichotomy between the two groups not only underscored their differing levels of readiness and familiarity with the temple but also set the stage for how each would face the trials and revelations that lay within. For the League, the temple was a well-known map to be followed; for the Roots, it was an unknown maze to be discovered, each path offering unique lessons and trials.

Within the hallowed darkness of the temple, the monks moved with an uncanny grace and precision that belied their inability to see in the traditional sense. Their movements were fluid and assured, reminiscent of bats skillfully navigating the tight confines of a cave or dolphins gliding effortlessly through the ocean depths. They had transcended the need for visual guidance, instead relying on a deeper, more intrinsic sense of their surroundings that came from years of attunement to the temple's spiritual energies.

The temple itself was a crucible of enlightenment, a sacred space designed not just to strip away the reliance on physical sight but to challenge and ultimately liberate its visitors from the deceptive allure of visual desires. It was here that one learned to perceive the world through spiritual eyes, to walk a path illuminated by internal light rather than external stimuli.

Each member of the Root group now separated and alone, embarked on a personal journey through this enigmatic darkness. The temple's energy seeped into them, whispering ancient secrets and revealing hidden truths about themselves and the universe. As they navigated through the corridors and chambers, each turn and each room presented a unique challenge or a lesson to be learned, tailored mysteriously to their individual needs and weaknesses.

These adventures were not merely physical trials but profound spiritual encounters designed to confront and resolve their deepest insecurities, fears, and desires. The darkness forced them to face these internal demons, to engage with them and, ultimately, to overcome them. With each step and each revelation, their minds grew clearer, free from the chains of their past and their perceived limitations.

As they progressed, their innate abilities began to enhance and evolve. The monks, ever present though often unseen, guided them subtly, providing support and instruction that nudged them toward self-discovery and empowerment. This process was intensely personal and transformative, leaving no part of their psyche untouched.

By the time each Root emerged from their individual voyages through the darkness, they were fundamentally changed. Not only had their mental and spiritual capacities expanded, but their physical abilities had also reached levels of proficiency and power they had never before imagined possible. The temple had reshaped them, not just as warriors but as beings of heightened perception and purpose, now truly prepared to face whatever challenges lay ahead, including the formidable demigods.

As the Roots ventured deeper into the enigmatic depths of the temple, the pervasive darkness that had once cloaked their surroundings began to subtly shift. Initially imperceptible, the change grew gradually, a testament to the temple's transformative power and its ancient, sacred purpose. It wasn't just a removal of light but a reshaping of perception, altering the very way they experienced their environment.

The darkness seemed to pulse with a life of its own, throbbing with an unseen energy that vibrated against their senses. Slowly, the Roots noticed that their reliance on traditional vision was diminishing. Instead, their surroundings began to manifest in new forms—shadows took on textures, sounds carried colors, and the cold stone beneath their feet seemed to hum with a quiet luminescence.

This sensory evolution was disorienting at first, as their minds struggled to adapt to the unusual influx of stimuli. But as they continued their journey, their initial confusion gave way to awe and a deepening understanding. The temple was teaching them to 'see' beyond the limitations of their eyes, to perceive the world through a fusion of senses that defied ordinary experience.

Shapes and outlines, previously obscured by the inky blackness, now appeared as contours of light and energy, painted not by photons but by a more profound spiritual radiance that the temple emanated. It was as if they were learning a forgotten language, the language of the divine and the arcane, which revealed the essence of all things without the deceit of appearances.

With each step, their new vision grew sharper, more attuned to the hidden depths of reality. They began to perceive the energy of life itself, the spiritual signatures of the monks who moved silently among them, and even the lingering echoes of those who had walked these paths before them.

This transformation was not just a physical enhancement but a spiritual awakening. The Roots found themselves shedding the superficial layers of their past perceptions, gaining not just the ability to navigate the darkness of the temple but also a deeper insight into the darkness and light within themselves and the world around them.

As Omni ventured deeper into the temple's heart, the ambient murmurs of the ancient stones and the subtle shifts of air seemed to blend into a chorus of whispers. It was as if the temple itself was alive, speaking in tones only the initiated could understand. The darkness around him was thick, a velvet curtain that seemed impenetrable to the untrained eye, yet alive with hidden forces.

Suddenly, from the enveloping shadows, a voice emerged— a shadowy whisper that seemed both everywhere and nowhere. "Welcome, Omni," it said, its tone resonant yet ethereal, as if the darkness itself had found a voice.

Startled, Omni paused, his senses peaking in alertness. The voice seemed familiar, yet alien, a paradox that made his heart quicken. He scanned the darkness, trying to locate the source, but found that the voice did not seem to come from any one direction but echoed around him, a spectral presence that was both unnerving and mesmerizing.

His training in the temple had taught him to confront the unknown, to find calm in the chaos. Gathering his composure, Omni responded cautiously, his own voice steady but curious. "Who speaks?" he asked, his words cutting through the silence that had briefly fallen after the greeting.

The shadows seemed to pulse gently as if considering his query, before the voice spoke again, this time a soft chuckle accompanying the words, adding a layer of enigmatic depth to the encounter. "One who has watched your journey with great interest," the voice replied, cryptically yet with an undertone of warmth.

Omni felt a mix of apprehension and intrigue. The temple was full of mysteries, each corner, each shadow holding stories and spirits of the past. That a guardian or an ancient spirit might reach out to him was not beyond belief, but it required a careful and respectful engagement.

Omni halted in his tracks, the air around him thick with anticipation and mystery. His hands reached out tentatively, feeling the subtle energies that swirled through the temple's darkness. The question lingered in his mind, stirring a blend of curiosity and caution. "How do you know my name?" he asked, his voice steady despite the uncanny nature of their meeting.

From the shadows, the figure of the monk gradually became discernible. The darkness seemed to part around him like a curtain drawn back, revealing a serene, aged face marked with lines of wisdom and peace. As Omni's eyes adjusted to the contrast, the monk opened his hand, and from his palm, a radiant light burst forth. It was not just a physical light but a manifestation of profound spiritual energy that filled the room with warmth and clarity.

"I have seen you come, and I have had this conversation with you already through meditation," the monk explained, his voice calm and resonant, suggesting vast spiritual experience. "I know what you desire, so join me in meditation, and I can show you the way." His words floated in the illuminated space, inviting and compelling.

With a graceful motion, the monk crossed his legs and settled into a meditative pose, the light from his hand dimming to a soft glow that continued to fill the room with a gentle luminance. He closed his eyes, his face a mask of tranquility, as he awaited Omni's decision.

Omni, moved by the monk's presence and the surreal yet profound connection they seemed to share, felt a deep pull toward the promise of understanding and enlightenment. He took a deep breath, releasing his initial hesitations with the exhale, and carefully mirrored the monk's position. Sitting opposite the sage, he crossed his legs, straightened his back, and closed his eyes, surrendering to the moment.

As he settled into meditation, the ambient sounds of the temple faded into silence, and a new world of sensory perceptions opened to him. The monk's guidance began to resonate in his mind, leading him deeper into a state of heightened awareness where time and space seemed to dissolve, revealing the layers of reality and consciousness that lay beyond the physical senses.

This moment marked the beginning of a transformative journey for Omni, under the guidance of a monk who had transcended the ordinary limits of knowledge and perception. Here, in the heart of the ancient temple, enveloped by darkness yet surrounded by light, Omni was poised to uncover the truths that would empower him and his comrades in the challenges that lay ahead.

Omni settled into his meditation posture, feeling the cold, smooth stone beneath him. As he closed his eyes, he took a deep, steadying breath, the monk's words echoing in his mind. "Do not think of nothing; imagine where you want to talk and take us there," the monk instructed with a serene confidence that belied the complexity of his request.

Confusion flickered across Omni's closed eyelids. The concept was unfamiliar, intriguing, yet daunting. How could one simply choose a location within the mind and transport both spirits there? The idea challenged his understanding of meditation and spiritual practice.

Sensing Omni's hesitation, the monk added gently yet with assurance, "Once you imagine the place, put the intent into my head, and I will follow." His voice was a guiding light in the shadowy depths of uncertainty that Omni felt.

Encouraged by the monk's calm certainty, Omni let his mind drift, searching for a place that felt significant, a landscape that resonated with his current journey. Slowly, an image began to form in his thoughts—a vast, tranquil lake surrounded by towering mountains under a starlit sky. This place, though a creation of his mind, felt deeply real, imbued with a sense of peace and possibility.

With the image clear in his mind, Omni focused on projecting this thought, this intent, toward the monk. He envisioned the idea traveling from his mind, through the space between them, and into the monk's consciousness. It was like threading a needle with a strand of thought, delicate yet deliberate.

As Omni held this image, the air around them seemed to pulse softly, the energy of the temple resonating with the power of their combined focus. There was a momentary sensation of movement, not through physical space, but through layers of consciousness, as if they were diving deeper into a shared dream.

Then, tranquility settled over them. In the mindscape they now shared, they sat by the imagined lake, the sound of gentle waves lapping at the shore, the crisp mountain air mingling with the scent of pine and earth. The monk opened his eyes within this mental construct, a smile playing on his lips. "Very good, Omni. Now, let us converse here, where your mind is free from the constraints of the physical world."

This shared journey into a mental sanctuary was not just a lesson in advanced meditation techniques but a profound exploration of the potential that lay within Omni's own mind. It was an initiation into higher levels of mastery, revealing that the path to power and understanding could be as boundless as the imagination itself.

As the serene image of the tranquil lake began to fade from Omni's mental landscape, he felt a pull toward a place deeply rooted in his past experiences—a hilltop where his journey into deeper self-awareness had once taken a significant turn under the guidance of the chief. This was not just any hilltop; it was a place of awakening, of pivotal moments and profound clarity.

With this new destination clear in his mind, Omni shifted his focus. He summoned a vivid memory of the hilltop, recalling the feel of the grass beneath him, the panoramic view of the valley below, and the expansive sky above. The details were crisp in his mind's eye: the way the wind danced through the trees, the scent of the earth after a rain, and the warmth of the sun on his skin.

Concentrating on this image, Omni began the delicate task of transferring this mental scene to the monk. He envisioned the thoughts forming a bridge between their minds, a conduit through which the image of the hilltop could travel. It was a process of deep intent and focused will, pushing the boundaries of his mental capabilities.

As Omni projected this scene, the monk, sitting opposite him in their shared meditative space, received the image with a nod of acknowledgment. His expression reflected a quiet appreciation of Omni's choice—a place symbolizing personal growth and introspection.

The transition was seamless. The environment around them shifted subtly at first, then more distinctly, as the imagined hilltop took form around them in the realm of their shared meditation. They were no longer in the temple or by the lake but were now sitting on the grassy hilltop, surrounded by the sounds and sights that Omni had so vividly remembered.

The monk opened his eyes, now looking out over the hilltop view, and smiled gently at Omni. "A place of learning and reflection," he observed, his voice carrying a hint of reverence for the significance of this location in Omni's spiritual journey. "Let us explore what this place means to you and how it shapes your path forward."

In this recreated hilltop setting, the monk began to guide Omni through a deeper exploration of his past experiences and current challenges. This was more than a mere recollection; it was an active engagement with his subconscious, a way to unlock deeper insights and empower his spiritual and emotional growth.

The hilltop, recreated in their shared meditative state, offered a panoramic view that stretched endlessly under a sky streaked with the soft colors of dawn. The tranquil surroundings, accompanied by the gentle rustle of leaves and the distant call of birds, formed a stark contrast to the dark, enclosed spaces of the temple below.

"This is peaceful," the monk observed, his voice carrying a tone of curiosity mixed with a hint of admiration. He turned to face Omni, his eyes reflecting the serene landscape around them. "Why do you bring us here?" he inquired gently, encouraging Omni to explore and articulate the significance of this particular mental and spiritual landscape.

Omni took a deep breath, the fresh, crisp air filling his lungs as he gathered his thoughts. This place, though a construct of his mind, was imbued with profound personal meaning. It was here, on this hilltop, where he had first truly connected with the elements and where he had begun to understand the depth of his abilities.

"This is where I learned to become one with nature," Omni shared, his eyes reflecting the hues of the landscape that enveloped them both. "The chief taught me how to become one with my body and not just my mind." His words carried a tone of reverence and gratitude, painting a vivid picture of his transformative experiences on this very hilltop.

The monk listened intently, nodding slightly as Omni spoke. The serene environment seemed to echo the sentiment of unity and balance that Omni described, with each element of the hilltop scene—from the whispering wind to the sturdy earth underfoot—serving as a testament to the lessons of harmony and integration.

After a moment of thoughtful silence, the monk posed a question, one that seemed to delve deeper into the essence of Omni's journey. "Do you know what your name means?" he asked gently, his voice soft yet carrying a weight that suggested the importance of his inquiry.

As the gentle breeze stirred the leaves around them, the monk observed Omni closely, taking note of his response and the slight shift in his demeanor. "No. No, I actually don't," Omni admitted, his voice carrying a hint of resignation mixed with newfound curiosity. "My mother said one of her sister's friends named me. So, I never gave interest in the meaning."

The monk nodded thoughtfully, taking a deep, relaxing breath before speaking, his tone soft yet encouraging. "Sometimes the names we carry are more than just labels passed down from others. They can be a compass, guiding us toward our destiny or reminding us of who we are meant to become," he explained, his eyes reflecting a deep well of wisdom.

He continued, "Understanding the essence of your name might provide you with insights into your path and the energies you are meant to harness. 'Omni,' encompassing all, suggests a capacity for vast understanding and connection. It speaks to potentiality, the possibility to be in tune with the myriad aspects of the cosmos."

Omni listened to the monk's words, sparking a series of thoughts and questions about his own identity and the deeper implications of his name. It was as if a door he had never noticed before was slowly creaking open, inviting him to explore what lay beyond.

"Perhaps," the monk suggested gently, "it is time to consider what your name means not just to the one who gave it to you, but to you personally. What power it might hold, what it might teach you about your own nature and capabilities."

The hilltop, with its expansive view and peaceful aura, seemed the perfect backdrop for such introspection. Omni felt a connection to his name deepen, realizing that it might hold the key to understanding more about his spiritual journey and his role in the universe. This unexpected shift in perspective was both daunting and exhilarating.

The monk's voice was calm and deliberate, each word carefully chosen to guide Omni through the layers of his name and its broader connotations. "Omni means all," he began, setting the foundation for the profound lesson he was about to impart. "But it is just the beginning. Have you heard of Omnipotent, Omniscient, and Omnipresent?"

Omni nodded, his interest piqued as he sensed the depth of what the monk was about to reveal.

"Omniscient is to know everything," the monk continued, his eyes locked onto Omni's, ensuring he grasped the full weight of each concept. "But knowing everything does not mean you can change everything, especially when dealing with other people. Knowledge alone isn't always enough to effect change; it must be paired with wisdom and understanding."

He paused for a moment, letting the idea settle in Omni's mind before moving on to the next term. "Omnipresent is to be present everywhere at the same time. Through the sense of nature, you will be able to feel for many things, but you will not be able to be everywhere. True presence is about more than physicality; it's about where you direct your energy and focus."

Finally, the monk addressed the last of the triad. "And Omnipotent is having unlimited power, being able to do anything. But such power is only attainable once you find your heart, once you align your immense capabilities with the true essence of who you are and what you stand for."

The monk leaned closer, his voice dropping to a whisper as if imparting a sacred secret. "These concepts are not just definitions; they are stages of spiritual evolution. They represent the journey you are on, Omni. Your name is not a simple label—it's a roadmap to what you can become."

Omni absorbed the monk's words, each sentence sparking a cascade of thoughts and revelations within him. The ideas of omniscience, omnipresence, and omnipotence—once abstract terms—suddenly took on tangible significance. They were not just powers to aspire to; they were aspects of a much larger journey toward self-mastery and spiritual enlightenment.

"Your journey," the monk concluded, "is about balancing these elements within yourself. Learning to know when to use knowledge, where to present your energy, and how to harness your power responsibly. Finding your heart is essential. It is the compass that will guide you through these vast potentials without losing sight of your humanity."

As the monk finished speaking, Omni felt as if the ground beneath him had shifted. The hilltop, the temple, and the deep meditative space they shared—everything seemed to echo the truth of the monk's teachings. Omni realized that his path was not just about acquiring skills or overcoming challenges; it was about evolving into the fullness of his name, embracing all aspects of being, and ultimately finding the harmony within that would unlock his true potential.

As the monk's words echoed through the serene hilltop, a sudden clarity struck Omni like a gentle yet profound revelation. The mention of a dream stirred memories deep within him, where visions of Finity intertwined with his feelings and aspirations. His heart momentarily lifted at the thought of her. "I think Finity is my heart," he confessed, a hopeful smile playing on his lips as he visualized her face, a symbol of love and connection in his journey.

The monk, observing Omni's expression change, responded with a gentle but firm correction, aiming to guide his understanding deeper. "No, she is a person, not a heart. You cannot look outside to find your heart." His voice was soft yet carried a weight that seemed to ground Omni's fleeting thoughts back to the core of their meditation.

"If you want to be happy, just be happy. Leave your selfish thoughts and your personal desires behind, and your heart will arise," the monk continued, his words flowing like a calming stream, washing over Omni's earlier misconceptions. "Love is not singular, and it does not belong to one person. Feel the love for all beings on Earth, and you will hear your heart beat like it never did before."

These words resonated within Omni, stirring a profound emotional and spiritual awakening. The monk's guidance was clear: true love was universal, expansive, and unbound by individual attachments. It was a force that connected all life, a fundamental vibration that echoed the very essence of existence.

"Once you hear it beat, let the sound of the beat lead you," the monk concluded, his eyes closed in meditation, his presence a calming force. The simplicity and depth of this instruction left

Omni to ponder, to let the concept of universal love and inner guidance sink deeply into his consciousness.

As they continued to meditate, the ambient sounds of the hilltop seemed to fade into the background, replaced by the emerging awareness of his own heartbeat. Omni focused, allowing each beat to resonate more clearly, more profoundly. Slowly, the external world dimmed, and he was left in a space where only the heart's rhythm existed—a rhythmic guide back to his true self, beyond the personal, reaching into the universal.

In this sacred space of meditation, Omni felt his earlier conceptions of love and connection broaden, transcending personal affection to embrace a love that was boundless and inclusive. The monk's teachings had opened a doorway to a deeper understanding of what it meant to truly love and be connected—not just to a person but to the life force that animated all beings.

Keem found himself enveloped by an oppressive darkness that seemed to thicken with each step he took deeper into the temple. The absence of light was not just a physical barrier but a psychological one, challenging his senses and his sense of self. As the familiar comforts of sight were stripped away, he felt increasingly isolated, his surroundings a mysterious void that seemed to pulse with unseen energies.

Lost in this tangible darkness, Keem's other senses began to heighten. The subtle sounds of his own movements echoed oddly in the space, making him acutely aware of his solitude. The cool air felt heavier as it brushed against his skin, carrying with it faint, unidentifiable scents that teased his mind, hinting at the temple's ancient secrets just beyond his reach.

It was in this realm of shadow and uncertainty that Keem's internal struggles came to the forefront. The darkness outside mirrored the darkness within—his fears, doubts, and unresolved conflicts. Each step became a test of his resolve, a journey not just through the physical space of the temple but through the more daunting labyrinth of his own psyche.

As he ventured onward, navigating by touch and the occasional sounds that reached his ears, Keem began to reflect on the reasons he was here. His initial goal to gain power and knowledge was now intertwined with a deeper, more pressing need to understand his own strengths and weaknesses. The temple, with its enveloping darkness and silence, offered a rare opportunity to confront these inner demons without distraction.

As Keem continued to navigate the enveloping darkness, a sudden burst of light momentarily startled him—a flame that appeared without warning and blazed with an intensity that rivaled the sun itself. It was not just any flame; it carried with it the aura and might of a dragon, pulsating with power and ancient energy. Keem stopped in his tracks, mesmerized and momentarily overwhelmed by the spectacle.

"The power of the dragon," remarked a calm voice nearby, breaking the silence that had fallen after the flame's appearance. Keem turned toward the source of the voice and saw a figure cloaked in the shadows, a monk whose presence seemed as timeless as the temple itself.

The monk stepped forward, his movements echoing the serenity and controlled strength that the flame itself suggested. "Haven't seen such a flame so bright in all of my life," he continued, his eyes reflecting the firelight. "Why do you seek power when you are already powerful?" His question was gentle yet probing, aimed at the heart of Keem's quest and the inner turmoil that accompanied him.

Keem, taken aback by the question, searched around him as if the shadows might hold an answer. The monk's question pierced through the facade of confidence and ambition that

Keem often projected. It forced him to confront a fundamental doubt about his pursuit of power and his understanding of what it truly meant to be strong.

Keem's response was tinged with a mix of frustration and curiosity. "Power is the only way to protect my people. I have met a lot of people who are stronger than me, so how can you say I have power?" His tone reflected his inner conflict—caught between his understanding of power as a means to safeguard and his experience of often feeling outmatched.

While Omni and Keem underwent their intensive training under the watchful guidance of their respective monks, Nakh found himself in a markedly different setting. He entered a large, expansive room, dimly lit yet clearly defined, filled with rows of ancient tables and chairs meticulously arranged to face the center of the space. Each piece of furniture was carved from dark wood, surfaces worn smooth by the passage of countless years and countless scholars who had once studied there.

The atmosphere in the room was thick with the scent of old paper and ink, a testament to the knowledge that had been poured over and preserved in this sacred place. Along the walls, shelves brimming with scrolls and books lined every available space, their spines a patchwork quilt of histories, philosophies, and arcane secrets.

Nakh felt a reverential awe as he stepped further into the room, his footsteps echoing softly on the stone floor. The silence was profound, broken only by the occasional flutter of a page in the draft of his passing. This was no ordinary library; it was a repository of vast wisdom, a place designed not just for learning but for understanding the deeper currents that ran beneath the surface of all knowledge.

Nakh's voice carried softly across the room filled with ancient texts and the heavy scent of knowledge long preserved. "Is anyone there?" he called out, more to the quiet air than expecting a response. The room seemed to absorb his words, the silence following his question feeling almost palpable.

"There is always someone everywhere," came a reply from a shadowed corner of the room, where the light barely reached. The voice was old, wise, and tinged with an air of mystique. A figure stepped forward, the outlines of his robes blending with the darkness until he was close enough for the faint luminescence of the texts to illuminate his aged face. "But that's not the question that you want to ask. You seek knowledge. Great knowledge."

Nakh turned toward the source of the voice, his curiosity piqued and his heart beating a tad faster with anticipation. The monk's presence was unassuming yet filled with an authority that seemed to echo with the walls of this sacred library.

"I've been there," the monk continued, his eyes reflecting a depth of experience, "In the city where the streets are gold and only books live in the homes. The City of the Great Library is what you seek." His words painted a picture of a place that Nakh had only envisioned in his most ambitious dreams, a city that seemed to promise the answers to the questions that had long burned in his mind.

"Come! Come meditate with me, and I will show you what you seek," the monk invited, settling down cross-legged on a small, worn rug that seemed to have been placed there for just such a purpose. His demeanor was inviting yet solemn, suggesting that the journey they were about to undertake was no ordinary one.

Nakh, driven by his thirst for the knowledge that might change the course of their quest, joined the monk on the floor. They both closed their eyes, the world around them fading away as they slipped into a state of meditation. The room, the temple, and the world they knew dissolved into the ether.

As they delved deeper into their meditative state, Nakh began to see visions of a city bathed in golden light, where the streets glimmered with the promise of untold wisdom. Towering shelves lined with endless books rose around him, each tome a gateway to new realms of understanding. This was the City of the Great Library, a metaphysical space that transcended physical boundaries, a repository of all the world's knowledge.

The monk's voice guided him through the streets of this visionary city, pointing out landmarks that were not places but ideas, theories, and philosophies that had shaped the course of civilizations. Nakh absorbed it all, his mind expanding with every detail, every word.

As they sat in deep meditation within the dimly lit confines of the temple library, the monk focused his intent, channeling the essence of the City of the Great Library into Nakh's consciousness. The transition was seamless, and soon, Nakh found himself walking alongside the monk down the shimmering golden streets of this metaphysical city, a place where knowledge breathed through the very air.

The monk's words floated around Nakh, blending with the ethereal ambiance of their surroundings. "To reach the Land of Gods, you must survive," he began, his voice both a warning and a wisdom. "Can you feel the molecules within your body? If you sit here and focus, I can teach you how to control your molecules and others. Even gas, liquid, and solid matter."

Nakh listened intently, the monk's guidance opening doors to possibilities he had never imagined. The idea of manipulating vibrations and molecules seemed daunting, yet the city around them, a manifest of such arcane knowledge, made it all seem within reach.

"The vibrations that you should be controlling are of great stature," the monk continued, his gaze intense, urging Nakh to grasp the gravity of his potential capabilities. "Connect your manipulation of vibrations with the molecules of the universe and become great."

As they walked, the monk handed Nakh a book, its cover worn but resonating with a profound energy. "This is Reiki," he explained. "It will allow you to use your energy from within to heal your friends. If you survive, the knowledge is yours." The statement was solemn, underscoring the serious nature of the powers Nakh was being introduced to.

As the vivid imagery of the City of the Great Library gradually receded from Nakh's consciousness, he slowly transitioned back to the reality of the temple's library. The transition was gentle, yet Nakh felt a profound shift within himself as if he had crossed an invisible threshold from one realm of understanding to another. He opened his eyes, the dim, ambient light of the library greeting him once more, a stark contrast to the golden radiance of the city in his meditation.

In his hands, the Reiki book he had received from the monk continued to resonate with the energy of their session. The book vibrated subtly at first, a sensation that might have been dismissed as a lingering effect of the deep meditative state he had been in. However, as moments passed, the vibration intensified, making the book appear as if it were shaking on its own accord.

Nakh gazed at it in awe and slight trepidation. The physical manifestation of the book's power was unexpected and slightly unnerving. He could feel the energy emanating from the pages, pulsing in sync with his own heightened awareness of the molecular vibrations around him. The monk's teachings echoed in his mind, reminding him of the connection he now understood between his own energy and the energies of the universe.

Hutch's path through the temple had been a silent, solitary journey thus far, his footsteps echoing softly against the ancient stone floors, a steady rhythm that seemed to sync with his heartbeat. The darkness, while initially disorienting, had gradually become a companion, its presence now a familiar shroud that enveloped him, sharpening his other senses.

As he ventured deeper, the sound of his footsteps began to change. The solid, echoing tap of stone was replaced by a softer, irregular splashing. Confused, Hutch paused, extending his hands to feel his surroundings. The air was cooler here, and there was a palpable humidity that clung to his skin. He took a cautious step forward and felt his foot sink slightly into a shallow puddle.

The realization dawned on him slowly—he was no longer walking on dry stone but was traversing through what felt like a series of small water pools. The sound of water, gentle and unassuming, filled the space around him, and he could sense the subtle shifts in the air as the coolness of the water mingled with the warmth of his breath.

Curiosity piqued, Hutch continued forward, his steps careful and measured. Each splash was a small reminder of the temple's complex nature, each drop of water a note in an unseen melody that seemed to guide him. The floor beneath his feet gradually became more uneven, and the shallow puddles grew deeper, compelling him to slow his pace and pay close attention to the liquid terrain.

Suddenly, his hand brushed against something unexpected—a wall, smooth and cold but covered in what felt like moss or algae. The sensation was strangely comforting, the natural growth a sign of life in the pervasive darkness. As he followed the wall, his fingers traced the outlines of intricate carvings and patterns that spoke of water's sacred role in the temple's design and mythology.

It became clear to Hutch that he had entered an area of the temple dedicated to the element of water, perhaps a sanctum where monks once meditated on the fluidity and transformative power of this essential element. Embracing the symbolism of his surroundings, Hutch allowed himself a moment to reflect on the fluid aspects of his own nature—the parts of himself that were adaptable, ever-changing, and yet as persistent and powerful as a river carving through stone.

With renewed resolve, Hutch continued to navigate through the watery pathway, each step taking him deeper into both the physical and spiritual depths of the temple. The water around him seemed to echo with ancient chants, a reminder of the countless seekers who had walked these paths before him, seeking enlightenment through the embrace of nature's most versatile element.

Hutch paused at the edge of the small pool of water, his reflection barely visible in the dim light that seemed to seep from the stones themselves. The pool was a still mirror, undisturbed and serene, contrasting with the uncertainty he felt within. As he contemplated the quiet surface, a voice suddenly broke the silence, reverberating softly through the chamber.

"What does the water tell you?" the monk inquired, his voice emerging from the shadows behind Hutch. There was a gentle curiosity in his tone, an invitation to explore deeper meanings rather than a mere question.

"Nothing at all," Hutch responded, his tone flat, a hint of frustration threading through his words. He turned slightly to glance at the figure of the monk who approached, his robes barely making a sound as he moved closer to the edge of the pool beside Hutch.

The monk's voice resonated with profound reverence for the element they discussed, casting water in an almost mystical light. "The water is all-knowing and all-powerful, like no other. It holds memories of the earth that will never fade away and possesses abilities that are unique to this world." His gaze was steady on Hutch, ensuring every word sank deep into his consciousness.

"You can feel the true pain of someone's life by feeling their teardrop," the monk continued, his voice soft yet filled with intensity. "You can obtain all the information you need from someone's sweat. These are not mere metaphors, Hutch. Water carries essence, it carries life and histories, and it binds all living things."

The monk gestured to the small pool, its surface serene and inviting under the dim light. "You must listen to the water and allow it to work within you. Understand its cycles, its patience, and its persistence. Notice the water's abilities and learn to emulate them. Water rises to the clouds as if it flies, transcending the confines of the earth in a cycle of endless renewal."

With a deliberate pause to let his words permeate the air, the monk concluded, "Now, taste the water you're standing on and tell me what you see."

Intrigued and slightly apprehensive, Hutch knelt by the edge of the pool, his reflection staring back at him from the surface. He cupped his hands, scooped up some of the cool water, and brought it to his lips. As the water touched his tongue, it was not just the coolness or the slight mineral taste that he experienced. It was as if with each droplet, images, emotions, and sensations flooded his mind—echoes of the water's journey through the earth, through roots and rivers, through rain and clouds.

As Hutch bent down to taste the water, a chill ran through him—not from the temperature but from the anticipation of what the monk had promised. With a small sip, he closed his eyes, allowing the simplicity of the act to transcend the ordinary. The moment the water touched his lips, his mind was flooded with vivid memories, each as clear and poignant as if he were experiencing them again.

The visions that swirled before him were of Dallas, his friend and companion through countless adventures. He saw laughter shared under the open skies, challenging moments overcome together, and the simple, quiet times that truly defined their friendship. Each memory was a snapshot of joy and camaraderie, rendered in the brilliant clarity that only the most cherished memories hold.

"Water is like energy. It cannot be destroyed," the monk's voice echoed through the montage of memories, grounding Hutch back to the lesson at hand. "As long as you know this, your memories will never be forgotten. Use this source of energy to power the world with the visions you see."

Hutch opened his eyes, the images of Dallas still dancing at the edges of his thoughts. The monk's words had struck a chord deep within him, intertwining the teachings of water's eternal cycle with the enduring nature of his memories and the energies they carried.

A smile broke over Hutch's face, born from the warmth of the memories and the comforting realization that those he loved and lost were never truly gone. They lived on in the world's cycle, in the energy of life that water symbolized, and now, in his understanding of how deeply interconnected everything was.

With newfound resolve, Hutch nodded to the monk, feeling a surge of gratitude for the profound lesson. "I see now how the energies we carry and share continue to influence the world, just like the water's cycle. I'll honor these memories and use them to inspire and energize not just myself but those around me."

The monk smiled back, a look of approval in his wise eyes. "Yes, let the flow of water inspire your path. Remember, just as water nourishes the earth and supports life, so too can the energy you channel nourish and uplift those around you. Your memories, your hopes, and your dreams are all part of the great cycle of energy that binds us."

Hutch stood by the water's edge a moment longer, reflecting on the monk's teachings. He felt a profound connection to the world around him, a sense of purpose renewed by the understanding that every action, every memory, had its place in the world's vast tapestry. Energized by this realization, he was ready to continue his journey, carrying with him the lessons of the water—endurance, renewal, and the indelible nature of life's energy.

As Finity ventured deeper into the temple's enigmatic corridors, her footsteps grew softer, her presence almost blending with the shadows that enveloped her. The temple seemed to respond to her movement, as if aware of her passage through its ancient halls. The darkness, a thick cloak around her, was not just an absence of light but a presence that felt almost alive, whispering secrets of the past in hushed tones.

Just as she adjusted to the near-total darkness, a subtle change occurred. Without warning, half of the room ahead began to illuminate gently. It was as if an invisible line had been drawn down the center of the space, one side bathed in a soft, ambient light while the other remained shrouded in mystery.

The contrast was startling, and Finity paused, her eyes widening as they adapted to this sudden shift.

The light seemed to pulse gently, casting soft shadows around the room as Finity stood beside the monk, their gaze fixed on the illuminated half. The monk's question lingered in the air, "You can see the light, my dear. Do you know why?" His voice was both gentle and laden with a wisdom that hinted at deeper truths yet to be revealed.

"No," Finity replied honestly, her voice a mixture of curiosity and apprehension. She felt the weight of the moment, sensing that the monk's question was about to lead her to a profound revelation.

"I'll show you," the monk said with a reassuring smile. He extended his hand toward the light, and as he did, the air around them seemed to shimmer, the boundaries between reality and vision blurring.

Before Finity's eyes, images began to materialize within the light—a vivid, lifelike vision that pulled her in. She saw herself, younger and carefree, with Pi and her father. They were in a place of breathtaking beauty, an idyllic realm that radiated peace and joy. The Land of Gods unfolded around them, a paradise that seemed to promise eternal happiness. The sight of her family, together and content, filled Finity with a warmth she hadn't felt in a long time. A smile spread across her face as she soaked in the sense of belonging and love.

However, the vision shifted suddenly, the light dimming as night fell. The peaceful scene was abruptly replaced by one of tension and fear. Finity saw a figure—Fie—sneaking into her room and kidnapping her. The tranquility of the previous images was shattered, replaced by a rush of confusion and fear that mirrored the emotions of that fateful night.

The vision ended as abruptly as it had changed, leaving Finity standing in the temple, her face contorted with anger and her fists clenched at her sides. The resurgence of these painful memories reignited the fury and hurt she had long harbored against Fie.

The monk's words lingered in the air, echoing softly as he turned to leave the room. "You can see through the darkness because you are from the light. You will find the peace you need once you return to the land you're from," he said, his voice steady and reassuring yet leaving a profound burden of thought in his wake.

As the soft sound of the monk's departing footsteps faded, Finity was left alone with the flickering shadows and the light that half-illuminated the room. She sat there, a solitary figure enveloped by the ambiance of half-darkness, half-light, reflecting the duality of her own emotions. The monk's parting words stirred something deep within her—memories of a homeland imbued with light and peace, now distant and tainted by the trauma of her abduction.

The serenity that had briefly touched her face during the vision vanished, replaced by a pensive, disturbed expression. Her mind replayed the scenes shown by the monk—the joyous times with her family in the Land of Gods sharply contrasted with the harrowing night of her kidnapping. Each memory, vivid and intense, was like a wave crashing against the shores of her current reality, pulling her back into the depths of her past fears and unresolved anger.

Sitting alone, Finity felt the weight of her history and her destiny converge. The monk's assertion that she was 'from the light' echoed not just a physical truth about her origins but a spiritual directive. It was a call to reconnect with her essence, to embrace her heritage not just as a place but as a state of being—of light, peace, and innate strength.

Her hands clenched and unclenched as she contemplated the path that lay ahead. To return to the Land of Gods meant confronting not only the physical journey back to a place she once called home but also the emotional and spiritual journey within herself. It meant facing the darkness of her past, understanding it, and using her inherent light to reclaim her peace and power.

The room around her, with its stark division of shadow and light, seemed to mirror her internal struggle. The shadows could hide much, but they could not completely suppress the light, just as her past could obscure but not extinguish her true nature. The realization was both daunting and uplifting.

With a deep, steadying breath, Finity rose to her feet. The decision to confront her past, to seek her homeland and the peace promised by her return solidified with each breath. Though disturbed by the resurgence of painful memories, she was also invigorated by the clarity of her purpose.

She exited the room not with the uncertainty with which she had entered but with a resolute step toward reclaiming her identity and her destiny. The journey would be fraught with challenges, but Finity was now armed with a deeper understanding of her own strength and the prophetic guidance of the monk: to find peace by returning to her roots and embracing the light from which she came.

In the depths of the temple, shrouded in near-perpetual darkness, the concept of time began to lose its grip on the Roots. The absence of natural light, along with the constant, unchanging environment of stone and shadow, made hours indistinguishable from minutes, and days melded seamlessly into nights. This disorientation from the usual measures of time encouraged a deeper, more introspective journey—a plunge into the realms of knowledge and self-discovery that each member had come to seek.

The darkness around them, though initially a cloak of uncertainty, gradually became a canvas upon which their innermost desires and quests were illuminated. As they delved deeper into their respective teachings—be it through meditation, combat training, or the study of ancient texts—the Roots found themselves more attuned to the rhythms of their own hearts than the ticking of any clock.

Finity, emerging from her encounter with the monk, carried with her the vision of her homeland and the peace it promised. Her steps were guided not by the passage of time but by a growing understanding of her purpose and destiny. Each moment spent in contemplation of her return to the Land of Gods brought her closer to reconciling her past with her future.

Meanwhile, Omni, taught by the monks to harness the elemental powers around him, learned to flow with the natural energies of the world as effortlessly as water flows around obstacles. Time for him was measured in breaths and heartbeats, each one bringing him closer to mastering the balance between strength and serenity.

Keem, engaged in the physical rigor and discipline of hand-to-hand combat, found his perception of time altered by the immediacy of each movement and countermove. His training transcended the need for a schedule, each session stretching endlessly as he pushed his body and mind to adapt, react, and integrate the monk's teachings on the true nature of power.

Nakh, surrounded by the wealth of knowledge in the temple's library, experienced time as a scholar does—a relentless pursuit of wisdom where one book leads to another, and one mystery unfolds into deeper mysteries. The scrolls and texts did not age or adhere to the temporal constraints of the outside world; they were timeless, and so they became his study.

For the Roots, the loss of conventional timekeeping was not a loss at all but a liberation. Freed from the tyranny of the clock, their spiritual and educational pursuits deepened, allowing each member to engage fully with the mysteries and challenges posed by the temple. They operated on a time known only to those on the path of true knowledge—a time that bends to the will of the heart and the mind's quest.

As they each honed in on the knowledge that their hearts sought, the darkness of the temple ceased to be an enemy. It became a trusted companion in their journey, a reminder that in the pursuit of profound truths, time is not a boundary but a bridge—and in the deepest shadows, the brightest lights of understanding can emerge.

As the Roots delved deeper into their respective paths of enlightenment and mastery within the temple's timeless shadows, the outside world was not idle. Tensions had been simmering, a slow boil that was now threatening to spill over. The war for the wall, a looming conflict that had been whispered about in shadowed corridors and sealed letters, was on the brink of eruption.

Unbeknownst to the Roots, their very presence and the powers they were honing had been calculated into the strategic plans of the Dynasty. The rulers and their advisors, having foreseen the inevitability of conflict with neighboring realms and the insurgent forces within their borders, had long been preparing. The temple, a place of ancient power and profound knowledge, was not just a sanctuary for spiritual seekers but a forge for creating the ultimate weapon—the Roots themselves.

Each member of the group, chosen not only for their unique abilities but also for their potential to transcend ordinary human limits, was integral to the Dynasty's plans. The leaders of the Dynasty believed that the eclectic blend of skills and the deepened spiritual and physical capabilities of the Roots could turn the tide in a war that was as much about ideology as it was about territory.

As the Roots continued their training, oblivious to the machinations of the political world, the stakes outside the temple walls grew higher. Scouts reported increased movements at the borders, and secret missives flew between the spymasters of the Dynasty and their agents in the field. Each report confirmed that time was running short and that the confrontation could no longer be avoided.

Meanwhile, in the temple, the monks, aware of the impending conflict but bound by ancient oaths, subtly steered the training toward skills that would not only benefit personal enlightenment but were also crucial for combat and strategy. They imparted knowledge of ancient martial techniques, healing arts, and the manipulation of natural energies that could be decisive in battle. Yet, they spoke nothing of the war, trusting in the wisdom that each Root must come to understand their role in the wider world in their own time.

Back in the capital, in the dimly lit chambers of the royal palace, the Dynasty's war council convened. Maps were unrolled, and strategies were debated. The Roots were discussed not by name but as elements of a grander plan—a secret weapon whose unveiling was awaited with both anticipation and anxiety.

As the drums of war began to beat louder, a messenger was dispatched to the temple with sealed orders. The time was coming for the Roots to step out of the shadows of their training and into the harsh light of the battlefield, where their mettle would be tested not just by their adversaries but by the moral and ethical dilemmas of using their newfound powers in the service of a war they had not chosen.

The war council room was somber, the air thick with tension and the heavy scent of impending conflict. Misery, her usually calm demeanor now edged with palpable anxiety, leaned forward over the large, scarred oak table that dominated the room. Maps scattered with markers and lines depicting troop movements and strategic points covered its surface. The flickering light of the oil lamps cast long shadows, mirroring the uncertainty that clouded the meeting.

"We do not know what to expect. War is crazy enough when you know your enemy and understand why you are fighting, but this feels like madness," Misery voiced, her words capturing the collective unease of the room. Her role as a seasoned strategist was well respected, yet even she seemed rattled by the unpredictable nature of the looming conflict.

Around the table, the other council members exchanged glances, their expressions a mix of resolve and concern. Each one was acutely aware of the stakes at hand, not just for their dynasty but for the realms that bordered their own. The unknown elements of the enemy's capabilities and the mysterious factors driving them added layers of complexity to their planning.

Perched high upon the craggy cliffs overlooking the turbulent seas that served as a natural border between the zones, Colu, the demigod and undisputed leader of the formidable army, surveyed his forces with a steely gaze. His stature was imposing, a commanding presence bolstered by his supernatural lineage, and his eyes burned with the fire of ambition and ancient power.

The army arrayed before him was unlike any other—creatures of war, each bearing monstrous qualities that made them both fearsome and awe-inspiring. They were hybrids, part human and part beast, crafted through dark magic and the whims of their demigod leader to be perfect soldiers for the battles they were bred to fight.

Some soldiers bore massive wings, feathers ruffling in the gusty wind, reminiscent of eagles or bats, allowing them to swoop down on their enemies or scout from high above. Others had the muscular build and ferocity of lions or wolves, their senses heightened, and their instincts honed for the hunt. Colu's army was a terrifying blend of strength, speed, and savagery, each soldier a testament to the dark arts that had birthed them.

Others were fused with the traits of terrestrial behemoths like apes and rhinos, their bodies fortified with natural armor and brute strength, capable of devastating charges that could break through almost any defense.

Among these hybrid warriors, the giants stood out for their sheer size and strength, towering over their comrades and ready to act as the vanguard in the upcoming siege. Their deep voices rumbled like thunder as they prepared their weapons, each eager to bring down the walls that had long stood between their realm and the territories they coveted.

Colu's naval commanders, hardened warriors who controlled the ships guarding the volatile waters, stood ready at his side. Their vessels were outfitted for war, the decks bristling with weaponry and crews of seasoned fighters who could navigate the treacherous currents and lead assaults from the sea.

With his army assembled and his strategies set, Colu dispatched emissaries bearing a message for the Dynasty— words crafted to chill the hearts of even the most hardened rulers. The message was clear: surrender the wall and negotiate peace or face the full might of his monstrous legion in a war that would spare no one.

As the emissaries rode out, Colu turned back to oversee the final preparations. His heart, if it could be called that, was set on victory. He knew the Dynasty had been training their secret weapons, the Roots, and though he respected their power, he believed no amount of training could match the raw, brutal force and the dark magic that fueled his army.

The air was thick with the electric tension of impending battle, the sky darkening as if to mourn the inevitable bloodshed. Colu raised his arm, signaling his generals to their positions, each movement precise and deliberate. This was more than a battle for territory; it was a declaration of his dominion over the natural and supernatural, a challenge to the old powers that had dared to oppose him.

As the war drums began to beat, echoing across the cliffs and over the turbulent waters, Colu's army roared their assent, a sound that was both terrifying and exhilarating. The wall would either fall or stand, but one thing was certain—the world would not be the same when the dust settled.

The bat, a dark silhouette against the twilight sky, darted with remarkable precision over the formidable wall that marked the boundary of the Dynasty's territory. Its wings beat silently as it flew tirelessly over the expansive desert, the dunes reflecting the last glimmers of the setting sun. It was a messenger of urgency, navigating the vast, barren landscape to reach the canyon that cradled the Dynasty's stronghold.

The ancient stronghold, carved into the living rock of the canyon walls, stood as a testament to the Dynasty's enduring presence and strategic prowess. The bat maneuvered effortlessly through the narrow window of the council's meeting room, a space hewn from the stone with arches that echoed the natural curves of the canyon.

As the creature swooped into the dimly lit chamber, the council members, deep in strategic debate, paused mid-sentence, their attention snapping to the unexpected visitor. With a swift motion, the bat released the scroll from its clutches, letting it flutter down onto the heavy oak table around which the council was gathered. Without missing a beat, the bat exited through another window, leaving behind a room charged with sudden, intense anticipation.

The members of the Dynasty exchanged glances, a mix of surprise and apprehension flickering across their faces. Lord Inertia, ever composed, was the first to react. She stretched out her hand and grasped the scroll, her movements deliberate, betraying none of the fatigue that caused her to yawn just moments before. Her eyes met those of her council as she passed the scroll to Misery, the room's tension palpable.

"What does it say, Misery?" Inertia asked, her voice steady yet tinged with the weight of the moment.

Misery, with hands that were steady despite the gravity of the situation, carefully unrolled the scroll. The room fell silent, every breath held as if the very air awaited her words. Her eyes quickly scanned the message, the script familiar yet foreboding.

Misery's voice filled the chamber, each word carrying the weight of the imminent threat, echoing slightly off the stone walls. Her reading of Colu's message was measured, her tone betraying none of the anger or concern that might have simmered beneath the surface.

"I seek more land for my people. You can either bow to me and make me your ruler, or you can get stepped on like the bug you are, and we take the land from under you. Putting up a fight will be futile. I have thousands of men at my disposal. I will wait for your response at the top of the wall when the sun rises." The finality of the statement hung in the air, a challenge laid bare, as brazen as it was menacing.

The council members absorbed the message, the reality of their situation settling upon each of them with heavy clarity. They shared glances, each look conveying a mix of resolve and unease. The silence that followed was tense, each leader contemplating the path that lay before them.

The war council room, usually a place of measured discussion and careful planning, was charged with a palpable urgency. Misery's words to Lord Inertia were spoken softly, yet they carried the weight of seasoned caution, "You cannot meet with him, Lord Inertia. If we are going to fight back, what would be the purpose of letting him know? We should just keep our distance."

Before Lord Inertia could respond, Ina, always the more aggressive among the advisors, could not contain her impatience. She stood abruptly, her voice loud and filled with a warrior's fervor, "If he wants to meet at the top of the wall, that will just make him vulnerable. You should let me attack him long distance. I will create enough weapons that he will have no escape." Her strategy was clear—turn Colu's proposed meeting into a trap, an opportunity to eliminate the threat in one decisive blow.

Lord Inertia, who had been listening intently, finally stood, her presence commanding silence from her animated council. For the first time that evening, her voice rose, not just in volume but in authority, "We do not know what they are capable of, so staying cautious is best." She looked around the room, her gaze settling on each of her advisors, ensuring her next words were clearly understood, "You are right, Misery. We do not accept their offer, so meeting them would be pointless."

Just as she was about to elaborate her thoughts, the door swung open with a purposeful push. Lona entered the room briskly, her expression serious as she led the group of Roots into the council chamber. Their sudden appearance caused a momentary pause in the discussion, drawing all eyes to them.

The atmosphere in the council chamber was thick with the weight of impending war, the dim light casting long shadows across the room's ancient stone surfaces. Keem, standing among the Roots, was the first to break the silence after the strategy session had convened with all key players present. His voice, steady and purposeful, carried a direct query that captured the urgency of their situation. "What is the plan?"

Misery, who had been reviewing a series of scrolls and maps since their discussion began, turned toward Keem with a determined look. She unrolled a large, detailed map across the table, anchoring its corners with small stones. The map depicted the terrain between their stronghold and the wall—a vast expanse of desert that served as a natural buffer and a challenging obstacle for any invading force.

"The wall is miles away from the canyon, across a large desert," Misery began, her finger tracing the route that any army would have to take to reach their lands. "We will let them destroy the wall and get halfway through the desert so we can see half of what we are up against. We fight from there." Her strategy was clear: to use the desert itself as a means to weaken and reveal the enemy before committing to a full engagement.

The Roots and the council members leaned in, studying the map as Misery pointed out specific locations and potential sites for ambushes. "The desert will sap their strength and slow their advance, giving us the advantage of fighting on our terms, on terrain we know well," she continued, her voice laced with a tactical sharpness that reassured her listeners of her deep understanding of warfare.

Lord Inertia nodded in approval, her eyes scanning the faces of her council and the Roots. "It's a risk to allow them through the wall, but it's a calculated one," she added, her tone imbuing the room with a sense of resolve. "Misery's plan utilizes our knowledge of the local geography and allows us to engage the enemy weakened, not at their fullest strength."

Keem, processing the strategy, looked back at the map. His mind raced through various scenarios, considering the implications of allowing the enemy to breach the first line of defense. He understood the logic—by allowing the enemy to extend themselves deep into hostile territory, they would inevitably stretch their supply lines and expose themselves to counterattacks.

Misery, sensing the need to solidify her plan with more details, elaborated further. "Once they are engaged in the desert, we will use our mobility to harass their flanks and cut off their retreat. The Roots will be crucial here; your unique abilities can turn the tide of any engagement."

As she spoke, Misery placed small markers on the map, indicating where their forces would be hidden and where the Roots could be most effective. The strategy was not just about defense; it was about controlling the battlefield, dictating the flow of combat, and using their home advantage to the fullest.

"We'll need a contingent ready to extract you should the need arise, and our scouts must keep a vigilant watch for any changes in enemy movements," Misery stated, her gaze sweeping the room, ensuring everyone understood the gravity of their roles.

She turned to Keem, her gaze firm yet filled with respect for his initiative. "Keem, you and the other Roots will take the lead at the wall, as you've suggested. But this is not a lone mission. You'll have the full backing of our forces, and at the first sign of overwhelming resistance, you will pull back. This is about reducing their numbers, not a last stand."

Keem nodded in understanding, the weight of the responsibility settling on his shoulders. His suggestion had been accepted, and now the pressure was on him and his fellow Roots to deliver a significant blow to the enemy forces.

In the strategy room, lit by the flickering light of lamps, the air was thick with the tension of impending conflict. As the Roots and the Dynasty's leaders continued their preparations, Hutch, whose heightened senses were tuned to the elemental shifts around him, suddenly spoke up, a note of urgency in his voice. "I can feel many ships arriving near the wall on the sea." His statement redirected the focus of the room toward the naval aspect of the invasion, underscoring the multi-front nature of the threat they faced.

Keem, standing beside the map that sprawled across the table, turned to Omni with a strategic request, reflecting the need for future mobility. "Omni! Can you create us a ship to carry us to the next zone when this war is over?" he asked, plotting their movements beyond the immediate battle.

Omni, whose abilities with the earth could easily extend to manipulating water and wood, nodded in agreement without hesitation. His skills would be crucial not just in the forthcoming battle but also in ensuring their escape and regrouping if the need arose.

As they discussed logistics, Misery, her face shadowed by concern, added to the conversation, her voice low and steady. "I doubt they know who they are coming for, but they wanted to meet on top of the wall to answer their question." Her strategic mind was always analyzing, always trying to predict the enemy's moves and motives.

Keem, intrigued and slightly confused by her statement, pressed for clarity. "What is their question?" he asked, his brow furrowed.

Misery opened her mouth to respond, but Lord Inertia, who had been quietly absorbing every piece of information, spoke first, her voice firm and filled with a leader's resolve. "Will we bow to them as they take over our land? Or will we be destroyed as they take our land?" She paused, letting her words sink in among those gathered. "We will not fold under their pressure. If they want a fight, we will give it to them."

Her declaration was met with nods of agreement from around the room. The sentiment she voiced was not just strategic but also deeply patriotic, reflecting the indomitable spirit of the Dynasty.

Inertia's leadership had always been characterized by her calm demeanor, but in moments like these, her warrior spirit came to the forefront, inspiring confidence and readiness among her people. As the meeting drew to a close, each member of the council and the Roots knew their roles and the stakes at hand.

In the dimly lit council chamber, the air heavy with the weight of imminent war, Hutch stood firmly as he outlined the battle strategy, his voice resonant and commanding. "Let us make plans for this battle. Omni, Keem, and Nakh can handle the first wave of enemies. From there, we all can handle close hand combat. Keem and a few other members of the Roots will be our air support, just in case they have anything up their sleeves. Once we pass the wall, leave the sea to me." His gaze swept across the room, meeting the eyes of his fellow warriors, ensuring each understood their role. "Our goal is not to push them back but to completely get rid of them."

The members of the council and the Roots listened intently, each absorbing the gravity of their assignments. The plan was bold, perhaps as daring as it was dangerous, reflecting not just a desire to defend but to decisively end the threat.

Lord Inertia, who had been overseeing the preparations, stood up with a solemn sigh, her expression one of both resolve and deep concern. She began to exit the room but paused at the threshold to deliver a parting command, one that underscored the seriousness of the dawn they faced. "Alert everyone. Tell them we fight at sunrise and make sure everyone gets eyewear to protect their eyes from the sand."

She turned back to face her people, her voice softening but filled with an intensity that drew everyone's attention. "Spend a long, meaningful night with your families and show them all the love you can because today could be their last. Prepare the families with evacuation plans." Her words hung heavy in the air, a stark reminder of the stakes of the battle that loomed.

"This war will determine our fate," Inertia continued, her tone imbued with a mix of hope and the harsh reality of their situation. "If we win, the bridge of knowledge will be restored. But if we lose, life as we know it will start anew." With that, she turned and left the room, her steps echoing softly down the hall.

The room remained silent for a moment, each person processing the weight of Inertia's words. Then, as if her departure had been the signal, the council and the Roots sprang into action, mobilizing with a newfound urgency.

Omni, Keem, and Nakh briefly conferred, discussing the finer points of their tactics for the first wave. Omni, whose powers would be critical in shaping the battlefield, nodded solemnly, ready to manipulate the earth to their advantage. Keem, designated for air support, checked his gear, mentally preparing for the aerial maneuvers he might have to execute. Nakh, always calm and collected, reviewed the intelligence reports one last time, ensuring no detail was missed.

As they left the council chamber, the atmosphere was charged with a mix of determination and somber reflection. The evening air felt heavy as Finity and Omni, along with others, headed toward their quarters along a dusty trail that wound through the encampment. The crunch of gravel underfoot seemed overly loud in the quiet that had descended among them.

"What do you think it will be like?" Finity asked, her voice tinged with a mix of curiosity and apprehension. She glanced at Omni, seeking not just his thoughts but perhaps a reassurance of some kind.

Omni, his face set in a thoughtful frown, replied, "I fought before, but not in a war. Not even in a big battle. But I'm ready!" His voice carried a resolve that was more to fortify his own courage than to convince Finity.

Finity nodded slowly, digesting his words. "I saw my father when I was with the monks. He is past the wall. I came along with you all for adventure. For a change. I do not want to kill anymore but I will do what I have to do to reach my father." As she spoke, her voice quivered slightly, and she lowered her head, her eyes brimming with tears.

Omni, noticing her distress, hesitated before adding, "This may not be the right time, but I believe I saw your mother before we met you." He watched cautiously as Finity wiped her tears away.

"She was looking for you," he continued gently, hoping to provide her with some comfort or perhaps a connection she might have thought lost.

Finity turned sharply to him, her grief momentarily replaced by surprise and a flash of anger. "How do you know that? You do not know me or my family!" she exclaimed, her voice rising as she wiped away the last of her tears.

"It could be a hunch," Omni replied, his confidence waning under her intense gaze. "She mentioned a loved one who had beautiful brown eyes. I didn't see those brown eyes of yours until that necklace was broken from your neck. Now I see."

The revelation did not have the effect Omni had hoped for. Instead of calming or comforting Finity, it only seemed to stir more turmoil. Finity looked at Omni, her expression hardened with frustration. "I appreciate you helping me, but like I said, you do not know me. Do not try to analyze me! You have helped enough now, and I do not need your help anymore!" Her words were sharp, and she turned abruptly, walking away from him down the trail, leaving a palpable divide between them.

Omni stood there for a moment, watching her go, feeling the sting of her words. He then continued to walk in his own direction, his thoughts swirling with the complexities of their impending battle and the personal conflicts that seemed as tumultuous as the war they were about to face. The world around him was indeed changing, and he was right in the heart of it, grappling with the realities of war, alliances, and the personal demons that each of them carried into the fray.

As dusk fell over the canyon, a soft blanket of twilight draped itself around the stronghold of the Dynasty. Despite the looming threat of war, there was a palpable warmth in the air—a bittersweet mix of anticipation and apprehension, as the people of the Dynasty gathered to cherish what could be their final moments of peace.

Throughout the encampment, lanterns were lit, casting a gentle glow that flickered against the sandstone walls, bathing the entire canyon in a soft, golden light. The night was filled with the sounds of laughter and music, a defiant celebration of life in the face of potential devastation. Soldiers, who had spent the day sharpening their weapons and fortifying their resolve, now set aside their armor to revel in the company of their loved ones.

In the central square, long tables were laden with food. Cooks and families had outdone themselves preparing dishes that were as much a feast for the spirit as they were for the body. There was bread baked with herbs from the gardens, meats seasoned with rare spices from distant trades, and fruits that glistened under the lantern light. It was a feast that represented the very best of the Dynasty's culture—a tapestry of flavors that told stories of seasons, of harvests, and of the many hands that had labored to bring such bounty to the table.

Children ran about with shrieks of delight, their laughter a light note floating above the deeper timbre of adult conversations. Husbands and wives exchanged glances loaded with unspoken words, their hands touching in brief caresses that spoke volumes of the love and fear that mingled in their hearts. Here and there, a soldier would lift a child into the air, spinning them around, their joyous yells punctuating the evening air like bursts of hope against the shadow of war.

Elderly members of the community, many of whom had seen the cycles of peace and conflict come and go, sat together, their stories weaving through the younger generations like threads binding the present to the past. Their tales were peppered with wisdom and sometimes with warnings, but tonight, they chose to speak of victories, of celebrations, of times when the strength of their people had been a beacon that led them through darkness.

Amidst it all, musicians played traditional melodies, the strains of flutes and drums rising and falling rhythmically, as if their music could ward off the impending doom or perhaps call upon the spirits of their ancestors for protection. Couples danced slowly, their movements graceful and laden with an intensity that only those possibly facing their last night together could understand.

And in quieter corners, warriors whispered to their loved ones, their voices soft but fierce with promises of return. They shared stories, not of battles, but of dreams—dreams of what they would build once peace was restored, dreams of children growing up under a sky unmarred by the smoke of war.

This night, under the stars of the canyon, the Dynasty's people came together not just to brace for battle but to affirm the bonds that made them a community—a family forged not just by blood but by shared hopes, shared fears, and the shared resolve to protect their way of life, no matter what the dawn might bring.

The night before, the battle unfolded in varied shades of camaraderie, reflection, and solitude for each of the Roots. Keem and Lona found solace in each other's company, sharing not just a meal but the quiet understanding and comfort that only those who face the same fate can offer. Their conversation was a soft murmur beneath the rustling of the tents and the distant hum of the canyon's nightlife, each word a testament to their shared resolve and burgeoning bond. As the night deepened, they retreated to a shared bed, seeking warmth and closeness in the face of uncertainty.

Elsewhere, Hutch and his cousin Nakh, along with the other members of the Root group, gathered in a circle under the open sky. Their figures were silhouetted against the soft glow of lanterns as they meditated. The practice was silent but for the occasional shift of robes against the sand or a deep, steadying breath. The air around them was charged with a focused energy, each individual drawing upon their inner reserves and seeking mental clarity and spiritual strength. Finity, passing by, felt the pull of their collective energy and, almost without thinking, joined the circle. Sitting among them, she closed her eyes, letting the rhythmic breathing of the group guide her into a state of deep contemplation, her earlier frustrations momentarily set aside.

Omni, however, found himself apart from the group. He walked alone through the winding paths of the canyon, his steps aimless but his mind racing. The cannabinoid plant he smoked created a haze around him, both literal and metaphorical, as he wrestled with thoughts of his role in the coming battle and the revelations about Finity's family. The quiet of the canyon was a stark contrast to the turmoil within him. Every step, every puff of smoke seemed to echo his internal quest for purpose, for understanding his place not just in the battle but in the broader tapestry of his life's journey.

As he walked, the stars overhead were a canopy of indifferent witnesses to his solitude. The soft glow of the moon lit his path, casting long shadows that seemed to dance with his doubts. Omni's contemplation was a lonely vigil but necessary, as he sifted through his emotions and responsibilities, trying to align them with the imminent reality of war.

Each of the Roots, in their way, was preparing for the dawn in a manner that reflected their personalities and needs. Together yet apart, they were a microcosm of the larger forces at play—individual stories woven into the fabric of a communal fate, each thread essential to the strength and resilience of the whole.

As the first pale light of dawn stretched lazily across the sky, there was a heavy, almost palpable pause in the atmosphere. The canyon, usually vibrant with the sounds of nature, seemed subdued, the usual chirping of birds and rustling of small creatures muted as if in anticipation of the storm to come. The sun's ascent was slow, grudgingly casting its light over the land, illuminating the faces of those who were awake and stirring, their expressions a mix of determination and the quiet dread that precedes battle.

The members of the Dynasty, including the Roots, gathered at the designated meeting point, their movements deliberate and their gear checked and rechecked. There was a sense of unity, each individual part of a larger whole, as they prepared to take the trail leading to the top of the canyon— their first waypoint in the journey toward the wall.

Commanders issued low-voiced instructions, their orders punctuated by the clinking of armor and the soft thuds of boots on the earth. Soldiers embraced their loved ones briefly, fiercely, the air tinged with the sweet pain of farewells that could be final. Among the Roots, there was a silent nodding of heads, an unspoken understanding of the roles they were about to play, their unique abilities crucial to the defense strategy.

Everyone was there, falling into formation, everyone except for Omni. As the first rays of the sun breached the horizon, casting long shadows over the gathered forces of the Dynasty and the Roots, a sense of urgency tinged the air. The assembly was almost complete, every member accounted for except one. Omni's absence became increasingly conspicuous as the time to move out drew nearer. Concerned murmurs rippled through the ranks, and a quick search was organized to locate him.

The Dynasty's commanders, already on edge due to the impending battle, speculated with growing frustration about Omni's whereabouts. Some among them, hardened by countless skirmishes and wary of any sign of weakness, voiced concerns that Omni had deserted, unwilling to face the horrors of war. "He must have run away," one commander said grimly, his voice a mix of disappointment and anger. "He did not want to be part of this war," another agreed, casting a shadow of doubt over Omni's commitment to their cause.

The Roots, however, held a different perspective. Knowing Omni better than the others, they were torn between concern for their friend and confusion over his sudden disappearance. "It's not like him to just run away," Keem argued, his voice laced with worry. "There must be another explanation." Despite their faith in him, even the Roots could not completely dispel the uncertainty that clung to Omni's absence.

Unbeknownst to all, Omni had not fled, nor had he abandoned his comrades. Instead, he was far closer to the enemy than anyone could have imagined. As the Dynasty and the Roots prepared to depart, Omni was already nearing the wall, not on foot, but being carried silently and swiftly across the desert sands. His unique abilities allowed him to merge with and manipulate the sand, creating a form of travel that kept him undetected by enemy scouts.

The sun climbed higher as Omni approached the imposing structure of the wall. It stood as a stark barrier in the landscape, the first line of defense and now a point of contention that might decide the fate of his people. As he reached the base of the wall, the sand beneath him shifted, lifting and propelling him upwards in a soft, swirling motion. This was the path he had chosen—direct and solitary, driven by a need to confront the impending threat head-on, perhaps to make amends for the doubts his disappearance had sown among his allies.

The sun was now fully aloft, casting long, stark shadows across the undulating sands as it bore down on the desert landscape. The tension among the Roots palpably grew with each step closer to the conflict zone. Rumors and concerns about Omni's whereabouts swirled among them, adding a layer of personal urgency to the looming battle.

As they navigated the rugged terrain leading to the top of the canyon, Keem's thoughts returned repeatedly to Omni, their absent companion whose unexplained disappearance had left many questions unanswered. Glancing over at Hutch, who seemed lost in his thoughts, Keem couldn't contain his concern any longer. "Do you think he is at the wall?" he asked, his voice tinged with both hope and worry.

Hutch, tightening the straps on his gear as he walked, replied without looking at Keem. "We told him not to go alone," he said, the frustration evident in his tone. It was clear that Hutch, like the others, felt a mix of irritation and concern for Omni, who had always been both fiercely independent and integral to their group.

Nakh, ever the voice of calm, chimed in, trying to alleviate the mounting tension. "I am sure he is not doing anything crazy," he stated confidently, though he couldn't completely mask his own doubt.

Finity, overhearing the exchange, turned her face away, her expression unreadable. The mention of Omni stirred a complex whirl of emotions within her, especially after their last conversation. She felt a pang of guilt and fear for Omni, wondering if her harsh words might have driven him to act recklessly.

Keem noticed Finity's reaction and sighed, his resolve hardening. "Come on, Nakh, we have to catch up to him and join him. We cannot continue to let him try to do things on his own!" he declared, his voice rising with determination.

Without waiting for further discussion, Keem and Nakh picked up their pace, their strides becoming more purposeful as they climbed the final stretch to the top of the canyon. Sand kicked up under their boots as they moved, each step propelling them faster toward the unknown. Behind them, the rest of the Roots quickened their pace as well, driven by a shared resolve to reunite with Omni and face the impending battle as a united front.

Meanwhile, at the wall, Colu was advancing with a formidable presence, the leader of a vast army that roiled like a dark sea beneath him. Thousands of men, creatures of war, awaited his command, their faces set and determined, ready to follow him into the heart of Dynasty territory.

As Colu reached the top of the wall, his eyes scanned the horizon, his mind calculating the best strategy to breach the defenses before him. He was unaware of the lone figure of Omni, who had positioned himself strategically, blending with the environment as he prepared to make his stand.

The scene was set for a confrontation of epic proportions, with the Roots racing against time to join forces and face not only the external enemy but also their internal conflicts and fears. The desert, vast and indifferent, watched silently as the pieces moved toward an inevitable clash.

As the sun arced higher, its rays casting an increasingly stark light over the vast expanse of the desert and the imposing structure of the wall, Omni reached the summit. There, amidst the ancient stones that had witnessed countless battles, he coaxed a cannabinoid plant from the arid soil. It sprouted swiftly, rolling itself into a perfect cylinder, an otherworldly manifestation of Omni's unique connection to the earth.

Just then, the heavy thud of armored boots announced Colu's arrival at the top of the wall. The demigod, towering and imposing, approached Omni with a mix of curiosity and disdain. His eyes, accustomed to scanning battlefields and commanding legions, narrowed slightly as he took in the sight of Omni, seemingly alone and unperturbed by the approaching danger.

"Are you the ruler of this zone?" Culo asked, his voice echoing slightly against the stone battlements, laden with both challenge and intrigue.

Omni, unfazed, lit the cannabinoid plant and took a deep inhale, the smoke swirling around him like a protective shroud. Exhaling, he replied calmly, "I am not the ruler of this zone. I am not even from this zone." His voice was steady, conveying a serene detachment that contrasted sharply with the martial energy emanating from Culo.

Culo laughed, a deep, resonant sound that seemed to vibrate the very air between them. "Did they hire you to stop me?" he asked, amusement coloring his tone as he eyed the smoking plant in Omni's hand.

"Not at all. I am here to reach the Land of Gods. But it bothers me that you want to leave from the same place I seek. Why do you want to leave?" Omni's question was genuine, probing beneath the surface of the conflict to understand the motivations of the man who sought to conquer his newfound home.

As he spoke, Omni extended the hand holding the cannabinoid plant toward Culo, an offer of peace and perhaps a gesture to establish a dialogue rather than a confrontation.

Culo paused, his expression shifting from amusement to a more contemplative demeanor. The offer of the plant, so unusual in the context of their meeting, caught him off guard. He glanced at it, then back at Omni, assessing the man before him not just as an obstacle to his conquest but as a fellow seeker of truths, albeit of a different kind.

As Culo contemplated Omni's offer, the brief pause stretched between them, filled with the tension of their conflicting aspirations. Finally, he reached out, accepting the plant from Omni with a deliberative gesture. Drawing a deep breath from it, he exhaled a thick cloud of smoke, his eyes narrowing as he pondered the weight of his next words.

"They are nothing like me," Culo began, his voice a mix of defiance and bitterness. "Everyone in the Land of Gods is seeking their light body. I do not care for that. I want to unleash the darkness inside of me, but they will not allow it. They do not treat me for who I am. It's like they do not see the evil within me," he confessed, his frustrations with his homeland spilling over into the smoky air between them.

Omni listened intently, his eyes locked on Culo's. "So why this land? What do you want with this land?" he asked, taking back the plant as Culo offered it to him.

"This land will be my land," Culo declared, his tone resolute. "This is where people who want to open up to darkness will be able to do so willingly. They have taught me to control my power, but with so much power, there is nowhere for me to use my abilities. I want to have a place where I can be acknowledged for who I am."

Omni passed the plant back to Culo, his mind racing to understand the depth of Culo's desires and the implications of his plans. "Were you scared to use your abilities on the people who taught you? Why take out your anger on these people just for acknowledgment?" Omni questioned, challenging the basis of Culo's justification.

Culo took another deep inhale from the plant, his gaze distant as he recounted his past actions. "I did. I attacked them every chance I got. But they would not attack back. They only defended themselves and dodged my attacks. As much as I hated them, they never showed their hate for me. My presence didn't even anger them." He paused, letting out a slow stream of smoke. "Now that I have told you my reasoning, do you wish to join me, or would you rather die here with these people in a land that you do not even come from?" he asked, crossing his arms, the plant hanging loosely from his mouth.

Omni absorbed Culo's words, the gravity of their discussion weighing heavily on him. After a moment of silence, he responded with a calm clarity that resonated with resolve. "My path is to reach the Land of Gods. Our paths are crossing but not for the best. I seek the love you fear, so I'll follow my heart and face your evil head-on. Now that I know your reasoning, I will not hold back."

With those final words, Omni transformed into sand, his form dispersing into countless particles that slid effortlessly off the wall. He flowed back toward the Dynasty's position, ready to defend the land and its people, armed with a deeper understanding of the enemy's motivations and a renewed commitment to his own journey.

Culo watched Omni's sandy form disappear, a rare flicker of uncertainty crossing his features before he turned away, preparing himself for the confrontation that was now inevitable.

The desert was a blur of shifting sands as Omni, in his unique form, flowed swiftly toward his comrades. The landscape around him buzzed with the tension of impending conflict, each grain of sand seeming to vibrate with the collective apprehension of the Dynasty's forces.

Keem and Nakh, having hurried from the canyon with urgent strides, were nearly breathless by the time they reached the appointed meeting spot. The sight of Omni's sandy form coalescing into his human shape before them was startling, causing both to instinctively step back in surprise. They watched, wide-eyed, as Omni took his final form, standing tall and composed, his face betraying none of the turmoil that had surely raged within him moments before.

"Are you ready?" Omni's voice broke the brief silence, his tone firm, pulling Keem and Nakh back from their astonishment to the reality of their mission.

Nakh, recovering from the initial shock, nodded, his expression one of relief mixed with resolve. "I'm glad you didn't just run off trying to handle things yourself," he replied, a subtle acknowledgment of their unity and shared purpose.

"We are ready!" Keem declared, stepping forward to shake Omni's hand, his grip firm and reassuring. The gesture was more than a sign of readiness; it was a symbol of their solidarity and mutual trust.

"It's going to begin now. Do not hold back," Omni stated, turning to gaze in the direction of the wall, where the enemy awaited. His eyes narrowed slightly as he considered the enormity of the task ahead. "Nakh! Tell us what you feel," he added, knowing well that Nakh's heightened senses could provide them with crucial insights into the enemy's movements and intentions.

Nakh closed his eyes for a moment, reaching out with his senses. The air was thick with the vibrations of countless feet and the heavy breaths of an assembled army. "Their numbers are vast, and they are restless," Nakh reported, his voice low. "But there is hesitation, too. They are waiting for a sign from Culo. Their resolve isn't as firm as they portray."

With this information, a new layer of strategy began to form in Omni's mind. If they could strike decisively before the enemy's resolve solidified, they might gain the upper hand.

As they prepared to move out, the sun climbed higher, casting long shadows that seemed to point ominously toward the wall. The moment was upon them, and with each second, the likelihood of peace dwindled to nothing.

"Let's go," Omni said, his voice a catalyst that spurred them into motion. Together, the three Roots advanced toward the wall, their strides purposeful and synchronized, their hearts braced for the battle that would determine not only their fates but the fate of the entire Dynasty.

Behind them, the land seemed to hold its breath, waiting for the clash that would shake the very foundations of their world.

As the trio approached the looming shadow of the wall, the sound of distant thudding and the murmur of orders carried on the wind. Nakh, his senses sharpening with each step closer to the enemy, paused. He drew his sword, a finely crafted blade that hummed slightly with latent energy. With a determined glance at his companions, he raised the weapon and brought it down hard against the sandy ground.

The impact was more than physical; it sent a surge of vibrations through the desert floor, a deliberate pulse of power that echoed Nakh's unique ability to communicate with and through the earth. The sand around them danced in response, rising and falling like the chest of a sleeping giant, each grain resonating with the force of Nakh's strike.

As the vibrations spread, they met the wall and the amassed forces beyond it, bending and bouncing back with echoes of information. Nakh stood perfectly still, his eyes closed, focusing intently on the returning signals that painted a vivid picture of the scene on the wall.

"They are at the wall, putting their strength together to burst through in one fell swoop," Nakh reported, his voice calm but laden with urgency as he relayed his findings to Omni and Keem. His brows furrowed slightly as he sifted through the sensory feedback. "Someone is further behind them, with many more flying beside him as if they were waiting or leading." His words hinted at a strategic reserve force, possibly led by Culo himself, poised for a decisive intervention.

Opening his eyes, Nakh looked at Omni and Keem, gauging their readiness. The information he provided was crucial—it meant they were facing not just a frontal assault but also a coordinated attack, potentially from multiple directions.

Keem nodded, absorbing the tactical situation. "We need to disrupt their formation before they can initiate their charge," he suggested, his mind racing through possible counters to the enemy's strategy.

Omni, ever the strategist, agreed. "If we can create enough confusion within their ranks, it might delay their plans or better yet, cause them to reconsider their assault," he added, thinking of how best to use their combined abilities to sow discord among the enemy.

The decision was made swiftly. Nakh would continue to monitor the vibrations and movements of the enemy, providing real-time updates. Keem would ready himself to take to the air, prepared to strike at the flying units that Nakh had detected, potentially throwing off their coordination. Omni, with his control over the elements, planned to manipulate the environment to their advantage, possibly creating barriers or traps to hinder the enemy's advance.

With their roles set and the enemy's strategy partially unveiled, the Roots readied themselves. They were a small team, but each was formidable in his own right. Together, they prepared to face the coming storm, their resolve as unyielding as the wall that stood behind them.

As they moved into position, the sounds of the enemy grew louder, the impending battle almost palpable in the air. But with Nakh's warning, they had a chance, a slim opportunity to turn the tide in their favor.

Omni's words cut through the air, sharpened by the urgency of their situation. The frown on his face was set, a reflection of the resolve hardening within him. "That's the one I talked to," he affirmed, his gaze fixed on the distant shapes and movements beyond the wall. The sense of gravity in his voice conveyed the seriousness of their conversation, underscoring the weight of Culo's intentions.

"They are coming with everything they've got. There is no going back for them, so do not give in," he continued, his tone resolute. The finality in his statement left no room for doubt or hesitation. It was a call to arms, a directive that bound the Roots together in their shared purpose.

Now standing shoulder to shoulder, Keem and Nakh absorbed Omni's words, their own expressions mirroring his determination. The reality of their mission was stark and clear—this was not just another skirmish or a defensive maneuver; it was a decisive confrontation, one that would determine the fate of their land and their people.

Keem clenched his fists, the readiness to engage flowing through him like a current. "Let's handle them and reach our destination," he echoed, his voice a blend of defiance and assurance. His eyes, always sharp, now glinted with the strategic calculation of a seasoned fighter ready to leverage his aerial skills to their fullest.

Nakh, usually the calmest among them, nodded solemnly, his hand resting on the hilt of his sword, a silent testament to his readiness. "We stand together," he stated, the simplicity of his words belying the depth of his commitment. It was a reminder of their bond, the unspoken pact among them to protect each other and push forward, regardless of the obstacles.

The moment the wall crumbled under the relentless assault of Culo's army, a thunderous roar echoed across the desert, a sound that marked the beginning of the onslaught. From the breach, a surge of hound-like men—ferocious, quadrupedal creatures with the keenest of senses—poured forth. Their forms were grotesque, a nightmarish blend of beast and man, engineered for carnage and tracking. Their noses twitched as they sampled the air, picking up the distinct scents of their targets with terrifying precision.

As the dust settled from the fallen wall, the ground vibrated under the stampede of these monstrous soldiers. Hundreds of them, their eyes wild with bloodlust, zeroed in on the scent trails left by Omni, Nakh, and Keem. With a collective howl that chilled the bone, they surged forward, their claws digging into the sand, propelling them at alarming speeds toward the Roots.

"They are coming," Omni stated, his voice calm yet edged with anticipation. He turned to Keem, his expression steely as he prepared for the imminent clash. He could feel the vibrations of the charging army, a relentless tide of fury racing through the desert sands toward them.

Keem, soaring above the chaos, extended his arms wide as he harnessed the power of the wind and sand around him. With a sharp motion, he swept his hands forward, orchestrating a fierce sandstorm that whipped across the battlefield. Grains of sand churned into a blinding maelstrom, a natural weapon aimed at disorienting and slowing the enemy. The storm howled through the breach in the wall, obscuring sight and turning the day momentarily into night.

However, Culo's army, bred for such conditions and driven by instincts beyond those of ordinary men, was undeterred. The hound-like soldiers relied less on their vision and more on their keen sense of smell, which guided them through the sandy fog. Their noses, sensitive to the slightest hint of their prey, kept them relentlessly on the trail of the Roots.

Unfazed by the visual barrier Keem had created, the creatures continued their advance, their pace unbroken, their growls and barks piercing through the storm. It became evident that the Roots would need to adapt their strategies, recognizing that traditional methods of warfare held little sway over these beastly adversaries.

From the ground, Omni witnessed the persistence of the approaching foes, realizing the challenge they faced. "They're tracking by scent!" he shouted over the roar of the wind, ensuring that Keem heard him even from above. This crucial piece of information necessitated a shift in tactics immediately.

Nakh, sensing the critical moment had arrived to escalate their defense, knelt and pressed his palms against the cool sand. His eyes closed in concentration, and he reached deep into his connection with the earth beneath, channeling his energy into its vast network of grains and minerals. With a deep, resonant breath, he sent his intention downward, where it spread through the layers of sand and stone.

Suddenly, the ground trembled violently. A localized earthquake erupted right beneath the advancing hound-like army, sending shockwaves across the battlefield. The soldiers, trained for combat but not for the capriciousness of nature manipulated by such potent forces, found themselves scrambling to maintain balance as the earth heaved and split.

Reacting quickly to the seismic disturbance, the creatures adeptly jumped from one patch of stable land to another, their agility a testament to their brutal training. However, Nakh was not finished. As the soldiers navigated the upheaving ground, he altered his strategy, focusing on the sandy terrain that surrounded the enemy.

With a subtle shift of his hands, Nakh caused the sand to behave unnaturally, its particles beginning to move apart and then together, creating a quicksand effect. The liquefied sand turned treacherous, ensnaring the feet of the hound-like soldiers. What moments before had been solid footing now became a trapping mire, pulling them down and slowing their frenetic charge to a desperate struggle for freedom.

The army's advance faltered as more and more of their number found themselves caught in the shifting, sinking sands. Their efforts to free themselves only hastened their entrapment, the sand clinging and dragging with merciless persistence.

As the battle raged and the ground beneath the feet of Culo's army continued to shake and shift, Omni, standing firm amidst the chaos, extended his control over the elements with a calm yet resolute focus. The sandy terrain that Nakh had transformed into a trap was now set for a critical maneuver that could decisively impair the enemy's capabilities.

Observing the enemy struggling to free themselves from the liquefied sand, Omni realized that further intervention could cement their disadvantage. Closing his eyes, he concentrated deeply, channeling his energy to intensify the trap. With a subtle motion of his hands, he directed his intent to the sandy quagmire where the enemy's feet were ensnared.

The loose sand around the feet of the hound-like soldiers began to shift more dramatically, each grain seeming to vibrate with Omni's will. Slowly, the sand thickened and tightened, its consistency changing from merely troublesome to downright perilous. The liquefied sand transformed into quicksand, increasing its suction and pulling the trapped soldiers further down.

The hound-like soldiers, already disoriented by the seismic shocks and the blinding sandstorm, found themselves completely immobilized as the ground beneath them turned hostile. Their attempts to escape became futile efforts, as the quicksand clung relentlessly, drawing them deeper with every struggle and movement they made.

Panic spread among the ranks of the trapped soldiers, their ferocious barks and growls turning into cries of alarm. The front line meant to breach and clear paths for the main force, was now sinking slowly into the desert, their strength and ferocity neutralized by the clever manipulation of the terrain.

From a tactical viewpoint, Omni's action was a masterstroke. It not only halted the advance of the first wave but also served as a psychological blow to the enemy, displaying the level of control and power the Roots wielded over the very earth they fought upon.

As the enemy struggled within the treacherous quicksand that Omni had masterfully manipulated, Keem hovered above, his body radiating an intense heat that shimmered in the arid desert air. The energy within him coalesced, channeling through his core and into his hands, which glowed ominously with a dark, crackling fire. This was not ordinary flame; it was a manifestation of his innermost power, a black fire that consumed not just flesh but the very spirit of whatever it touched.

With a fierce cry that echoed across the battlefield, Keem unleashed the inferno. The black fire surged downward in a devastating blast, targeting the trapped hound-like soldiers. It engulfed them in a searing, unnatural heat, their cries of agony briefly overpowering the roar of the battle. The sand around them, superheated by the intensity of the flame, fused into sheets of jagged glass, further complicating the terrain for any who dared traverse it.

The horrific spectacle of soldiers burning and the ground itself transforming into a glassy trap marked a grim but necessary tactic. The enemy, witnessing the fate of their vanguard, hesitated, their advance faltering as they navigated around the newly formed glass barriers. The sight of their comrades, half-sunken and charred, served as a dire warning of the formidable defenses arrayed against them.

Despite this, the resolve of Culo's army did not completely break. Driven by their ferocious leader's will and the sheer numbers at their back, more soldiers pressed forward, emerging through the sandstorm that still raged at the hands of the Roots. Weapons were drawn, gleaming with malice and intent, they advanced toward Keem, Omni, and Nakh, who stood ready to meet them.

Omni, observing the relentless approach of the enemy, knew that the battle was far from over. He reached deep into his connection with the earth, preparing to shift the battlefield once again to their advantage. Nakh, standing firm beside him, readied himself for close combat, his sword humming with the same vibrational energy that he had used to shake the very foundations of the desert.

Keem, after the exertion of his powerful attack, descended to the ground, joining his comrades. His hands still smoked slightly from the black fire, a stark reminder of the destruction he could wield. Together, the trio formed a formidable front, their combined abilities creating a dynamic defense that adapted fluidly to the shifting tides of battle.

As the enemy drew closer, the Roots launched into action. Omni manipulated the sand to create swirling barriers, disorienting the approaching soldiers and forcing them into choke points where Nakh's swordsmanship could be most effective. Keem, recovering his strength, prepared for another surge of his dark fire, targeting clusters of enemies to break their morale and thin their numbers.

The battlefield had transformed into a chaotic theater of sand, glass, and fire, with the Roots at the center, commanding the elements with a fierce determination to defend their homeland. The air was thick with the sounds of battle—cries of pain, the roar of fire, and the relentless howling of the wind.

Omni, standing amidst the swirling sands, orchestrated the granules like a maestro, each movement of his hands directing another wave of sand to rise and strike at the hound-like soldiers. The sand clutched at their limbs, pulling them off balance and hurling them through the air with the force of an invisible giant. The desert itself had become their ally, turning against the invaders with a vengeance.

Keem, taking the lead as Omni and Nakh regrouped, stood tall with his hands lifted high, summoning the winds to his command. His eyes burned with the intensity of battle, focused on the swirling sands at his feet. With a powerful outward thrust of his arms, he manipulated the gusts, whipping the sand into a series of formidable tornadoes.

These were no ordinary twisters; they were ferocious cyclones supercharged by Keem's elemental magic. They roared across the battlefield, their cores dense with sand and debris, engulfing enemy soldiers in their path. The hound-men, caught in the violent updraft, were sucked into the vortex, losing any semblance of control as they were spun mercilessly and then expelled at lethal speeds, flung far from the heart of the conflict.

The sight of these sand tornadoes hurling enemies across the desert was both awe-inspiring and terrifying, a testament to the Roots' mastery over nature and their unwavering resolve. Keem moved with a dancer's grace, his body attuned to the winds and sands, every gesture fluid and potent.

As Keem directed the tornadoes, Omni used the opportunity to regroup with Nakh. Together, they surveyed the battlefield, ready to adapt their tactics to any new threats. Nakh's eyes narrowed as he monitored the enemy's movements, his hand gripping the hilt of his sword, ready to engage at a moment's notice.

The Roots' display of power had a visible effect on the morale of Culo's forces. The enemy soldiers, though numerous and relentless, began to show signs of hesitation, their formations breaking as they witnessed the destructive capability of just three defenders wielding the raw forces of nature.

Yet, the battle was far from over. Even as some of the enemy were scattered or incapacitated, others regrouped and pressed forward, driven by their own commanders and the unyielding will of Culo. The Roots knew this was only the initial phase of what promised to be a protracted engagement. They prepared for the next wave, each man aware that their endurance, as much as their power, would be tested in the hours to come.

As the dust settled momentarily and the echoes of the sand tornadoes faded, the Roots stood together, a formidable trio against the horizon, their resolve as unbreakable as the elements they commanded. The battle for their land, their people, and their very way of life continued to rage around them, each moment defining the legacy they would leave behind.

As the battlefield churned with sand and wind, Omni further honed his control over the earth elements. His focus intensified, and with a series of sharp gestures, he manipulated the sand to ensnare more of the hound-like creatures. The granules of sand acted like countless tiny hands, gripping and lifting the enemies with an unyielding grasp. As Omni controlled these sandy appendages, he flung the captured soldiers directly into the swirling maelstroms created by Keem.

Each throw was precise, designed to maximize the disorientation and disruption among Culo's forces. The creatures, caught in the powerful grip of the sand, found themselves helplessly tossed into the raging sand tornadoes. The tornadoes, now loaded with enemy combatants, became even more chaotic and destructive.

Keem, seeing the effectiveness of their combined efforts, pushed his abilities to the limit. His arms rose and fell in dramatic arcs, directing the tornadoes with expert precision. The winds howled louder, filled with the energy of his command, as he steered the swirling columns toward the wall— the very structure that had been breached by the enemy earlier.

The tornadoes moved like sentient beings across the battlefield, each step they took marked by the screams and the clatter of armor from the soldiers trapped within. As they reached the wall, the tornadoes unleashed their fury, hurling members of Culo's army against the broken remnants of stone and earth. The impact was devastating; armor dented, weapons scattered, and the cries of the injured filled the air.

After delivering their chaotic payload, the tornadoes began to lose their energy. Spent from the effort of containing and transporting such destructive forces, the columns of wind and sand started to dissipate. The last remnants of their presence flickered out, leaving behind a scene of disarray along the wall where many of Culo's soldiers lay scattered and disoriented.

With the immediate threat temporarily mitigated, Omni and Keem took a moment to assess the battlefield. They stood back to back, their breathing heavy but controlled, their eyes scanning for the next wave of attacks. The lull was short-lived, but it provided a crucial moment for them to regroup.

Culo's surprise turned into fury as he watched his meticulously assembled force being thrown about by the elemental fury conjured by the Roots. Standing high atop a dune, overseeing the chaotic scene, he barked orders to his lieutenants, his voice a thunderous echo across the battlefield. "This couldn't be possible. Get me my land!" he roared, unwilling to accept any outcome but victory. His eyes burned with resolve as he signaled for reinforcements.

With a ground-shaking rumble, a new wave of troops surged forward, led by hulking giants whose very steps caused the desert sands to shift and quake. Towering over their comrades, these behemoths of war moved with surprising speed for their size, their eyes fixed on the horizon where Keem, Nakh, and Omni stood resolute.

As the giants approached, the air trembled with the weight of their footsteps, sending vibrations through the sand that could be felt even at a great distance. Keem tightened his grip, his previous encounter with the tornadoes having drained some of his energy, yet his spirit remained unbroken. "We have to hold up! We cannot let them pass us now," he shouted over to Nakh and Omni, his voice firm despite the approaching threat.

As the battlefield became a canvas for Omni's elemental artistry, his control over the sand evolved into a more lethal form. With a deft motion of his hands, he transformed the soft desert floor into an array of sharp, jagged spikes. They jutted out from the ground like deadly spears, strategically placed to impede the relentless advance of the hound-like creatures.

The first wave of hounds, driven by instinct and the scent of their enemies, approached at breakneck speed. Anticipating the danger, a few of the more agile beasts leaped over the initial row of spikes. However, their relief was short-lived. As they cleared the spikes, Omni's focus shifted, and with a subtle manipulation of his powers, the spikes dissolved back into a flowing river of sand.

The sand moved with predatory precision, quickly reforming into grasping hands that clutched at the legs of the hounds that had just evaded the spikes. The creatures' triumphant leaps turned into desperate struggles as the sand wrapped around their limbs and dragged them downwards. Confusion and panic spread among the hounds as they were pulled under, their ferocious barks and growls muffled by the sand closing over them.

This deadly trap not only halted the charge of the leading hounds but also sowed chaos in the ranks, following closely behind. The remaining hounds skidded to a halt, their instincts now warily alert to the shifting sands that could spell their doom. The hesitation rippled back through the ranks, giving the Roots a crucial moment to regroup and plan their next move.

As the tumultuous battle unfolded across the sands and skies, Culo, driven by desperation and the indomitable will to conquer, unleashed the full might of his remaining forces. With a commanding roar that reverberated across the battlefield, he sent forth his army, a massive wave of soldiers that surged past the battered wall and into the open desert.

The air filled with the sound of beating wings as a large contingent of Culo's forces took to the skies. These were not mere foot soldiers but elite warriors capable of aerial combat, their bodies equipped with gliders and wingsuits, turning them into deadly predators of the air. As they swooped down toward the Roots, the sky darkened with their numbers, casting a foreboding shadow over the battlefield.

Keem, his eyes scanning the horizon, was the first to notice the swarm of flying soldiers. "We've got a large number coming in from above!" he shouted to his comrades, his voice tinged with urgency. Positioned strategically, he prepared to counter the aerial assault with his own fiery abilities.

Omni, deeply connected to the earth, felt the vibrations of countless feet pounding across the sand. "I can feel a large number coming through the sand as well," he confirmed, his brow furrowed in concentration. The dual threat from land and air presented a new challenge, one that required a swift reassessment of their tactics.

Facing overwhelming numbers and the coordinated assault of Culo's army, the Roots made a tactical decision. "We need to retreat and regroup," Omni stated, his voice calm but resolute. The decision was strategic, aimed at preserving their strength for a more defensible position where they could better leverage their elemental powers.

As the Roots executed their strategic retreat, Omni's mastery over the earth element came to the forefront. With a commanding gesture, he caused the sand beneath his feet to ripple and rise, forming a swift-moving wave that carried him across the battlefield with impressive speed. The sand shifted under his control, propelling him back toward the main forces of the dynasty, where reinforcements awaited.

Beside him, Nakh demonstrated his own profound connection to the elements. Concentrating deeply, he manipulated the molecules of the air around him, harnessing their vibrations to create a lifting force. With a sudden surge, he lifted off the ground, the air swirling visibly around him as he soared through the sky. It was a remarkable display of his power, enabling him to join Omni in their rapid retreat without touching the ground.

Keem, witnessing the inventive escapes of his comrades, couldn't help but flash a brief, wry smile amidst the chaos. He then launched himself into the air, using powerful gusts of wind to propel himself forward, his body cutting through the air with the grace and speed of a falcon. Together, the trio made their way back to their army, each using their unique abilities to retreat efficiently and regroup for the coming stand.

Behind them, the relentless march of Culo's army painted a stark picture. The vast sea of warriors had crossed more than half of the desert, their numbers appearing as an unending tide of malice and determination. With each step, they closed the distance, driven by Culo's unyielding ambition to conquer and claim the land as his own.

The sounds of the advancing army were a constant, ominous rumble, a reminder of the threat that loomed ever closer. As they breached the halfway mark of the desert, their pace quickened, spurred by the sight of the retreating Roots. They pushed forward with renewed vigor, their eyes set on the prize that seemed within their grasp.

Upon reaching the defensive lines of the dynasty, the Roots quickly briefed their commanders on the situation. The urgency of the moment was palpable, as preparations were rapidly made to strengthen their defenses. Omni, Nakh, and Keem coordinated with the military leaders, sharing insights from the frontline that would be crucial in shaping the defensive strategy.

The dynasty's forces were rallied, with soldiers taking up positions along the prepared defenses. Archers climbed to higher vantage points, their quivers full, while infantrymen sharpened their blades and braced for the clash. Omni took charge of fortifying the terrain, creating sand barriers and traps that would hinder the enemy's advance. Nakh focused on enhancing the sensory capabilities of the lookout posts, using his ability to manipulate air molecules to detect even the subtlest vibrations of the approaching army. Keem, meanwhile, prepared to unleash his elemental fury, setting up positions where his fire could be most effective against the onslaught.

As the enemy drew near, the air was thick with anticipation and resolve. The dynasty's forces, bolstered by the return of their elemental warriors, stood ready to defend their homeland against the invaders. The stage was set for a confrontation that would determine the fate of the land, a battle between the unyielding force of Culo's ambition and the immovable object of the dynasty's will to survive and protect their realm.

The battlefield, now a maelstrom of elemental forces and determined warriors, was alive with the sound and fury of an epic confrontation. As Culo's army continued its relentless advance, the Roots responded with their own display of power and ingenuity.

Omni, standing firm on the front lines, focused his energy on the sandy terrain beneath his feet. With a series of fluid motions, he conjured multiple clones from the sand, each one a perfect replica of himself. These sand clones, imbued with a portion of his own elemental spirit, moved forward to meet the enemy, multiplying the defensive efforts and confusing the attackers with their numbers.

Beside him, Hutch, feeling the urgency of the moment, tapped into his deepest reserves of power. His breath visible in the air as he concentrated, the temperature around him dropping sharply. With a forceful exhale, he summoned a series of ice clones, each one forming from the moisture in the air and freezing instantaneously. These clones, armed with crystalline ice weapons, joined Omni's sand replicas in a phalanx of frost and sand, ready to intercept the oncoming foes.

In the midst of this, Finity, who had been engaged in her own skirmishes on the flank, caught sight of Omni. Relief washed over her face, replaced quickly by a determined smile. Seeing Omni alive and wielding his powers with such command bolstered her spirit, and she redoubled her efforts, her own abilities flaring to life as she manipulated the light around her to dazzle and blind her opponents.

Meanwhile, Keem, recognizing the need for a dramatic shift in the battlefield's dynamics, prepared his most ambitious creation yet. Standing atop a dune, he drew deeply from the elemental air around him, his hands weaving complex patterns as he gathered the winds. With a thunderous roar, he unleashed a massive tornado, far larger than any before. This colossal whirlwind of sand and air tore across the desert, a titanic force of nature directed squarely at the heart of the enemy's formation.

The battlefield, already a scene of epic conflict, escalated to a new level of elemental chaos as Keem poured his fiery essence into the vast tornado. Standing firmly, his eyes narrowed in concentration, he directed his inner fire toward the swirling mass of sand. Sparks of black flame, dark and intense, began to emerge from the tornado's base, quickly multiplying and rising through the vortex. As these black flames intertwined with the swirling sand, the tornado transformed into a spinning pillar of destruction—a massive cyclone of black fire that roared across the desert with a fearsome, crackling sound.

This formidable fusion of wind and fire created a spectacle of awe and terror, a black spinning death that carved through Culo's forces with ruthless efficiency. The heat from the flames scorched the earth, leaving a trail of glassy sand in its wake, while the swirling winds carried embers far and wide, igniting anything in their path.

Amidst this chaos, Omni, driven by the need to amplify their defensive efforts, tapped into the deeper layers of his elemental power. As he ran toward the fiery tornado, his body underwent a stunning transformation. His limbs thickened, his stature grew, and his flesh turned into glowing, molten rock. The ground beneath his feet cracked and sizzled as he moved, his form becoming that of a magma monster, a titan of rock and fire.

With a thunderous roar that matched the intensity of the transformed tornado, Omni leaped into the heart of the fiery cyclone. As he merged with the black flames, his magma body acted as a catalyst, intensifying the heat and adding a molten core to the already fearsome tornado. The combination of

Keem's black fire and Omni's magma form created a superheated vortex that blazed through the battlefield, an unstoppable force of nature that consumed and obliterated everything in its path.

From a distance, Nakh and Finity, alongside the rest of the dynasty's forces, watched in awe and horror as the fiery tornado, now pulsating with a core of molten lava, rampaged through the enemy lines. The sight of Omni, transformed into a creature of raw elemental power, underscored the lengths to which the Roots would go to protect their land.

Keem, his energy somewhat drained but his resolve unshaken, watched as his creation, now magnified by Omni's intervention, became a symbol of their defiance. "Hold the line!" he shouted to the soldiers around him, his voice carrying over the roar of the flames. "Let no one pass!"

Expelled from the seething heart of the black fire tornado, Omni, still radiating with molten energy, was propelled with great force toward an approaching giant. His trajectory was a perfect line of fury, his fist clenched and glowing with residual heat. As he neared the massive adversary, he unleashed a powerful strike, his burning fist connecting with the giant's chest with a sound like thunder cracking. The impact sent a wave of heat across the battlefield, visible even through the swirling sand and flames.

The giant, caught off guard by the sudden and intense assault, stumbled backward, its thick skin smoking and charring under the extreme heat of Omni's touch. Without pausing, Omni surged forward, driven by the momentum of his flight and the urgency of the battle. He delivered another devastating blow, this time aiming for the giant's face. His fist, encased in layers of glowing magma, struck true, melting away the features on one side of the giant's face, leaving it grotesquely deformed and partially incinerated.

Around them, the battlefield was a vortex of chaos and destruction. The enhanced tornado, now a lethal weapon of wind and flame, continued its rampage. It swooped across the enemy lines with predatory grace, its path marked by the screams and the scorched armor of Culo's soldiers. Men caught in the tornado's path were lifted off their feet and sucked into its fiery core, where they were consumed by the intense heat, their cries silenced almost instantly as the flames engulfed them.

With the battlefield now a torn and charred testament to the ferocity of the conflict, the remaining forces of the Dynasty saw an opportunity to press their advantage. As the great tornado crafted by Keem began to wane, it nonetheless served as a powerful deterrent, pushing back the remnants of Culo's disorganized army. The enemy soldiers, battered and disoriented by the elemental onslaught, found themselves temporarily at a disadvantage.

Seizing the moment, the Dynasty's reinforcements surged forward. The ground troops, led by the valiant Nakh and the resolute Hutch, charged with renewed vigor. Nakh's presence on the battlefield was like that of a storm—swift and devastating. Each swing of his sword was both a strike and a symphony, the vibrations from his blade cutting through both air and armor. Beside him, Hutch wielded his icy abilities with precision, crafting spears of frost from the moisture in the air and hurling them with deadly accuracy at the enemies still struggling to regroup.

Above the fray, Keem and Mo took to the skies, their figures outlined against the harsh desert sun. Mo, another master of the elements from the prehistoric zone, joined Keem to form a formidable aerial duo. Together, they summoned gusts of wind and torrents of fire, their combined powers weaving a tapestry of destruction that rained down upon Culo's forces. Their tactics were not just about brute force; they were a display of strategic mastery, cutting off enemy escape routes and funneling attackers directly into the path of the Dynasty's ground forces.

Joining the fray were members of the Root from the prehistoric zone, warriors who had long mastered the art of combining raw physical prowess with elemental magic. These seasoned warriors, veterans of countless battles through the ages, brought skills and tactics that were both ancient and effective. Their presence bolstered the ranks of the Dynasty, their unique abilities adding layers of complexity to the battle strategy.

As the combined forces of the Dynasty pushed forward, the battlefield dynamics shifted markedly. The ground troops, energized by the leadership of Nakh and Hutch, moved with a cohesion and determination that were palpable. Each unit fought not just as individuals but as part of a larger organism, their movements synchronized, their attacks orchestrated with a precision that spoke of extensive training and unshakeable camaraderie.

The enemy, meanwhile, found themselves steadily pushed back, their initial numerical advantage waning under the relentless assault of the Dynasty's coordinated attacks. Culo's forces, though still formidable, began to show signs of faltering morale, their lines breaking where the Dynasty's assault was most intense.

In the thick of battle, the Roots and their allies became symbols of resistance, emblematic of the fierce will to protect and prevail that drove the Dynasty. Each clash of swords, each burst of elemental power was a declaration of their refusal to yield, their commitment to defend their land against any who dared threaten it.

As the sun began to dip toward the horizon, casting long shadows across the desert, the outcome of the battle still hung in the balance. Yet, the resolve of the Dynasty's forces remained unbroken, their spirits bolstered by each small victory within the larger chaos. With Keem, Mo, Nakh, Hutch, and their allies leading the charge, they pressed on, each step forward a testament to their bravery and their unyielding desire to secure the future of their land.

The desert became a forge under the might of Omni and Keem, each employing their elemental powers with devastating precision. As the giants, formidable in size and strength, lumbered toward the Dynasty's lines, Omni met them head-on with a calculated strategy. Recognizing their vulnerability to terrain manipulation, he deftly twisted his hands, palms pressing toward the earth. The ground beneath the giants' feet transformed, turning into treacherous quicksand that swallowed their steps and halted their advance. Their massive forms struggled against the pull of the earth, their movements becoming labored and slow.

With the giants momentarily stalled, Omni seized the opportunity for a more aggressive assault. His form glowed with intense heat as he scooped up handfuls of sand, transmuting them into molten magma before hurling them at the ensnared foes. The air hissed as the magma rocks struck the giants, their skin sizzling and smoking upon contact. Cries of pain echoed across the wind-swept dunes.

Above the fray, Keem's battle was a spectacle of raw power and fierce determination. His hands, transformed into black fiery fists of fury, became lethal weapons. Each strike delivered with his blazing fists left searing holes in the bodies of Culo's soldiers, the smell of charred armor and flesh permeating the battlefield. Not content with merely striking his foes, Keem embraced the full ferocity of his fire-based abilities. Grasping enemies in his fiery grip, he transformed his entire form into a spinning ball of black flames. He moved through the ranks of

349

the enemy like a meteor, each contact reducing his foes to ashes and leaving a trail of destruction in his wake.

The combination of Omni's control over earth and fire with Keem's fiery onslaught created a dynamic front that Culo's forces struggled to penetrate. Each Root's attack not only inflicted physical damage but also terrorized the morale of the invading army, their advance faltering under the relentless elemental barrage.

Meanwhile, Nakh and Hutch coordinated the Dynasty's ground forces, exploiting the openings created by their comrades' powerful displays. Nakh's mastery of vibration and sound turned the battlefield into a resonant echo chamber, disorienting the enemy, while Hutch's icy creations provided barriers and traps that further hampered enemy movements.

As the battle raged into the late hours, the desert landscape transformed. Areas once dominated by sand were now glassed over from the intense heat, and craters pocked the battlefield, remnants of the fierce clashes. The air was thick with the scent of ozone and burnt earth, a testament to the ferocity of the conflict.

Amidst the chaos, the Roots moved with purpose and unity. Their combined efforts not only held back the tide of invaders but also pushed them back, reclaiming ground with every counterattack. Their powers, though draining, were wielded with a precision that spoke of their deep commitment to protecting their homeland.

The battlefield had transformed into a chessboard upon which Nakh and Hutch orchestrated their masterful strategies. Nakh, his awareness heightened to the molecular vibrations around him, took a deep breath and extended his hands forward. Concentrating deeply, he began to manipulate the very molecules of the air surrounding the advancing enemies. His powers, subtle yet profound, slowed the molecules to a crawl, causing a noticeable deceleration in the movements of Culo's soldiers. They staggered, their motions becoming sluggish as if moving through a viscous fluid, their faces contorted in confusion and frustration at their sudden impotence.

This temporal manipulation created a perfect opening for the Dynasty's forces. With the enemy slowed almost to a standstill, they became easy targets for the waiting warriors. Nakh's manipulation of molecular vibrations was not just defensive but a prelude to a more aggressive assault. His allies capitalized on the advantage, striking with precision and ferocity, cutting down the bewildered invaders who could barely raise their weapons in defense.

Parallel to Nakh's molecular mastery, Hutch wielded his icy powers with equal finesse. His hands moved in elegant, sweeping gestures, summoning the cold from the depths of the earth and the chill of the wind. With a powerful exhalation that misted in the desert air, he unleashed a wave of frost that spread rapidly across the battlefield. Enemies caught in the frost's path were instantly encased in ice, their bodies frozen mid-motion, expressions of alarm and pain etched forever on their faces.

Around Hutch, his ice clones mirrored his actions, multiplying the effect of his freezing assault. They moved through the ranks of immobilized soldiers, shattering the frozen forms with ruthless efficiency. Each strike of Hutch's and his clones' icy weapons sent shards of ice mixed with armor and flesh scattering across the sand, a chilling testament to their lethal precision.

The combined efforts of Nakh and Hutch, leveraging their control over molecular motion and ice, dramatically turned the tide of the battle. The field was littered with the slowed and frozen, a testament to the strategic dominance of the Roots and their allies. As the Dynasty's soldiers moved through the ranks of their disoriented and immobilized foes, the morale of Culo's army plummeted, and their once fearsome advance reduced to a desperate crawl.

As the sun dipped below the horizon, casting the desert into twilight, the remnants of Culo's forces were in disarray. Many attempted to retreat, scrambling back across the sand that had been their pathway to conquest but now served as their grave. Others, still trapped in the slowed time field or encased in ice, met their end on the battlefield, overwhelmed by the relentless assault of the Dynasty's forces.

In the fading light, the Roots stood among their comrades, their faces marked by exhaustion but also by fierce satisfaction. They had held their ground, protected their land, and decimated an enemy who had underestimated the power of those bound to the elements of earth, air, and water. Nakh and Hutch exchanged a look of mutual respect, their combined efforts having proven decisive.

The battle, though brutal, showcased the strength and unity of the Roots and the Dynasty. As they prepared to deal with the aftermath, their hearts were heavy for the fallen but also filled with resolve. The war might continue, but they had sent a clear message this day: their homeland was guarded not just by soldiers, but by masters of elemental forces, ready to defend it against all threats.

In the midst of the chaos, Finity's role became crucially tactical. Her abilities, mystical and elusive, played on the disorientation already inflicted by her comrades. With the battlefield awash in the aftermath of elemental fury, she became a wraith-like presence, her movements almost ethereal against the backdrop of war.

As enemy soldiers recovered from the assaults of Nakh and Hutch, they found themselves confronted by Finity's mesmerizing gaze. Her eyes, glowing subtly in the twilight, held a compelling power. Those who met her gaze found their minds clouded, their senses betraying them, leading to a maelstrom of confusion. Misunderstandings and paranoia quickly spread among Culo's ranks, as soldiers, gripped by an inexplicable fear, turned against one another. Accusations flew, swords were drawn, and the cohesion of their units began to crumble from within.

Finity, capitalizing on the chaos she sowed, vanished into smoke each time an enemy soldier tried to confront her. She moved like a shadow across the battlefield, her form dissipating and coalescing with the ease of a practiced illusionist. Each time she rematerialized, it was behind or beside an unsuspecting foe. Her strikes were swift and silent, leaving her targets collapsing before they could scream, further contributing to the panic spreading through the enemy lines.

Her tactic was not just about inflicting physical casualties; it was psychological warfare, perfectly executed. As she weaved in and out of visibility, the tales of a ghostly warrior spread rapidly among the remaining invaders, chilling their resolve even further. Her ability to appear and disappear at will, striking without warning, became a legend whispered in the ranks with hushed tones and fearful glances.

Finity's mysterious and deadly dance through Culo's forces turned her into a spectral figure of retribution. Each disappearance into smoke, each unexpected strike, eroded the will of the invaders, turning their own numbers against them as mistrust and fear took root. The psychological impact of her actions was profound, serving as the perfect complement to the more overt displays of power by her fellow Roots.

As the tides of battle ebbed and flowed, the appearance of Lord Inertia on the battlefield marked a crucial turning point. Her presence alone was a significant morale boost for the

Dynasty's forces, and her entrance was both strategic and theatrical, emanating a powerful calm amidst the chaos.

From the back of the formation, Lord Inertia walked with deliberate slowness, her every step measured and purposeful. The soldiers around her parted ways, creating a clear path as she moved toward the front lines. Her calm demeanor contrasted sharply with the frenetic energy of the battlefield, drawing the attention of both friend and foe alike.

As she reached a central vantage point, Inertia paused and lifted her head slightly, her eyes closing in deep concentration. The brief moment of stillness was palpable, charged with anticipation. Then, in a blink, she disappeared, her body transforming into a blur too fast for the naked eye to follow.

Utilizing her incredible speed, which bordered on the speed of light, Inertia became a whirlwind of movement across the battlefield. Her approach was surgical and precise, her targets barely registering her presence before feeling the impact of her attacks. She moved through the ranks of Culo's forces like a phantom, each strike dismantling their defenses and sowing further disarray among the enemy.

In her hands, Inertia wielded fine needles, each one a slender filament of concentrated power. As she darted among the enemy ranks, she used these needles with expert precision, targeting critical pressure points on her opponents' bodies. Each strike was calculated to disable rather than kill, rendering her foes incapacitated with minimal effort.

The effect of her technique was immediate and devastating. Soldiers collapsed where they stood, overwhelmed by sudden paralysis or intense pain as their bodies' nerve clusters were expertly manipulated. This method of attack not only efficiently reduced the enemy's combat effectiveness but also sowed confusion and fear among their ranks, as soldiers witnessed their comrades falling en masse to an unseen assailant.

Inertia's methodical and rapid strikes across the battlefield shifted the momentum significantly. With each soldier she disabled, the Dynasty's forces gained ground, bolstered by her support and the decreasing resistance. Her ability to move at such extraordinary speeds allowed her to cover a wide area in a short time, maximizing her impact on the battle's outcome.

As the enemy struggled to understand the source of their sudden incapacitation, the morale among Culo's forces plummeted. The sight of their peers being swiftly and silently neutralized without a chance to defend themselves was demoralizing, and the cohesion of their strategic formations began to crumble.

Inertia continued her assault with calm efficiency, her face an impassive mask of focus. To the Dynasty's soldiers, she was a spectral avenger, a guardian angel whose intervention was both awe-inspiring and terrifying. Her actions not only demonstrated her formidable prowess but also her strategic acumen, choosing to disable rather than destroy, preserving the core tenets of mercy and restraint.

As the battle reached its climactic moments, the dwindling enemy forces became increasingly desperate. The giants, towering and formidable, pushed past the front lines in a last-ditch effort to turn the tide of battle. Omni's strategic disappearance into the sand was a spectacle of his mastery over his elemental powers, demonstrating his ability to evade and reposition with a cunning that matched his raw power.

Omni's reformation from swirling sand into solid form next to Finity was both a protective maneuver and a striking display of his bond with her. As one of the giants lumbered dangerously close to where Finity was strategically positioned, Omni materialized between them, his stance resolute and his intent clear. He positioned himself protectively, his arms outstretched with his back to Finity, forming a human shield against the approaching threat.

The giant, undeterred by the loss of many of its comrades, raised its massive arm, preparing to bring down a crushing blow aimed at Omni and Finity. The ground trembled with each of the giant's steps, a physical reminder of the imminent danger they faced. Omni's eyes narrowed, focusing on the towering foe before him, his body tense and ready to respond.

Behind him, Finity's expression was a mix of concern and determination. While Omni's protective stance gave her a momentary respite, she was far from helpless. Her hands glowed with a subtle, radiant energy, ready to unleash her own powers should the need arise. The bond between Omni and Finity, forged in countless battles and moments of shared peril, was evident in their seamless coordination.

The battlefield became a tableau of raw emotion and elemental power as Finity's wrath reached its zenith. Her transformation into smoke was not just a defense mechanism but a declaration of her escalating fury and her mastery over her abilities. With Omni as her steadfast guardian, she moved with purpose, a specter of vengeance gliding effortlessly through the chaos of battle.

As she approached the giant, her form ephemeral and untouchable, the creature's massive fist swung through her smoke-like body, connecting with nothing but air. The futility of its attack only heightened its confusion and fear, emotions it was unaccustomed to feeling. Finity, seizing the moment, surged upward directly into the giant's head, her smoky form infiltrating his senses, enveloping his mind.

Inside the giant's consciousness, Finity unleashed a storm of psychic energy. The giant clutched its head, overwhelmed by an intense onslaught of pain and disorientation. This wasn't just a physical attack; it was a deep, invasive manipulation of his neural pathways, rendering him incapacitated. His roars of agony filled the air, a sound so primal and pained that it momentarily stilled the fighting around him. He stumbled, his massive frame shaking the ground as he fell to one knee, his fist pounding the earth in a mix of rage and desperation.

As silence finally claimed him, his eyes rolled back, a dark, smoky essence swirling within their depths. The transformation was profound—Finity's powers had not only subdued him but had turned him into something other. When he rose, the black smoke clouding his pupils marked a dramatic change; no longer just a giant, he was now an avatar of the power Finity had unleashed.

Facing the new giant approaching from behind, the transformed giant stood up, his stance altered, his demeanor more ominous. The black smoke in his eyes was not just a sign of his defeat but also a symbol of his new allegiance. Finity, through her incredible powers, had bent his will, redirecting his immense strength to serve the Dynasty's cause.

As the dust settled and the clamor of battle died down to an eerie quiet, all eyes were riveted on the transformed giant, his eyes swirling with dark smoke. The tension in the air was palpable as friend and foe alike watched this new entity, a being reshaped by Finity's formidable powers, take center stage in the battlefield drama.

The smoky-eyed giant advanced toward another of Culo's giants, an ominous figure whose fists were primed for destruction. With a deliberate, menacing poise, he drew back his massive fist and unleashed a powerful blow. The impact was thunderous, echoing across the battlefield as it connected with the opposing giant's jaw, sending him reeling backward. The struck giant crashed to the ground with a force that shook the earth, his enormous body tumbling onto several of Culo's soldiers who had been too slow to clear the path. The sound of armor and bone crushed under his weight marked a grim turning point in the fight.

This display of sheer power from their former ally sent a wave of panic rippling through Culo's forces. What had once been a formidable invasion force now crumbled under the weight of fear and uncertainty. As the smoky-eyed giant strode across the battlefield, each step was purposeful and devastating. He used his colossal fists to deliver ground-shaking blows that obliterated clusters of Culo's troops attempting to regroup or flee.

The sight of such unstoppable force caused the remaining soldiers of Culo's army to break ranks completely. The retreat turned into a rout as they scrambled to escape the wrath of the transformed giant. His massive footsteps crushed those too slow to evade, and his ground pounds sent shockwaves through the ranks, dispersing the invaders like leaves in a storm.

With the enemy in full retreat, the battlefield quieted, leaving behind the echoes of battle and the scars of conflict. The Roots, along with the Dynasty's forces, watched in a mixture of awe and relief as their new ally ensured no enemy remained to threaten their victory. The battle, which had once seemed a dire test of their resolve, had turned in their favor through a stunning display of power and strategic manipulation.

As the chaos of the retreat unfolded, Keem, with a keen eye for tactical advantage, intensified the disarray among Culo's forces. Recognizing the moment to seal their victory, he conjured a massive sandstorm at a strategic point near the wall. His control over the winds whipped the sand into a blinding frenzy, cloaking the battlefield in a dense, swirling haze. The wall of sand effectively obscured the vision of Culo's retreating army, disorienting them further and cutting off any view of potential escape routes. This maneuver not only slowed their retreat but instilled a deeper sense of panic within their ranks.

Nakh, observing the chaos and sensing an opportunity to further incapacitate the enemy, took a calculated risk. With precision born of his deep connection to the vibrational energies of the battlefield, he hurled his sword toward the far wall—the very structure the enemy had initially breached. The sword, empowered by Nakh's unique abilities, struck the wall with a resonant impact, sending a powerful wave of vibrations coursing through the stone.

The effect was immediate and devastating. The already weakened structure could not withstand the intense vibrational force; it shuddered and then collapsed, burying under rubble those enemies unlucky enough to be near it without an escape route. The wall's collapse served as a symbolic and literal crushing of any remaining hopes Culo's forces might have harbored of a regrouped assault.

In the midst of this turmoil, as the sandstorm raged and the wall crumbled, Culo himself made a dramatic appearance. Rising above the chaos, levitated by an unknown power, he emerged from the sandstorm, his figure a stark silhouette against the turbulent backdrop. His sudden ascent into the air was a desperate bid for control, a visual rallying call to his scattered forces.

Culo's presence aloft was a powerful image, his face marked by rage and determination. Even as his army faltered, he sought to embody defiance and command. His voice, amplified by fury and the mystic energies at his command, boomed across the battlefield, attempting to reassert his authority and stem the tide of retreat.

As the winds of battle calmed and the dust settled around them, Finity took a deep breath, her focus intensifying as she released her control over the giant's mind. The smoky essence that had clouded his eyes began to dissipate, returning the giant to his own consciousness. With a gentle nod of gratitude toward Finity for her intervention and guidance, the giant looked around, visibly confused but no longer under the spell of manipulation. His gaze fell on the remnants of his fallen comrades, and a sense of realization washed over him—a reflection of the chaos he had unwittingly contributed to while under her influence.

Finity herself faded into smoke, her form becoming ethereal and translucent as she moved away from the front lines. She rematerialized near the Dynasty's forces, her presence comforting to her allies who acknowledged her with nods and murmurs of respect. Standing among her comrades, she turned her attention toward Culo, who, hovering in the air, had become the focal point of the battlefield's remaining tension.

Culo, elevated above the ruin and despair of his defeated army, was a figure of defiance against the inevitable. His voice, imbued with a mixture of rage and desperation, echoed across the battlefield, reaching friend and foe alike. As his form began to shrink, his declaration echoed ominously, his words laced with a deep-seated yearning for recognition that transcended mere conquest.

"What point do you think you are proving? If you kill all of them, I will still pass through and get the respect I desire. I do not care for the land if I have no people to give it to. They wanted the land; I just want to be acknowledged for who I am.

I want everyone to see what I see when I look in the mirror. This world will see me for me," he proclaimed, his arms raised in a gesture that seemed both defiant and resigned.

As Culo's voice echoed across the battlefield, his form continued to shrink, encapsulating his desperation and desire for recognition in a visual that was as startling as his words. His transformation was not just physical but symbolic, revealing the vulnerability and desperation underlying his quest for acknowledgment and respect.

As Culo vanished into thin air, shrinking until he was no more than a whisper of his former self, the battlefield fell into a brief, puzzled silence. The Dynasty's forces, momentarily stunned, quickly regained their focus. The sandstorm that Keem had conjured still swirled around the wall, obscuring vision but not determination. The soldiers of the Dynasty charged forward, spurred on by the urgency of the situation and the potential opportunity that lay just beyond the chaos.

Omni, his senses attuned to the shifting sands and the movements of the retreating enemy, communicated his observations to Hutch as they ran. "I feel them running to the sea," he said, his voice steady despite the rush. "There are ships waiting for them. If we hurry, we can take their ships and use them to get to the Land of Gods. But there are more ships headed this way," he added, noting the approaching reinforcements that threatened to complicate their plan.

Hutch nodded, processing the information quickly. "We need to act fast then. Securing those ships could be our best chance to reach the Land of Gods before Culo regroups or reinforcements complicate our path," he responded, his eyes scanning the horizon for any sign of the enemy fleet.

As they strategized, Keem suddenly flew past them, a determined look on his face that caught Hutch's attention. "I will meet back with you all on the sea," Keem called out as he accelerated. His thoughts were on the precious egg he had left behind in the canyon, a responsibility he could not abandon even in the heat of battle.

"What is wrong?" Hutch called after him, concern lacing his voice.

"I cannot leave my egg here in this zone," Keem shouted back over the roar of the wind and sand. His attachment to the egg was not just emotional but bound by duty, a testament to his deeper connection to the life he had nurtured.

Lona, who had been following closely behind, overheard the exchange. Her decision was swift, driven by a mix of adventure and allegiance. "Take me with you!" she exclaimed, her voice carrying through the storm.

Without hesitation, Keem reached out his hand, grasping Lona's and pulling her close. Together, they veered off, flying against the tide of soldiers and sand, heading back toward the canyon where Keem's future, encapsulated in the egg, awaited.

As Keem and Lona disappeared into the distance, Omni and Hutch continued their sprint toward the sea, each step bringing them closer to the ships that held the key to their journey to the Land of Gods. Behind them, the sounds of the battlefield faded into the background, replaced by the pounding of their hearts and the shared resolve to seize the moment, knowing full well that the path ahead would demand every ounce of their courage, strength, and unity.

As the dust of battle settled and the armies began the process of withdrawal and regrouping, Lord Inertia called Nakh and Finity aside for a momentous conversation. Their silhouettes cast long shadows in the fading light, a testament to the gravity of their discussion.

"We must not follow you all," Inertia began, her voice steady but laden with the weight of her decision. "Now that the enemy is defeated, we must rebuild our land here in the desert.

This army is as confused with life as my children once were."
She opened a locket she wore around her neck, revealing a
picture of herself with Stats and a baby Otto—images of
simpler times.

"We must let the surviving soldiers speak with the monks
and see if they would like to help us rebuild and start a new
civilization. They were led by someone with their own selfish
needs and desires. With them being at such a low number now,
there is more than enough land for all of us to share," she
explained, her plan reflecting a deep commitment to healing
and integration rather than continued division.

Finity, ever vigilant, voiced her concern as Inertia turned
to leave. "But do you trust them? They still have giants."

Inertia paused, her back to the setting sun, casting her in a
halo of dusky light. "If you can stop them, then so can I," she
responded confidently. "There was no mercy shown to my
husband when he died to the first attackers. A giant came to
our village in the desert and was greeted by my husband. My
husband welcomed him before the giant attacked and killed him
in front of all of us. My husband's last words were to avenge
him. He told me to protect everyone and hide the knowledge.
Build a wall and kill all that come close."

She sighed, the weight of past decisions heavy in her voice. "I protected the wall, and my children collected bounties to keep the protection and wealth of our civilization stable as we moved them to the canyon. The killing began to lose its purpose, as most of the enemies didn't seem to be attacking but more so as they needed help. Now I see they just wanted to be accepted like my husband tried to do."

"Every one of them is not the same, and yet we treated them as if they were all evil. I feel we should take on what my husband was trying to do before he was looking death in the eyes. Although he was a man of peace, their presence showed him only one side—a side of evil that we related to all of them." Inertia's voice grew firmer with resolve. "I must head back to the canyon. Take some of my warriors with you to the Land of Gods. They are already aware of who is going, so just lead them."

With those final words, Inertia turned and ran toward the canyon, her speed a blur faster than lightning, leaving Nakh and Finity to ponder her profound reflections and the path forward.

As Omni and Hutch reached the shore, the scene before them was chaotic with members of Culo's defeated army scrambling to board ships, hoping for a swift retreat from the shores they had so fiercely fought to conquer. However, their escape was about to be thwarted by the determined Roots.

Standing firm on the sandy beach, Hutch extended his hands toward the sea, his eyes narrowing in concentration. Slowly, he began to levitate, his focus intensifying as he manipulated the elemental forces at his command. With a deft movement of his hands, he manipulated the water surrounding the ships, causing the sea to recede from around the hulls, effectively trapping the ships on mere puddles amidst a suddenly dry seabed.

The water, obeying Hutch's command, formed towering walls around the ships, a clear and intimidating display of his control over the element. The soldiers aboard the ships, realizing their predicament, were thrown into a panic. Their frantic movements turned to desperation as they saw the immense bodies of water held at bay by Hutch's will, the potential for a catastrophic deluge looming ominously over them.

Meanwhile, Omni, observing Hutch's effective blockade, decided to add his own show of force to ensure the enemy's surrender. Spotting a large boulder nearby, he used his earth powers to lift it from the ground, creating a platform for himself. With a powerful leap, he landed atop the boulder, which he then propelled through the air toward Hutch and the stranded ships.

Confronted with the overwhelming display of elemental powers and the strategic control of their only means of escape, the members of the army began to surrender. They threw down their weapons and raised their hands, their pleas for mercy echoing across the now-still waters. The sight of water walls poised to crash down upon them should they attempt any aggressive action convinced even the most stubborn fighters that their situation was hopeless. Landing his boulder beside Hutch, Omni stepped down, his expression serious as he surveyed the scene. Together, they faced the surrendered soldiers, their combined presence a clear statement of authority and control.

As Hutch's voice trailed off, a critical moment unfolded on the sandy shore. Omni, realizing the gravity of their actions and their potential impact, intervened with a plea for compassion and understanding.

"STOP!!!" Omni's voice boomed across the beach, full of urgency and conviction. "They have nowhere to go. They just want somewhere to call home. They have been following the wrong lead, and now that their head is missing, they have no purpose." His words echoed in the sudden stillness, a stark contrast to the sounds of desperation and fear that had filled the air moments before.

Gently, Omni manipulated the earth beneath him to approach Hutch more closely, his eyes earnest, seeking to convey the importance of mercy in this pivotal moment. "We have a chance here, not just to end a battle but to end a cycle of violence. Let's offer them a chance to find a new way forward."

Hutch listened, his expression torn. The memories of battle, loss, and the aggression they had faced were fresh, and his instincts toward defense and retribution were strong. "So we should show them mercy? We should let them live even though they wanted to kill everybody? What will they do if we let them go? They have no purpose, so we should just do away with them. And..." Hutch's voice was firm, his hand wavering as he maintained control over the massive bodies of water surrounding the ships.

As he spoke, the water began to rise ominously around the ships, the threat of destruction palpable in the air. The soldiers on the ships, realizing their peril, began to panic, their cries adding to the tense atmosphere.

"There are more coming!" Hutch suddenly exclaimed, his attention shifting as he sensed additional ships approaching. In a reflexive move driven by concern for the immediate threat, he let the water crash down, the force of his elemental power smashing into the ships below. The structures buckled and broke under the weight of the water, splintering wood and cries of men lost in the roar of the destruction.

Omni, shocked by the sudden escalation, reached out, trying to mitigate the impact, but it was too late. The ships were destroyed, and the potential for mercy was lost in a moment of preemptive defense. The realization of what had happened—what they had done—settled heavily on both of them.

As the water settled and the debris floated on the now calm sea, Omni and Hutch stood in silence, the consequences of their actions unfolding before them. The beach was quiet, save for the soft lapping of waves and the distant cries of the survivors struggling in the water. Omni, perched upon the rock, wore an expression of stoic sorrow, his face mirroring the icy chill that seeped into his soul. The devastation below, caused by the elemental fury unleashed by Hutch, played over in his mind like a haunting refrain. He watched helplessly as the waters settled, revealing the aftermath of their decision — the floating debris, the struggling survivors, and those lost to the depths.

The sight of the soldiers, who had moments ago harbored hopes of escape or redemption, now battling the unforgiving sea, etched a deep scar in Omni's conscience. Each cry for help, each plea that went unanswered, intensified the ache in his heart. His eyes, usually a wellspring of resolve and strength, now reflected profound internal turmoil — the pain of witnessing unnecessary death, and the burden of his own power and its consequences.

This moment of introspection was more than just a reflection on a single tragic event; it was a pivotal point that challenged his understanding of justice, mercy, and his role in the war. The coldness that gripped him was a stark contrast to the fiery battles he had endured; it was the chill of doubt, questioning whether the path of destruction they had chosen was the only way, or if there had been another path they could have taken — a path of compassion and understanding, even for their enemies.

The silence around him was punctuated by the soft lapping of the waves against the shore, a gentle but constant reminder of the lives disrupted by the day's violence. As Hutch joined him, a heavy silence fell between them. It was clear that the events had also shaken Hutch, leaving him to grapple with the immediate impact of his decisions.

In this shared silence, a bond was tested and tempered. For Omni, the resolve to never let fear dictate their actions became a new cornerstone of his philosophy. For Hutch, the incident was a harsh lesson in the weight of power and the importance of temperance.

Together, sitting amidst the quiet aftermath, they faced the horizon. The setting sun cast long shadows, wrapping the beach in hues of orange and red, a visual reminder of the day's fiery conflicts and their cold consequences. In this light, they made a silent vow: to strive for a future where power would be guided by wisdom, and where their abilities would be used to forge paths to peace rather than the destruction they had witnessed today.

Upon their arrival, Keem was immediately drawn to a circle of children gathered around an object of profound importance to him—his egg. The children, who had been curiously observing and perhaps even guarding the egg in his absence, looked up with bright eyes as he approached. Keem's expression softened as he neared, his heart swelling with relief to see the egg unharmed and the children safe.

Lona, meanwhile, sought out Misery to relay the news of the battle's outcome. She found Misery overseeing the community's daily activities, her leadership evident in her calm demeanor and the respect she commanded from those around her.

"The war is over," Lona announced, her voice carrying a mixture of relief and exhaustion. Misery's reaction was measured, her eyes reflecting the weight of the news. She listened intently as Lona described the events, the destruction, and the dramatic turn of events that led to the enemy's retreat.

As they discussed the implications of the battle's end, Inertia appeared, her approach almost as sudden and forceful as her personality. She joined the conversation with a sense of urgency that underscored her leadership role.

"Inertia," Misery greeted her, nodding in respect.

"We need to act swiftly," Inertia declared, her tone commanding. "Misery, gather some troops together. We have many wounded on both sides that need our help. We must show them that we are not just conquerors but healers and builders of peace."

Misery nodded, understanding the importance of the task. "We'll start immediately," she assured, turning to organize the necessary aid.

Meanwhile, Keem knelt by his egg, the children clustering around him with curious and excited whispers. He gently laid his hands on the egg, feeling the life within stir—a poignant symbol of new beginnings and the potential for renewal even in the wake of destruction.

"This egg," Keem explained to the children, "represents hope. Just as it will soon bring forth new life, we too will help bring new life to our lands and our people after the ravages of war."

As Misery mobilized the troops to assist the wounded, Inertia coordinated with other leaders to ensure that their efforts were not just about healing physical wounds but also mending the broken spirits and communities affected by the conflict.

The canyon, with its tranquil beauty and the promise of protection it offered, became a center of recovery and reconciliation. The children's laughter mingled with the sounds of preparations, a reminder that life continues and that resilience is built not on victories in battle but on the actions taken in its aftermath.

In this renewed focus on healing and community, the residents of the canyon—led by figures like Misery, Inertia, Keem, and Lona—began the slow but hopeful process of building a future defined not by conflict but by compassion and a collective will to forge a better, more inclusive world.

The moment Keem's hands touched the egg, it began to crack more visibly. Thin lines spread like a spiderweb across the surface, and soft sounds emanated from within. Each crack released a bit more of the energy that had been building inside, hinting at the life eager to emerge.

Keem, sensing the imminence of the hatching, gently cradled the egg, his expression a mix of awe and tenderness. The children inched closer, their breaths held in quiet suspense, their faces illuminated by the glow of the breaking shell.

As Lona and Inertia approached Keem, the tension of recent battles seemed to momentarily lift, replaced by the shared wonder of the hatching egg. Keem, holding the egg gently, conveyed his intentions to Lona with a mixture of resolve and awe in his voice. "It's hatching. It's actually going to happen. But we have to get back to the others. I'm going to take it with me and watch over it. I'll stay out of the fight and protect it unless they need me," he explained, his protective instincts for both the egg and his comrades clear.

Lona, supportive and understanding, nodded in agreement, her hand resting reassuringly on Keem's back, symbolizing her readiness to help. However, before they could finalize their plans, Inertia interjected with a decisive tone, her leadership qualities shining through. "No. You will be joining your friends in battle. You will take Lona with you, and she will watch the egg. She has taken so much interest in you, I believe that this is the start of her journey," Inertia declared, redirecting the course of action with a clear vision of how each should contribute.

Keem and Lona exchanged a look, a silent communication of mutual respect and budding feelings that had been nurtured by shared experiences and now, a shared responsibility. Their smiles were a mix of nervousness and excitement about the path unfolding before them.

Keem carefully placed the egg into his backpack, the weight of its significance not lost on him. He handed the backpack to Lona, entrusting her with the care of their future hope. Together, they prepared to leave the canyon, Lona now bearing the egg and a new purpose, and Keem ready to rejoin the battle, knowing that part of his heart was safe with her.

As they departed, Misery was already moving toward the battlefield, gathering troops for what might come next. Her figure was resolute, a beacon of the determination that had sustained them through dark times. Her actions underscored the ongoing necessity of readiness and vigilance, even as they hoped for peace.

The journey back to the rest of the Root group was filled with anticipation. Keem and Lona, each stepping into their roles within the larger tapestry of their community's struggles and dreams, were symbols of the Root's evolving dynamics— warriors, protectors, and now guardians of new life. This balance of fighting for peace while nurturing growth encapsulated the essence of their journey, a poignant reminder of the cycles of conflict and renewal that defined their world.

Nakh and Finity hurried toward the beach where Hutch stood watching the horizon, his thoughts likely tangled in the recent events and their ramifications. As they approached, the weight of the recent battle hung heavy in the air, evident in Hutch's solemn demeanor.

Meanwhile, Omni was nearby, engaged in a task that was both meditative and practical. He worked in silence, focusing on constructing ships. Each movement was deliberate, channeling his elemental powers to shape and assemble the vessels from the natural materials around them. The ships, built with the precision only Omni could muster, were more than mere vehicles for travel; they were symbols of hope and means of journeying toward new horizons.

As Nakh and Finity approached the shore, Nakh noted to Hutch, "Everyone is here except Keem." He continued, detailing the recent decisions made, "Inertia has allowed her warriors to join us and has decided to spare the surviving enemies. She's taking them in." Hearing this, Hutch lowered his head in contemplation.

Omni completed his work on the ships, each vessel a testament to his meticulous craft and elemental control. As he rejoined the rest of the Roots, there was a palpable shift in his demeanor. He approached a member of the group, quietly took a scarf, and wrapped it around his neck, covering his mouth and nose. His actions seemed deliberate, hinting at a deeper, unspoken burden he carried.

The group watched him, a mix of concern and confusion in their eyes, as he turned and made his way toward the newly built ships. His solitary figure against the backdrop of the sea painted a poignant image of resolve tinged with isolation.

Finity, noticing the unusual solemnity in Omni's actions, turned to Hutch and asked, "What's wrong with him?"

Hutch, observing Omni's retreating back, remained silent for a moment, lost in thought. He understood the weight of leadership and the personal sacrifices it entailed better than most. Finally, without a word, he too began to walk toward the ships, signaling that now was not the time for explanations but for action. The group, sensing the unspoken gravity of the moment, followed suit, each member processing the silent exchange in their own way.

As Nakh and Finity exchanged puzzled glances, they took the lead, guiding the rest of the Roots toward the fleet of ships that Omni had meticulously prepared. The silent tension lingering from Omni's demeanor was palpable, yet it only solidified their resolve as they proceeded with the preparations to set sail. The atmosphere among the group was a blend of anticipation and the undercurrent of unanswered questions that hung in the air.

Together, the Roots boarded the ships, their silhouettes against the setting sun a symbol of their unity and determination. As the vessels began to pull away from the shore, the group looked ahead, their eyes fixed on the distant lands that awaited them. With the sails catching the evening breeze, the ships moved forward, carrying the Roots toward new adventures and the unknown promises of the Land of Gods.

As the Roots' ships cut through the waves, the tranquility of their departure was quickly overshadowed by a looming threat. The sea ahead churned, not just with the natural rhythm of the ocean, but with the approach of a new enemy— a faction distinct from any they had previously encountered. This new adversary, unlike Culo's land-hungry forces, was driven by a fervent dedication to the sea itself. To them, the ocean was sacred, a realm to be defended against all intrusions, and they viewed themselves as its staunch protectors.

These guardians of the waters believed it was their duty to shield the pathways to the Land of Gods, a mission that Culo had manipulated to his advantage. Before his defeat, Culo had communicated to them a dire warning: that he was contending against forces that threatened not only his quest but the sanctity of the Land of Gods itself. Although skeptical of his broader motives, given his history of disdain for allies and enemies alike, they had nonetheless seen fit to support him. Their loyalty to the cause of protecting the Land of Gods outweighed their doubts about Culo's character.

Their decision to aid Culo was not born out of affection for him but rather a cautious strategy to safeguard their cherished realms. Culo's message had stirred enough concern that they dispatched reinforcements, albeit reluctantly. They were prepared to continue his mission posthumously if needed, driven by a deep-seated commitment to their cause rather than personal loyalty to Culo.

As the Root fleet sailed onward, the palpable tension was broken by Hutch's unusual behavior. His usually steady demeanor gave way to visible anxiety, his eyes darting across the ocean's surface as he sensed an unseen presence. The water around them seemed ordinary to the others, but Hutch felt something lurking beneath, something ominous and invisible that approached their ship and then, just as suddenly, disappeared.

Nakh noticed Hutch's distress and approached him, placing a steadying hand on his shoulder. Concern furrowed his brow as he observed Hutch's uncharacteristic unease.

"What is wrong? Why are you shaking, Hutch?" Nakh asked, trying to catch his eye and understand the source of his sudden fear.

As the strong, unseen presence in the water intensified, Hutch's reaction grew more severe. The robust and calm demeanor he usually exhibited was replaced by an uncontrollable tremor, and his words faltered into a stutter. The energy emanating from beneath the waves was unlike anything he had encountered before, seeping fear deep into his bones and rendering him momentarily paralyzed.

The rest of the Roots watched in growing concern as their typically unshakeable friend struggled to regain his composure. The sight of Hutch, so visibly affected, sent a ripple of unease through the group, underscoring the gravity of the threat lurking unseen beneath their vessel.

As the atmosphere grew tense with heavy, ominous clouds rolling in to obscure the setting sun, the situation on the ship became even more urgent. Omni quickly joined Nakh beside Hutch, both trying to physically and mentally stabilize their friend, who was still grappling with the overwhelming presence emanating from the depths below.

Omni placed his hands on Hutch's shoulders, giving them a firm squeeze to ground him. "Hutch, you need to come back to us now," Omni said, his voice both commanding and supportive. Nakh, meanwhile, held Hutch's gaze, trying to pierce through the fog of fear that had enveloped him.

Hutch's eyes, wide with terror, fixed on the water beneath the ship. He couldn't move, couldn't speak. The silence was deafening. Whatever was down there, it was getting closer.

Omni's hands shook slightly as he gripped Hutch's shoulders tighter. "Hutch," he said softly, his voice trembling, "you need to come back to us. Now."

But Hutch couldn't. The presence... the weight in the water... it was rising.

The last sliver of light slipped beneath the horizon, and the ship rocked as the waves began to churn beneath them.

To be continued...